THE ODDS JOB

THE ODDS JOB

Galbraith Case Files - Book 1

WILLIAM BOULANGER

William Boulanger

DEDICATION

Thanks to the original *The Odds*: S.A.M.M., Jeremy, and Carson. Our silly adventures live on in these pages.

Special Thanks to my first editor: Natalie Bilski

Extra-Special Thanks to those who supported the crowd-sourcing campaign that almost published this book. I had to find another way, but you all gave me the light to see it was worth finding.

Load Playlist Track: Dedication

As I write Einar for the first time, I reach out for the Deep Djugga. Finding it not of this world, but of the worlds in my mind, I seek inspiration. I seek for that music that I imagine Einar listens to. I imagine him, in each chapter of his life, listening to music that is real and now - but historical to him.

I imagine he turns his wrist-computer to face him and says "Load Playlist Track" and a name of a song and a band.

And I do the same.

And I write.

I don't have the rights to the music and the lyrics. I can only legally mention the name and invite you to "Load Playlist Track" and join me, and Einar, on our musical journey.

This Dedication is to every musician I heard as I wrote the chapter they are listed on. Thank you for your music and I hope it lasts to 2250 to play on the wrist of some future space detective.

PROLOGUE

Load Playlist Track: Dead Kennedys, When You Get Drafted

I tapped my foot in the air to the beat of Foreigner's "Feels Like the First Time" on my ear buds, humming the chorus to myself on the second round. It wasn't the first time I'd listened to it, but it wasn't one I'd heard often. I was exploring music outside my normal Punk choices, but sticking roughly to the same era.

The lights of my hotel room were out and I'd pulled the curtains closed to conceal myself as I peeked on the room parallel to mine with the zoom lens of an antique point-and-click film camera.

It was hard to steady myself for a clear shot. I kept drifting slightly to my right due to the space station's higher mass in that direction. I grabbed onto one of the red curtains, a straight length of fabric which ran between runners above and below the window, and rotated myself so that drift was below me.

Now that I was floating perpendicular to the layout of the room, I could steady my hand for shooting. I didn't want to get any blurry shots, having that film created and processed wasn't cheap – but it couldn't be intercepted or deleted either. There wasn't any gravity aboard the Hotel Europa thanks to it being built almost two hundred years ago. But, it was a classic hotel with a romantic story. It was number four in the Solar System for romantic getaways, right behind the Taj Mahal in India back on Earth.

That's what brought me here in search of my target. I'd tracked Mr. Weyland to the Europa, which floated over the moon by the same name.

His wife was convinced he was having an affair, coming to the space station twice a month on "business meetings".

I hadn't found any proof he was cheating on her yet. Just that he kept a lot of secrets and that, yes, he spent two weekends a month at the Europa. So, this was my last chance to catch him in the act.

If I didn't, sure, I'd still get my hourly stipend I was charging her, but I wouldn't get the rent-paying bonus I was promised if I couldn't name his paramour.

I floated there, all almost-six-foot pasty-white me, naked in the darkness of my room. The only light present reflected off of Jupiter somewhere out of sight, blocking out all starlight. It was a good thing we weren't in one of the hotels closer to Earth. There, the windows were tinted heavily to protect against the sun's direct light.

All the access I was getting from the more transparent windows here was the view of an elderly husband getting a full body massage in the indulgence of zero gravity. I'd expected the attractive blond dressed as a masseuse to be a cover for some more illicit encounter.

Unfortunately, for my objective, and my rent, it seems the old corporate tycoon was innocent of cheating on his young, third wife. He was just a wheelchair bound old man enjoying the freedom of zero gravity and the rejuvenating cares of a luxury rub down.

I tapped the holo display for record that glowed in the air about an inch above the wrist computer I normally wore, but had left dutifully floating in the air by me. Three beeps coincided with each of the small glowing numbers counting down where I'd placed my finger.

On the final beep I recorded a message that I had programmed for weekly uploads to my secretary. I relied on her for reminding me of things when I was back in the office.

"Velma, it's 8:00 AM Greenwich Mean Time." I said into the air. "After sufficient observation, I've determined that Mister Weyland is not cheating on his wife. I'm linking this message with the tracking information for the film processor I use. She should have the physical photographs in a week or so. No bonus on this one, I'm afraid."

Sure, the masseuse was hot, but the old man wasn't doing anything I could call cheating.

I snapped a final shot with the zoom-cam, popped the film canister out and into the mail canister I'd prepared when there was a stirring in the room behind me.

"Einar...?" A woman's pouty voice said from the bed as she spoke Galactic Common Tongue, but with a German accent. "Where did you go my *liebchen*?"

One of the best escapes in the system for lovers, paid for on the client's dime. Would have been a shame to not bring some company, right?

I'd met Sofie on the flight in. She was a flight attendant aboard the real-space slow-flight cruise ship that I'd followed Mister Weyland on. She was due for some time off and I was due for a much more believable cover. Weyland had some serious security and they would have been paying attention to who was within his proximity.

So, checking in *single* at one of the most romantic spots in the solar system would have raised some alarms.

"Ah well." I said to myself as a mutter in my native Icelandic. "Let the old man be the odd ball for this hotel. I'm not going to get my full paycheck anyway. I might as well enjoy my trip."

I was halfway back to bed when my wrist computer blinked and lightly illuminated the dark room, showing I'd received a message from my secretary all the way back on Earth. Earth messages take close to an hour to reach me here and she knew I was on a case.

I reached over for my floating wrist-comp and played the message as I reached the bed, which was a padded tube full of loosely floating blankets. In the center of one of those blankets, protruded the blond short-cropped hair of Sofie Whose-Name-I-Don't-Remember.

"Boss." My secretary's voice spoke in GCT with a business-like tone. "Sorry to bother you on a case, but we have a high paying client asking for you."

"High Paying." I said to myself as I navigated in through the white soft blankets, through an obstacle course of legs, over a diamond belly button ring, and over a pair of floating mountains to pursed lips and a face illuminated by the glow of my now adorned wrist computer. "My favorite kind."

"You need to get back to Earth, quick." My Secretary's voice became secondary in my head. "An ambassador for the Parliament. Says he'll pay you whatever your current fee is to drop the case you're on to take his, plus his case. Oh, and the shop called to say that The Snowball was ready for pick up."

I kissed Sofie on those demure lips. "I'm sorry Sofie. I have to get back."

"But we have the room for another night." She curled her fingers into my Lincoln beard. "I don't want to go yet. I don't have a flight to work until the next morning."

She was tempting. But my rent was behind and Mrs. Weyland's all-too-small payment just got outbid. "Sorry, doll. Keep the room. It's paid for."

"Keep an eye out for me on your flights?" She said as I floated over to the locker with my clothes in it.

"Oh yeah." I said. I was lying, but I suspected she knew it. There's an etiquette to 'two ships passing in the night' that private dicks, flight attendants, and other transients knew – even if we didn't speak of them. Sure, I'd love to have another float through a zero-gravity space bed with her, but I'd probably never see her again.

But nice girls don't settle down with guys like me, private detectives who travel around the galaxy chasing down lost items, stolen goods, cheating husbands, and the occasional life threatening kidnapper on a missing persons case the law had given up on.

Nah, she was better off.

"At least tell me your whole name and where I can look out for you." She said from the bed-tube, spinning slowly and looking at me with a wicked smile.

I blushed. Was she really that into me? Sure. Why not.

"Einar Galbraith." I tipped my red fedora at her as I put it on my head. "You can find me on New Reykjavik, Earth, here in Sol. I'm in the book."

"In the book?" She said confused. No one used actual phone books anymore. Hell, people didn't even really use phones. Even when they were still called cell phones, they were just computers you could talk through. Not much different than my wrist computer, just more primitive.

"Look me up if you're on Earth." I said as I floated through a pair of sliding doors that opened with the "swish" from one of those old science-fiction shows and kicked myself off a wall toward the hangar where I'd parked. There was probably still enough time to catch a ride back home on the ferry transport.

Some gigs don't pan out. Maybe this one would.

"Velma," after a new series of beeps, "it's 8:15 AM GMT. I've decided to drop the Weyland case in favor of our new client. I'm going to forward all of my notes as a courtesy to Mrs. Weyland. You'll probably have them all, and this message, by the time I'm aboard the Earth transport. Please forward me my destination and I'll divert once I get to the *Earth-port* in a few days."

I

⤜❧❧⤛

CHAPTER ONE

Load Playlist Track : The Dead Milkmen, Punk Rock Girl

A month and a half later, above me, the pitch black of night was awash with the subtle light blue glow of the Milky Way, pierced further with pinpricks of stars. Somewhere behind the horizon, I knew there would be a planet rise – this small moon's host planet, a gas giant.

"No light pollution or air pollution on this little moon." I said under my breath, taking in the clarity of night and smell of the air. It wasn't at all like back on Earth, still a hundred and fifty years into the clean up after The Collapse, a breaking point for our world's ecosystem that humanity wouldn't have overcome without the help of the Hegemonic Imperium, usually referred to by GCT speakers simply as "the Expanse."

Interestingly enough, nearby lights were interrupting the serenity of the moment. Not just lights, mind you, but the brutal, yet haunting savagery of an alien music that had grown popular throughout the Western Spiral Arm that Earth resided in.

I swiped my hand from my wrist computer to a nearby window and a girl's image came up onto the screen of the white repulsor mini-pod I traveled in. She was aborigine, from Earth's continent of Australia. Thanks to also being half Scottish, her blue eyes stood out. She was a diplomat's runaway child obsessed with a particular band that was performing tonight on this unknown little backwater.

I waved my hand in the air in front of me and the girl's image was replaced by an itinerary my secretary had acquired. It showed my target had booked passage from the Sol System, where her father worked, and made her way out here through a variety of stops onboard freighters and haulers.

Despite the very agricultural moon I was on, this system was heavily industrialized - most ships coming here were not nearly as luxurious as a rich diplomat's daughter would have been used to.

I looked over to the entrance of the cargo container that was parked in the middle of the field. Shifting neon lights and smoke poured out of the front door in a weird synchronicity with the thumping music within.

"Not exactly a luxurious club either." I said to myself as I got out of my pod, which I called Snowball. "She must really like this band to risk ending up in that dump."

I locked Snowball up and made my way to the entrance of the club to find out.

MOUSE CLUB!!

The name on the container identified it in the alphabet of the Hegemony, but the spelling and pronunciation was in the interstellar "street language" of Galactic Common Tongue, or GCT, used by just about everyone who wasn't in government or a member of the nobility.

I paid my fifteen credits to the colossal four-armed blue bouncer at the entrance to the Mouse Club, an interplanetary sideshow housed in a large space-born cargo pod converted into an on-the-go night club. It was run by a minor two-bit gangster called The Mouse; an ironic name for a hulking lardball of a Delosian that made his bouncer of the same species look like a human swimsuit model on a diet.

I had never met him personally, but he had a reputation in my sector of the Rim Worlds of the Galaxy. Maybe the girl wasn't here for the band? Maybe she or her father owed some kind of debt.

Past the front airlock of the club, the sound of popular Galactic Rim underground music thumped with drums and the strum of electronic harpsichords in a weird visceral sound that's hard to explain; but for you sheltered types, I'll try anyway.

It was like Old Earth Electronic Dance Music and Dark Matter Death Metal had a baby that grew up to be a transgenre mishmash of Dubstepped Swing and InterWorld Gypsy Music, with some intense fusion of raw primal rage and happening Jazz they called the Deep Djugga.

Deep Djugga's roots were in the Voltch system, with Voltch-Djugga performed by the dual-throated, white-furred, and four-armed dwellers of the system's primary ice planet. It was rocked to by Nordic Earthlings soon after our species met, and then exploded into the cosmos like a supernova, a timestamp matching humanity joining the Expanse.

Every world and species that picked up the style reforged and renamed it - Nordic Earth-Djugga, Terra-Martian Smooth Sol-Djugga, Pop Luna-Djugga. Even the musically inept Pyqian machines cobbled together what they called Binary Pyqia-Djugga.

But this Deep Voltch-Djugga was primal. The band played it on electric versions of the classic instruments and with singing by a gaggle of the species emulating the throat singing of the Voltch'i, but with a collective of growls and strangely concordant matching harmonies.

This was the edge. The very subculture of the galactic trend. The music of a social rebellion rising against the Galactic Expanse and its imperialist, centralized government.

It was the new Punk. The deep frothing mouth of a feral generation of spacers living on the Rim, spitting their lyrics of freedom and individuality and conflict into the faces of the System Lords and their puppet Parliaments.

Even as I paid my credits, I couldn't help but bob my head slightly to the rhythm and tap my leather booted foot to the beat. It wasn't normally my kind of music. I'm into classical music from the twentieth century, Old Earth Punk mostly. But, considering the rebellious attitudes of that style, I couldn't help but respect the instinctive counter culture of the Deep Djugga.

The Delosian bouncer ham-fisted some hard credits back to me - my change. You didn't see material credits much anymore. They didn't have the convenience of a cred stick, which almost anyone could accept and didn't have to bother with the act of figuring out how many Galactic Expanse Credits equaled how many of whatever local currency might be in place, if any. The Delosian bouncer wrinkled its pig-like nose and glowered its meaty, hairless brow at me upon having given me my change. Then, as if reluctantly, he nodded for me to go in.

"Thanks," I read the name embroidered on his four-armed security T-shirt. "Mook."

He glowered again, snorted a deep big snort, and urged me in again.

The Mouse Club was off the books in the tax system, an interplanetary speakeasy of sorts. And clearly the owner preferred hard credits because they weren't traceable. I could respect the anonymity, even if it did make you question the type of business going on.

Still, it felt somehow reassuring to hold the cold metal coins in my fingers. Their weight, unlike virtual credits on a cred stick, was reassuringly real. I was a bit of a tactile person. I found comfort in traditions and things I could hold on to, the older the better. And it didn't get much older than the exchange of cold hard cash for what you wanted.

I slipped the octagonal flat chits with their cameo headshot of the Empress Wren'lar, an elfin-eared humanoid of the Hegemonic Imperium, into the inside pocket of my leather trench coat. Then, before I made my way farther inside I stepped aside for others entering the club,. Knowing I was about to deal with people on business for the first time since I left Earth over a week ago, I took a moment to bring my wrist computer online and set the camera on myself. I had already touched myself up inside my mini-pod, but I still felt run down from travel and double checked myself.

A two-dimensional holographic image of myself came up like a reversed reflection. My hair had grown out long enough to put in a ponytail, even my bangs. That took annoyingly long to do and required in much wearing of hats so people wouldn't suspect I was attempting to bring back the mullet. Those were dark times.

I still had an old-style, reddish-brown Lincoln beard. My hair was dark brown with hints of red, if you caught it well in the light, but in the low lighting of the club it wouldn't have been as obvious. My hazel eyes were hidden except for the reflections of the club's light displays pinging along with the music. I was thin, and tall.

"Alright you wiry fuck." I said to myself. "Let's get that hair fixed in case there are any lovely ladies inside. You never know when a little 'side businesses might come up on a job."

After a brief moment of grooming with a comb - vintage Earth plastic, all black and still with all its teeth, the silver painted letters of the manufacturer profusely faded on it. If it were mint condition enough for legibility, I wouldn't be using it. I'd make a month's rent by selling the relic. As it was, I'm not the kind of guy who collects toys to keep them in the box. I like old and I like using old, as I said.

I glanced quickly into the club, switching off the self-image and paused once more before heading in. My fingers pressed against one of the buttons on the side of the wristcomp.

"Velma," I clicked off a new three beeps. "It's just after nightfall locally on Arcturis Minor. You'll have to check the timestamp on the record for accuracy. You know how I am about keeping time straight when I've got space lag. I'm at the Mouse Club. This is my kind of seedy joint. You'd probably like the band. Remind me to find a new plastic comb. The teeth on this one are getting a little fragile and it might be time to sell it on the antiques market."

I gently strummed a little string of notes across the plastic teeth, still bobbing my head to the primal rawness of the Deep Djugga and delved into the club proper, parting the smoky air beyond the doorway like a curtain, it smelled of second-hand tobacco smoke with a hint of sweet opiates.

"Incense! Burning with the *mooja!*" The Tilarian sang, if I got the lyrics right, as she danced in sheer white cloth. "Dripping roof of ice, snow all around!"

Through the almost silken material, firm breasts shifted distractingly as she moved, obscured only by a white halter top with the band's logo on it – a pair of polyhedrons with unlucky symbols on them.

She spun in place, her ankle-length hip hugging almost translucent white skirt elevating to show legs that went all the way up. I checked to be sure before she'd finished and dropped to one knee to practically yell the next line of the song while she stared directly into the eyes of a mesmerized fan.

The Tilarian was an almost-human female with skin the color of a blood orange and the contouring of a tangerine. The sweat dripping on her body made her look ripe and I found my mouth watering a little. A pair of color-matched horns curved skyward from her forehead and a mane of dreadlock-like prehensile tendrils draped down to below her shoulders. Her serpentine "hair" appeared to be looking about the room, like a freshly opened basket of headless snakes unaware of their blindness.

She swayed to the music like a cobra to some sort of hypnotic death metal clarinet. It was the smooth writhing of a belly dancer with the occasional pop and lock reversal of a possessed woman. As I became increasingly entranced by her movements, looking at the curves of her hips and the cut of her midriff, each of the tendrils, one by one, turned toward me...followed soon after by her eyes, which met mine.

An aroused, yet frightened, chill rippled down my spine.

As she danced along with the music, you could see why she doubled as the band's eye candy. But she wasn't just looks. Her melodic and al-most hypnotizing voice added an alto affect to offset the visceral growls of the large ginger-brown furred Grothrark roaring beside her.

"Mooja!!!" he growled the word, I think it was what he said, in his own bestial language when the Tilarian said it. He growled something else in sync with various words she sang, and if I understood the genre of music correctly, he was saying the same thing she was.

The feral looking alien stood nearly three meters tall, towering over the Tilarian and his other band mates. As he rocked back and forth, in a motion that looked like a full-body head bang, , you could see through the sweat matted long fur the definition of strong lean muscles; anyone with common sense knew those arms could crush almost any human if he got them wrapped around you.

Dressed in some heavy leather kilt-like garment, he was otherwise unclothed, as was typical of Grothrarks. I did not check to see if his legs went all the way up.

Among their own kind, modesty was an alien concept, one they only adopted for the well-being of more sensitive creatures, like humans...and most of the rest of the galaxy. So, I was pretty sure I wouldn't see anything up there I wanted to see.

He had a short, spiked metal plate over one side of his skull where the fur was missing, which looked intimidating as he growled into the crowd and played the electric *gerawl*, a sitar-like instrument traditionally played from the lap, that he slapped and jammed on like an electric bass guitar.

Singing together, his fierce growl and her strong harmonics allowed the two singers to emulate a single Voltch'i throat singer, who could produce both the deep growls and alto from a single mouth.

The two singers were in a bazaar vocal dissonance, that came together more in the mind than the ears, while a voice-synthesizing robot wrapped around the Grothrark's throat sang an almost operatic alto in sync with the voice of the human in the group; a scarred-up former warrior playing a sort of lead guitar known as a *staan'g* growled like a Dark Matter Metal lead singer.

He was the next step in looking for the diplomat's daughter. He was the one I'd come to see, the soldier with the past and more than a few names depending on who knew him; "The Stranger", "The Trooper", "The Hunter". Simple monikers tossed at him - because he never shared his actual name when he used to adventure before retiring to this Deep Voltch-Djugga band. But, according to my files, he was simply CT-R138, his designator as a manufactured human when he was in the service of the Expanse, and the now rogue and traitorous System Lord, Wilfred Archimedes the Third.

Like all of his "brothers", he was manufactured from a genetic template that pretty heavily borrowed from every culture of Earth humanity – and you'd be surprised how many types of "humans" there are in the Expanse. As such, he had even, olive-brown skin. He still wore his black curly hair short, cut and faded like the soldier he was raised to be. He was heavily scarred over his right eye, which appeared blind, down all the way to the right side of his neck.

It looked like the kind of damage that comes from an explosion.

The Trooper played his *staan'g* in perfect rhythm as he roared his lyrics in the Galactic Common Tongue, along to the beat of the *kresh'i* bongo-like drums being managed by a human drummer I had no data on. The drummer was in a red shirt with a yellow "5" written on it. The poor kid looked like he was having trouble keeping up. But then, the *kresh'i* was intended to be played with four hands.

I made my way through the busy crowd to the bar, doing my best not to start a fight with those that I had to effectively shoulder check.

Before making my way to the stage exit, I ordered a glass of SynthaScotch and Soda on-the-rocks from the robot bartender painted up like a suited butler.

Out of the way of the small crowd that was dancing and slamming into each other in the center floor, I sipped on my drink, feeling the base rolling out at me from the speaker near my head, expecting I'd have a slight ringing to my hearing tonight as I tried to sleep.

The drink didn't taste right, too smooth and lacking the earthy elements of an oak barrel. Besides, real scotch, not some synthetic or generically labeled whiskey, has to be made in Scotland, on Earth. That means there are two types who get to drink real Scotch; Earthers, especially those from Scotland, and really rich beings.

The former I got lucky with. Although my ancestors were from Scotland, I wasn't. But New Reykjavík, my home, floats not too far off the coast once a year as it cycles along the Atlantic Circuit. I take a trip to the island chain that makes up what used to be the United Kingdom whenever I can to tour the remaining highland distilleries.

The industrial city was made up of subaquatic laborers, mostly immigrants from water-based worlds. The behemoth mechanical island supported a population of transients riding along on the harvesters that did everything from local underwater mining, food collection and farming, to scientific research for sustaining the planet's ever-chal-lenged ecosystem and food needs.

It was the cheapest rent I could get and still live there. So - clearly, I wasn't going to get scotch by being a rich off-worlder. If I was, I wouldn't be in an illegal transient dive bar in the far reaches of the Galaxy getting paid by the day plus expenses.

Once the set was done, the band bowed and thanked the small cheering crowd before abandoning their instruments to make their way to the stage exit where I was waiting. I shot down my drink and set the glass on a nearby ledge.

The lithe Tilarian woman, "Vi'xiri the Vixen", made her way down the stairs, slipping into a pair of sandals on the way. It was hard not to watch her do it, her legs were supple like those of a seasoned dancer. She noticed my gaze and responded with a full- violet lipstick smile and winked an equally violet-shadowed eye at me. I felt her eyeless tendrils keeping tabs on me somehow as she made her way by.

I don't normally go for non-human, not that I hadn't once or twice, but she definitely made me consider rethinking my boundaries. Don't get me wrong, cross-species relationships, between sentient species any-way, wasn't generally a big social issue in the eyes of the Alpha Sensuo Kingdom, where Earth was located. But there are some risks involved that are hard to predict.

Don't ask me how I know.

The Grothrark, whose name was Khaleef-graa, said something to her in his bestial tongue as he came down behind her and the robotic thing on his neck translated it to GCT in a posh British woman's accent, "Kliff says that you didn't shake your ass enough for those young men in the front row." Khaleef-graa growled angrily and slapped the neck collar robot, who then adjusted his statement, now in a monotone ro-botic voice, "I meant to say that *Khaleef-graa* believes you didn't seem up to your usual self with the crowd today and hopes you'll get over your flight lag soon."

"Kliff," The Trooper said from the stage, "Stop forcing Diva to be lit-eral whenever she says what she knows you actually meant."

"So," I thought to myself, "he goes by Kliff. I wonder if that's like the old metal musician. He does have similar style, and they both play bass."

The Trooper, making his way down third, snorted and laughed. His skin was darker than it had looked in the light of the stage, except for the much lighter scars, and his one good eye was jovial as he slapped Khaleef-graa on the shoulder. He turned to me, his pale right eye, lazy looking and out of sync with his brown one, somehow locked on me first. The older warrior stopped a step up from me, maintaining the high ground, and studied me with furrowed brows.

Maybe it was the fact I wasn't a drunk groupie, maybe I was giving off an air of business, or maybe I have more of a tough guy vibe than I give myself credit for. Not that I couldn't handle myself in a fight, but, despite my height, I was more a dodger than a hard hitter.

"Can I help you?" he said as his other eye turned to me.

"Colonial Trooper, Regiment Thirteen, Number Eight?" I said solidly, not wanting to show him any fear.

He stood there looking at me, assessing me, contemplating what to answer. After all, he was a wanted man by more than a couple gangsters and by a very resentful System Lord, whose forces he had deserted.

"Hey, Eight," the bland human drummer in the red shirt said to him from above. "This guy giving you trouble?"

"So," I thought to myself, "he prefers to be referred to by Eight among his band. Got it."

Eight raised his hand in warning to the kid and then spoke to me. "Are we going to have some trouble here?"

I shook my head and held out my holo-badge that identified me as a private investigator. "Not a hunter and not interested in telling anyone where I found you Tr...um...Eight. Just looking for some information."

His eyes narrowed on me. He knew that I could sell out his location, no matter what he said. He'd done a few years as a bounty hunter himself, and not the legitimate type that took assignments from the System Lords. But I needed to find a missing girl, a Djugga groupie daughter of a well-paying client, that his band likely encountered, and I already knew that the two non-humans, runaways themselves, weren't likely going to talk to me about her. I needed him to trust me.

"Listen, Eight." I said, putting the badge away and ensured I continued using the name his band mate used. "What say I buy your band a round, pick up some of your merch, pay a few credits for some downloads, and we can talk?"

"Hey, I like those odds!" the kid in the red shirt punned, for that was the name of the band, The Odds. "Come on, Eight. We can't let down a paying fan, right?!"

Eight looked up to the drummer waiting to come down the stairs. "This was a try out for you, kid. You don't get a cut, so you don't get a say."

He looked back to me, "But he's right, the customer's always right. You get the time it takes to finish our drinks and then we'll see if I can help, or if you're trouble that I don't want."

By then Kliff, the Grothrark, sensing the tension, had menacingly made his way up beside Eight, his claws extending out from his fur a little. The Vixen had backed away, putting a table between her and the potential fight, her tendrils all seemingly "aware" of the situation.

"I'll make it two rounds of drinks then," I said. "This could take a bit."

"Oh goody," the operatic translator robot on Kliff's voice said on its own. "We're getting to the 'band getting drunk' stage of the night's entertainment. I suppose I better pay attention in case I have to remind everyone what happened tonight. What is your name, sir, for my records?"

I showed the badge again to its large photoreceptor, which my files had identified as the band's unofficial member, "Diva". An out of date holo displayed of me, from back when I had short hair and goatee. My credentials displayed above my image.

"My name is Einar Galbraith, P.I." I said, "Stolen Property Returned, Runaways Found, Dirt Dug Up, and Problems Solved."

A light from the bot's photoreceptor scanned over the holo and it declared my credentials legitimate.

The Odds led me to a large booth in the back while The Vixen waved over a scantily clad waitress wearing too little to call it an actual uniform. It became obvious that trying to deal with Eight meant I was dealing with the entire band.

"Tommy," Vi'xiri said with a silken voice that purred to the red shirted drummer. Her voice still resonated as if she were singing, a subtle frequency that somewhat changed the way the words felt rather than how they sounded. "Vould you do me ah favor an' go get my robe from ze dressing room vhile ve talk to zis detective?"

Well, maybe not the entire band.

The kid, clearly crushing on the Tilarian, hurried off with a smile and a "Sure thing, Vi!"

He wasn't more than a few tables away before she rolled her eyes and her tendrils shook with disgust. "Please tell me ve ah leaving 'im on this novhere planet?"

Kliff growled his assent and the droid accurately translated for him in a stereotypically robotic voice. "No shit. He sucks."

The Trooper finished placing his drink order and said with a chuckle, "Yep, number five down. Going to have to make a shirt with a six."

Vi'xiri leaned in across the table and raised her voice as the robot disc-jockey started playing some Pop Luna-Djugga to keep the now mingling and drinking crowd entertained. "Ve haven't had a regular drummer in over a year. Ve keep going through them."

Kliff laughed in a series of short mutted barks and said something. Diva spoke up for him. "Eight gives each drummer a numbered shirt and convinces them that since he goes by 'eight' that their shirt represents their 'number' in the band when we're done growing it to full size."

The Trooper shrugged. "But really, it's the number of drummers we've gone through. Only two more until the joke doesn't work anymore."

Kliff snorted and barked something and Trooper laughed, clearly getting the joke.

"Oh my, that's rude." Diva said.

"What'd he say?" I asked.

"He said that drummers aren't real musicians anyways." The Trooper said with a wicked grin, "A classic guitar joke. Makes bassists feel better about themselves."

Kliff grumbled something again and Diva replied, "Oh no. I'm not repeating that."

The Trooper laughed as the drinks arrived. He grabbed his from the tray while the rest were handed off by the waitress. Everyone raised their glass in a silent toast, and then after a quick swig, he set his glass down and looked to me.

"Ok, space dick," He drawled. "Your time starts now. What do you want?"

I pulled a small silver disk from my pocket and placed it on the table. A push of a couple touch sensitive controls and a clear glass emitter at it's center projected a hologram waiting symbol. I pressed some controls on my wrist computer and queued up an image of a human girl, maybe just in her early 20s in classic Central Systems ambassadorial white garb. Although the hologram was paler than reality, due to not projecting onto an actual surface and being slightly translucent, her medium-length black hair that would be curly if not done up for her station, and she had blue, maybe green eyes, and a particularly dark complexion. Being in her early 20s, she was barely legal to enter government service for a human – the concept of true adulthood shifting as humanity lived longer and longer, as it had throughout our history.

"This is Neridah Blooming-Star," I said. "She's the daughter of Ambassador Angus Blooming-Star from the Sol System and was interning as a Page to a parliamentarian from the central systems. She went missing two full cycles ago, right around the time the *Mouse Club* passed through her minister's constituency in the Charon Sector. She was a pretty big fan of Djugga and your band, I'm certain."

Eight looked at the girl. "I don't know her. Why are you talking to me instead of Mouse? It's his club."

I swiped through to an image of her personal files. "She had your tour schedule downloaded from the Black Net, since your Mouse doesn't officially venue anywhere...or pay his taxes. But, the reason I'm talking to *you* is because she had this image in her files."

Again I flicked a finger through the hologram and a new one swiped in of a full squad of Colonial Troopers appeared, all of them some genetic variation of to the other. I highlighted number Eight of Twelve of the squad.

"That one's you." I said, "I believe she came looking specifically for you, for some reason. I was hoping you could tell me why; or maybe her whereabouts."

Eight was stoic. So much so, I don't think that his companions even noticed the subtle, but profound, emotional shift his eyes made at the sight of his old squad. His pupils had dilated suddenly by more than half, a fight or flight response. His right index finger flexed slowly a few times, like a memory, as the rest of his hand curled casually into a pistol grip atop the table. But his breathing remained the same – controlled and careful.

"'ow do you know she is looking for Eight and not one of ze others?" Vi'xiri said, her Talerian accent fascinatingly not unlike a French pronunciation of GCT. "Other than he's the one in a Djugga band, I guess..."

The former Trooper pursed his lips. "Because I killed all the others."

"Pfft. And 'ow would she know that?" The Vixen leaned in, almost purring as she looked closer at the younger Eight. "'ou did not 'ave the scars zen. Sexy. But, I like you better now."

Eight let out a sigh, unfazed by the compliment, but clearly coming back to the moment. "She's a Page. That gives her access to diplomatic and government records. It'd be in my file."

The table got silent and his eyes looked more through the hologram than at it. "It was in the last year of the War. I was perhaps two years old at the time, speed grown and wetware trained, but already a veteran with a year of non-stop combat behind me. My unit was out front, hard and heavy, just days ahead of the arrival of *The Sacrarium* in what was supposed to be an easy victory against the last of the Nether. We were going to wipe them out and be done with it. Word from com-

THE ODDS JOB ‑ 15

mand was that we'd have it done within another week. Then everything...changed..."

I breathed in at the mention of *The Sacrarium*. It was the head of the Royal Armada, a Temple Ship carrying vast numbers of Holy Inquisitors and Purifiers armed with relics older than human civilization, but logistically supported by Pyqian advisers.

There are entire holovids dramatizing the invasion of Nether occupied space lead by the cathedral ship in concert with the fleets of the Five Sensuo Kingdoms. That was the battle the former Emperor sacrificed himself, with a handful of Shamans and Totem Masters that had survived that long, to help seal them in.

The Trooper was there for that – the greatest mobilization in galactic history.

He tossed back the rest of his drink, "Half your time is up, pal."

I'd been running around the Charon Sector accessing, sometimes infiltrating, records through the files of no less than three Parliamentary Systems along with the entire Galactic Expanse trying to nail down what was so special about this guy, and why a Page, even if she was just some Deep Voltch-Djugga fan girl, would go out of her way to seek him out in an illegal wandering club.

So - after some more digging into the illegal Mouse Club where they performed at, I learned that the ship that transported the club belonged to another defector from System Lord, Archimedes.

"I figured out she's heading to you," I said, "because you know former Lieutenant Nephiri Tora and you've been flying with her ever since you escaped your service to Archimedes."

"What does she have to do with this?" the droid translated monotone and lifeless for an otherwise defensive sounding Kliff, "She's a woman of honor."

I nodded. "People of honor are the types that would have left the service of Archimedes. But, she somehow ended up on a world of slavers and drug dealers, a hub in a galaxy of crime."

The Trooper downed most of his second drink, leaving only a sip and his ice -"And...?"

"And," I said to finish up, "when she, a diplomatic pilot, left, she escaped with her ambassador's ship. That ambassador was Neridah's uncle, a Totem Master who was killed during The Betrayal."

The Trooper paused just before drinking the last of his dark rum and set down his glass, his eyes distant. I can't imagine what details he was remembering. As a Colonial Trooper under Archimedes, he would have been there for The Betrayal, perhaps even participated in it.

Unlike all the other System Lords whose armies were selected from volunteers within the civilian population in exchange for the right to vote as citizens, Archimedes the Third had his grown. They weren't exact carbon copies of one another. Cloning was illegal in the Galactic Expanse and was right up there with slavery as a crime against Sentient Kind.

They were all created from the same parental genetic materials and grown in vats using accelerants to shorten the timeline of their biological maturity. Using Pyqian transorganic technology, they each had a lifetime of virtual reality experiences implanted to coincide with the pace of their rapid growth. There had easily been over a million soldiers, each and every one of them a brother to the other.

I heard that sometimes, a random mutation would occur and a female would be produced. No one I'd heard that from knew exactly what happened to them. Some say they weren't speed grown like the males and were just shipped off to orphanages. Others say he did grow them, keeping them for less savory purposes. I heard one conspiracy theory that after speed growing them, they were made to undergo Pyqian-like training and then secreted away.

The Betrayal was programmed into the Troopers during their virtual life, a simulation and brainwashing that, according to the tyrant's legality claims to the System Council, would still result in those perfectly human and non-slave beings having all the rights, choice, and free will of any other civilian of the Expanse, with the right to choose or deny service in the Colonial Troops. Regardless, every trooper chose to become good voting citizens through "Service to the System."

The other System Lords, on advice from their parliaments, and even the Hegemony they ruled their systems for, accepted this as truth from Lord Archimedes.

And, as far as I knew, every one of his Troopers participated in The Betrayal, a holocaust massacre of every Shaman and Totem Master of every species within Archimedes' Systems before he blew a hole in reality with the first, and hopefully last, Hyperspace Warp Bomb, an explosion that opened a hole between our galaxy and that of another one, releasing nearly unspeakable ancient horrors into "Real Space" from somewhere else, perhaps even Warp Space itself.

Somehow the extra-galactic, or maybe even extra-dimensional, monsters were part of the plan. The details are fuzzy, and largely classified, by the Hegemonic Imperium. Either way, they worked with him on his push for conquest.

The metaphysical nature of the creatures from that mysterious place we call "the Netherverse", along with their material existence as chaotic biological lifeforms, proved to be almost insurmountable for the combined armies of the Galactic Expanse to repel and hold off inside the rebel System Lord's domain before the rift between galaxies healed itself.

But, it became obvious during the following ten year war that The Betrayal was a deliberate act and that Archimedes had aligned himself with those extragalactic horrors in a push for power in the Galaxy. How he even knew of their existence is still a mystery.

Nearly all of Archimedes' troopers, over the course of the war, had consented to mutant conversion by the chaos beings of the Nether; a choice that the civilians of his Systems didn't have.

They fled his space, died trying to maintain their individual species' forms, or were mutated into half-being horrors. They became part whatever-they-used-to-be and part Nether; a physical transformation that the Shamans say began within their souls – if such things existed.

"Ok." The Trooper said, "What can I do to help?"

"I need to find Nephiri Tora." I said. "I'm hoping the reason you don't recognize her is she didn't need to find you. That maybe she found your ship's captain first. I figured she'd have parked your ship nearby – in which case I wouldn't have bothered you."

Eight nodded just as the drummer made his way back to the table with The Vixen's robe.

"We like to minimize association of the ship with the club." Eight said, "Too many people after each of us."

"Slavers for me." Vi'xeri took the robe. "And for Kliff. Xanadu pirates, mostly. Zey used him in ze fighting pits. They used me...as a...performer."

She paused for a moment, a shudder before that final word.

"And, of course," she continued, "Archimedes for Eight's treason on him, and the entire Expanse after him for Archimedes' Betrayal."

"And your Captain went AWOL after the Betrayal too." I had read her data sheet as well. "The War got too much of her I guess?"

"Grawel-grrr." Kliff responded with a repeat by Diva. "We escaped with the honorable captain's help. Whereas her time in the War –"

"Ask her yourself." Eight interrupted, "It's no one's place to tell others' war stories. After our next set, we'll take you to the ship. But for now, jam out to some Deep Voltch-Djugga; as smooth as a baby's bottom with the kick of a fifth of vodka."

He winked and I laughed. Wasn't exactly my speed, but I liked the charisma of it.

I dropped five credit chits on the table for the downloads of their latest album and ordered another round to pass the time until they performed again.

II

CHAPTER TWO

Load Playlist Track: Jim Carroll, People Who Died

The bright half orb of an orange gas giant ate up a third of the sky as the night side of the inhabitable moon, Arcturis Minor, faced the planet's meridian. White and orange ribbons stretched along its gaseous atmosphere until it met at a brownish orange super storm. Amidst the top of the storm, the largely automated gas-mining space station cast its disc-like shadow upon it.

The size of the old Manhattan Island on Earth, the Arcturis Corporation's mining platform siphoned and filtered out the exotic illudium gas needed to power Hyperspace Warp Engines and Capital Scale starship blasters for three nearby System Lords, their Parliamentary Navies, and the fleets of the Five Sensuo Kingdoms that served under the Hegemony of the Expanse. That made this galactic-rim star-system strategically valuable. Although unseen in the night sky, there were likely naval vessels in close proximity.

The Odds had left Red-Shirt Number Five back at the Mouse Club to secure the band's equipment for the night. In a loose formation, over the open plains and low hills of the agricultural moon, they cruised at a decent clip on their repulsor bikes. It took some effort for me to keep up in my twenty-year-old Micro-Pod.

Micro-Pods weren't built for speed, or comfort, or anything but a cheap price, and they'd fallen out of fashion nearly a decade ago. But, they were remarkably easy to maintain, and cost almost nothing if you could get ahold of parts at some junk dealership. More important than that, the little scratched-up, egg-shaped repulsor carriage was also capable of a full vacuum seal. That made the faded white vehicle a rarity for most repulsor vehicles, regardless of age.

That means, with some very limited modifications, it could also act as a local space transport; assuming you could get it into space.

It would never take off from a planet's surface. Hell, I doubt I could milk thirty meters off the ground on a standard one-gravity world like this. But, I could use it to get between space ships or even nurse it around within a star system if I were willing to take close to a month to get from point to point. Not that it had that kind of oxygen reserves. The best I could hope for was maybe enough oxygen to get to Sol Prime's lunar colony from Earth if I got dropped just far enough outside the planet's atmosphere to not get stuck in its gravity well.

Still, it was useful for clandestine transport off the books inside a star system. That, and its relatively durable hull had saved me on a case more than once.

The problem with private detecting is that you tend to piss people off, regularly, and there is no more a dangerous place to do that than in space; which is what most of the Galaxy is made of.

The Odds, after a handful of kilometers, made their way into a gulch that looked like it was only awash once or twice a year. There, in between what would occasionally be high-rising river walls, was parked an old *Wayward Class* medium transport. It was a flying brick of a ship with an engine system jutting out twice as wide as the ship itself.

Where the extra engine section stuck out was a clamp-system designed to lock onto the back end of a cargo pod. Effectively, *Wayward* transport pilots were interplanetary space truckers; moving a medium amount of cargo, maybe the equivalent of two or three, five-bedroom houses, from star system to star system.

Usually, they were used by shipping companies for food or building supplies.

My investigations so far had taught me that, prior to The Betrayal, the very frugal and somewhat strange Ambassador Blooming-Star's brother, Conner, also an ambassador at the time, had converted a cargo pod into a mobile constituency. He literally lived in the thing and kept his offices there.

It was genius really. Instead of expecting his voters to come to him for a personal audience on whichever world in his jurisdiction, he would travel from planet to planet and inhabitable moon to moon on a schedule, giving everyone a chance for a Town Hall.

Also, as a Totem Master, allegedly capable of summoning the Spirits, he could bring guidance to the entire System as a wise man. I'd heard stories of the supernatural things they were capable of, even seen some strange things that I couldn't explain at the hands of lesser Shaman, but I don't really buy all the scientific data about the spiritual energies of the living and their interaction with the material world; something to do with quantum entanglement and observation-based reality shifting.

But, over half the Galaxy's sentient species believed in some sort of afterlife and supernatural power, with half of that believing in the Shamans' and the Totem Masters' powers. So, bullshit or not, they mattered to how things worked in the Galaxy and to any day-to-day interactions as a detective.

The Legacy's Façade, the current name of the ship, still had the red ambassadorial striping on it along its more rigid edges. The painted lines were faded, dull, and partially scratched off; not just from a lack of maintenance, but also a half-hearted effort to remove them.

The bridge lights were on and the boarding ramp was down with white light spilling out into the dark chasm of the little valley where the ship was parked in.

I'd spent the drive out to it listening to some of the downloaded music of *The Odds's* latest album, which, roughly translated, was titled *Dank Turf Growing*. The song at the moment told an organic tale of a seed growing from under the pressure of waste to burst out and replace the woods above. The metaphors were pretty typical of Kliff's arboreal species, which had evolved from some sloth-like sapient species in a star system not far off from Sol.

The trio parked their bikes outside the ramp and dismounted as I pulled up and powered down.

Now that I was outside The Mouse Club, which had a weapons scanner at the door, I slipped my little Holdout blaster into my right boot holster under my pants leg. Holdout was an Earth Corporation and made really low profile blasters at the cost of both impact and firing charges. The thing I liked about Holdouts was that they afforded you some portable protection without giving off a begging-for-a-fight vibe.

Now, I prefer classic weapons too. Back on Earth I kept an old, slug-throwing, six-shot revolver. That bad boy couldn't do the kind of damage to ablative armor that a blaster could, but it also wouldn't be stopped by a high-powered energy shield like a blaster would. However, a classic old-world slug-thrower makes considerably more noise than a blaster, which isn't necessarily quiet itself.

I don't want to invite a fight, and I don't want to draw too much attention when one happens, typically.

Too many species in the galaxy were looking for a fight if you were asking for one. "Subtle" is better than not.

As we approached the ramp, a shadow cast down on us from above like some ominous gatekeeper. After a second, my eyes adjusted and I saw that the large person at the top of the ramp was really a short, stubby, humanoid robot with a white, almost plastic-looking shell, and a pair of red illuminated eyes.

"Halt!" it boomed in a menacingly deep voice, holding a rod forward in its hand like a gun, "Who goes there?!"

"Jesus 'uman Christ," Vi'xiri said on the way up the ramp with her alien accent. "Are your photoreceptors broken? You know who ze hell ve are, Tree."

I was giggling to myself at her alien take on a human expletive and then looked over to Eight. "Tree?"

"It's how the little shit pronounces Three." He shrugged following The Vixen, "RT-3, this guy is with us. Let him pass."

The little white robot looked me up and down, made some sort of scoffing sound and asked, "What did you do, get the other drummer killed already? It's only been two nights. That's a record."

I looked over at Kliff with wide eyes. He just shrugged and rolled his big black eyes as if embarrassed.

"What the hell do you people do to go through drummers so fast?" I asked while following him up.

He growled some incoherent response followed by a barking sound that was definitely a laugh.

"Music is just our cover," The Diva responded for him poshly, something I started to get the feeling only happened when the translations weren't exact. "But, despite his jest, they *are* better at smuggling than Djugga....considerably."

The Grothrark pulled the droid off his neck and tossed it to the floor. The ring that had been wrapped around his throat opened up into a set of eight spider-like legs and started clicking along the metal hull into the ship past the diminutive robot.

"Hi," I said to the little bot. "I'm Einar."

"Hello number six!" He barked at me like a drill sergeant, "I will show you to your quarters and have your band shirt manufactured!"

"He iz not in ze band, Tree!" yelled back Vi'xiri as she made her way into the next room of the ship.

"Ooooh!" The little robot's voice suddenly shifted to one similar to a polite British butler. "A guest. I'm sooo sorry, sir. Welcome aboard the *Legacy's Façade*. Please follow me and I'll introduce you to our captain."

"Finally, some progress." I said to myself.

I followed the little robot down a short hall that quickly opened up to the galley of the ship, where the crew were quickly moving to familiar lounging positions and passing around bottles of booze.

Tree turned with a strange little march, like that of a parade leader, moving his faux-gun baton up and down in rhythm with his steps. I continued to follow him down a longer thin hallway, past closed doors to what were obviously crew quarters, until we reached a metal stair-case that lead to another bulkhead door that could only have led to the bridge area of the ship.

It took the little droid some effort to climb up each step. He looked like a toddler holding the railing and having to get each foot onto a step before making the effort for the subsequent step. It's bland, white, bald robotic head bobbed and paused, bobbed and paused, bobbed and paused.

Finally, only five steps up, we made our way to the door and he tapped it with his rod.

"Excuse me, Captain." He announced with sickeningly sweet over-tures. "We have a guest of the crew on board. I am following protocol and introducing you so you can decide if he should remain onboard be-fore I eject him into the darkness of this moon's creature-filled night."

I looked down and frowned at the droid's obvious glee at threaten-ing me.

The door slid open and a middle-aged human woman poked her head out of the cabin. She was of Asian descent, but observably not pure blooded. Something in her cheekbones and nose indicated she had some Middle-Eastern in her.

"But, honestly," I thought to myself, "Who really was of a pure racial bloodline anymore? I may be predominantly Scottish by way of Iceland, but even I have some African and Ukrainian in me."

Her hair was jet black and, despite the records aging her a decade older than me, she looked like she could easily pass as slightly younger. Her eyes were impossibly jade and could only have been augmented.

"I'll have to look into that, if I remember." I told myself. "Are they only a cosmetic enhancement or do they come with some special tricks to them?"

She wore a cropped orange flight jacket with small, blaster armor-plates on the shoulders and elbows. Her fingerless gloves were black with matching orange accents. Underneath she had a white uniform shirt of some sort and a pair of black, formfitting pants that were high on the waist with a single white stripe down each seam. On her knees were another pair of blaster armor-shells. Across her hip was a gun belt with a blast pistol I had yet to identify.

Not subtle at all. Maybe that's why she was on the ship instead of out in public.

"Vi' told me you were coming," She said. "And Eight gave me some of the background on what's up. Can I see the holo of the girl?"

With some formality I extended my hand. "It's nice to meet you, Captain Tora."

She eyeballed my gesture for a moment, the looked me in the eyes as if evaluating me, and then took a deep breath in before hesitantly shaking it.

"Ok. Here she is." I reached into my pocket and pulled out the holo emitter and projected Neridah Blooming-Star's image. I would have just shown her with my watch, but the small silver disk projected larger and clearer resolution images.

"She looks like him a little." She replied.

"Her father?" I asked.

Tora nodded. "Yeah...but not the man she thinks is her father. The man she's probably looking for; the man she thinks is her Uncle."

That took me back a bit. Her father, who hired me, didn't mention anything about the girl actually being his niece. That was important information and would have saved me some of my guesswork before meeting the Odds.

"So, you've seen her?" I asked.

"Not yet." Captain Tora answered. "Though I knew this day would come. I'd only met her once, when she would have been too young to remember me. Back just after..."

She paused and shuddered.

"The Betrayal?" I finished the sentence for her.

"Yes." The Captain answered. "Neridah was little more than a baby and her mother had died in childbirth. I went to her biological uncle's estate to deliver the news about her father to his brother and wife. They'd been watching over her while we were on a mission."

"Shit." I thought to myself. This girl was the daughter of a Totem Master. The gifts they supposedly had were genetic. And this girl had grown up her whole life never having been taught about them, or knowing that she was the daughter of one.

"What do you think would have clued her into the truth?" I said, assuming the girl likely found out and that's what set her off looking for more information.

"Honestly?" Captain Tora raised her eyebrows and looked at me like I was about to find her really crazy.

"Um...sure..." I braced myself.

"Her father probably did." She said, as if it was some big secret.

"Her father could have told me that before sending me off looking for her." I said annoyed.

"No. Not him." She waited for me to realize what she was implying.

Her real father? A ghost showed up and told her about himself?

"Bullshit." I answered my own question, and the one that was on her face, out loud.

She shrugged her shoulders with her arms out and palms up, "He was a pretty powerful Totem Master and Shaman. I bet he could. I'd heard others had that level of power in the old days."

"Superstition and bullshit." I said "You have anything more?"

She started walking back to the galley and waved The Trooper to follow us to the exit of the ship. The little droid followed behind trying to be menacing, patting the baton in his open hand. I eyed him like a potentially ravenous Chihuahua.

"However she knew," Captain Tora said as we walked to the ramp. "Neridah would have started off looking into what happened to him probably by starting with looking for me. I'm betting she found out Eight and his band were traveling on an old Ambassadorial ship. It wouldn't take much research to find out mine was missing during the war. There was no record of where her father was murdered. Just that he was on assignment with me when it happened."

"How would she know he was traveling on an old ambassadorial ship?" I said.

"Well," she responded, "If she's actually a Djugga fan and knows much about the band's underground scene, it wouldn't take much to nail down how they're getting around."

I nodded, "That makes sense. It's part of how I found you as well. So, she either would have come after you looking for revenge or just...ah, I see."

She would have backtracked *The Legacy Façade's* steps since the war to figure out where her father was killed and go from there.

"Where do I go?" I said. "Since she's having to work backward, I can maybe get there ahead of her and be waiting."

"I wouldn't go all the way back there if I were you." She warned. "It'll likely get you killed. Her too."

Aw shit, the entire Betrayal took place inside what is now effectively Netherspace. It was Mutant territory at best, straight up Nether creatures everywhere otherwise.

"Ok, where in the Netherspace do I have to go?" I said.

The Trooper took my wrist and turned on my computer. He plugged in some Black Net data and brought up a set of coordinates in the middle of nowhere.

"Xanadu." He answered. "Good luck."

III

❦

CHAPTER THREE

Load Playlist Track: Ramones, Beat On The Brat

Less than an hour later, I sat in my motel room near the spaceport waiting for my flight back to Earth, which was about as close as I could get to Xanadu's location without either a ship of my own or a charter.

Xanadu appeared to be in a location that all official star charts deemed empty; a place no one would bother looking or travelling to on their own. It was the perfect place to park the heart of a criminal enterprise. It was also dangerously occupied. Mutants were people who had been partially converted by the Nether, but somehow managed to retain their individuality and spirit. Expanse scientists and shamans believe the ability to retain themselves is proof that some Nether-mutated peoples loyal to Archimedes could be reverted back to their previous selves.

That's better than the other type of Nether creatures resulting from the corruption by the alien monstrosities: Netherspawn weren't just some mutated or corrupted natural being, they were the offspring of a Nether creature with any other sentient race. The elements of a species responsible for producing and carrying offspring were kept by the

Nether forces, even when they couldn't be corrupted into mutants or become fully turned servants of the Nether.

The Nether can breed with any biological being. The genetic code of an offspring overwrites the ordered DNA provided by the parents' species into the chaotic nightmare forms of the Nether. The parent is then forced to survive until the offspring is born on this side of the closed rift to bolster their numbers.

The various crime organizations and pirates that operate at Xanadu consist of the mutants that had resisted being overtaken by the Nether. But, in a galaxy biased against all things Nether after the war, these people were forced underground for their own safety. Now, they've become a different threat than the one assigned to them by bigotry. They had become the scourge of the outer systems of the Expanse.

In a few hours, not even enough time to justify sleeping, a bulk freighter carrying illudium to the Terran shipyards would be leaving. I had to be on that ship if I wanted to make it back sooner than a few months from now.

The Arcturis System, like Earth, was a rim system out on the edges of the Galaxy. Its name, in fact, was after one of the moon's of the Sol System's planet Jupiter. However, most of the ships traveling to and from the mining system went coreward, delivering the hyperspace and weapons fuel toward the centers of the Expanse, stopping at each System Lord's holding between the two points.

But, much more rarely, a shipment made its way along the Rim to the poorer worlds. Worlds like mine – Earth and the rest of Sol Prime, capital of the Benighted Final Spiral Arm of the Expanse.

Less than a thousand galactic cycles ago, my species, like all successful species, figured out how to spread out from their home world. They discovered Hyperspace and the ability to warp space.

Warping space is done with what we humans call the Alcubierre Equation. I don't know the math of it, don't ask. But, the idea of it was that you could achieve speeds faster than light by bending space around a vessel. This somehow prevented issues with relativity, allowing the passengers in the vessel to exist at the normal rate of the universe.

I really don't follow that stuff. Nowadays, we just replace a module in a ship. I just know it works and we'd figured it out some time before Earth had a world government and before it was assigned a System Lord by the Expanse.

But, faster than light travel simply isn't good enough for pragmatic travel throughout the galaxy – it's too slow. Sure, you can speed up a vessel to reach another nearby star system within your lifetime. You might even get back in the same lifetime.

I was about to travel about 10,000 light years back to Earth. Though both locations are in the Orion Arm of the Galaxy, which isn't the almost insulting name that the Hegemonic Imperium calls it, that's the equivalent of almost a quarter around the edge of the Galaxy. That kind of distance needed Hyperspace travel.

Hyperspace is another dimension of existence. It's been around and known for longer than the Galactic Expanse; which has been around for almost as long as humans have been identifiable as humans. I don't think even the Expanse has records on who came up with it.

But, the idea is that a Hyperspace Drive Engine, or HDE, pulls a ship into an entire parallel dimension of the larger more quantum universe. Theoretically, there are an infinite number of universes; many of them alternatives to our own where different choices were made. No one has figured out how to cross between those yet as far as I know. But, in between each universe is a buffer zone to keep them separate; a dimension that acts as a barrier of sorts, like the way a light radiation barrier exists around a planet, or a buffer of matter and energy sits around an entire star system; a film between states of existence.

That's what Hyperspace is. There, the rules of distance and speed don't work the same. You can travel faster without difficulty, and when paired with space warping, it gets even easier. When you're warping hyperspace though, you effectively create another dimension of sorts. That pocket dimension around a ship in hyperspace is simply called "The Warp."

When Archimedes the Third set off his Hyperspace Warp Bomb, he warped an entire rebellious world...somewhere else. And in its place was a scar in the universe, a doorway between our Galaxy and what we call the Nether; where creatures of the same name came through, leading to the First Galactic War.

I finished packing my clothes into my duffle bag and carried them out to The Snowball

The captain of the freighter had agreed to let me store her in their maintenance bay. She was going to be my bed for the next few days.

The small egg-shaped craft was a two-seater with just enough stowage room in a compartment in the rear for my duffle bag, a backpack, and some basic gear. It was a very reliable repulsor vehicle, despite its age. At the front and rear of the base of the body were the grey steel repulsor engines. The white paint was scratched up in spots and faded from too much direct sunlight in the vacuum of space during one my jobs.

Despite the faded paint, the roundish shape and color prompted me to give it the Icelandic name "Snjóbolti." But, as my partner and I speak to one another almost exclusively in GCT, she refers to it in what translates to "THE Snowball." After a while, despite the small black cursive sticker with her proper name on it, I started calling her THE Snowball as well. Both Velma and I are protective of it; me because I own it and Velma because I usually stick her with having to get it repaired.

I had just finished stowing the bag into the small compartment when I heard footsteps in the gravel parking lot. It was the kind of movement that set off your instincts of danger. The sound was made up of those soft, slow movements of someone on the balls of their feet trying, and failing, to be quiet.

I saw the movement in the reflection of the rear window just in time to duck.

Whatever they were swinging hit the window right about where my head would have been and smashed it. Considering The Snowball could survive minor hits from space debris, whatever it was would have exploded my head like a blood sausage.

From the ground, where I'd thrown myself, I was faced with my attacker's large stubby and booted legs. The street lights were behind him and cast the rest of his mass in shadow. But, I could tell, the rest of his body was proportional to the large legs.

He arched his body upward, holding whatever he was about to swing above his head. I finally got a look at his full figure. He had four arms and was blue. The bouncer, I thought, from The Mouse Club.

I rolled my way under the mini-pod as a large metal club crunched into the gravel where I'd been prone. The Snowball lifted a little, shifting against my mass – which left a tingling feeling on my body from the repulsor field. I'd never really taken the time to learn how those worked and despite the danger, I found myself briefly reminding myself to learn since I'm once again putting my ride in danger.

The club was shaped similar to a baseball bat, if that baseball bat was twice as long and got wider and wider until it was six inches across at the tip. Also, it was studded along its five flattened sides. The air hummed around the club's half-spheres.

It was a repulsor-club, designed to use the same energy used by a hover bike or my mini-pod to move against the planet's mass to stay off the ground. But in such a club, it was designed to move force against your mass.

I had a feeling that wouldn't cause just a tingle on the surface of my skin.

Along with the mass and acceleration of the club, that meant...
BANG!!!!

He'd slammed the club against the side of The Snowball and knocked it a few feet off the ground and to the side, leaving me exposed.

"Holy shit!" I yelled in shock, "Sonofabitch! That's my ride, man!"

I rolled out of the way again as The Mouse Club's bouncer, again, brought the repulsor-club down into the gravel where I'd been splayed. The rocks went out in every direction, some of them pelting me with enough force that I could expect a spray of bruises up my body on the back side.

The four-armed assailant cursed in his native Delosian, his blue lips in a sneer and his yellow eyes rolling back in annoyance, "Settle down, ape. I promise if you give up I'll end it quick."

"Fuck that!" I said scuttling back and spreading my legs where the club went into the ground once more. I winced as another spray of rocks stung from my ankles to my groin. I wasn't getting out of this without fighting back.

With all the haste I could muster I jumped up, simultaneously dodging back to miss his swipe at my midsection.

I slipped off my trench coat and held it in my hands in front of me. The cool air of Arcturis' night washed over my sleeveless arms and into the open parts of my hooded sweatshirt.

I kept the jacket out, ready to catch the next swing of the club. Based on the amusement in his face, the Delosian wasn't impressed.

He swung at my midsection again.

I jumped backward, but rather than try and wrap my jacket around the club, like I'd feinted, I tossed the jacket over my attacker's face.

In the brief moments between his surprise and pulling the jacket out of his vision, I managed to drop to one knee and snatched up the hold-out blaster from my ankle.

The annoyance at my trick turned to one of surprise when he took three shots from close range to the center of his chest.

Delosians are like many of the sapien-type species in the area of the galaxy Earth was from. Evolution tended to follow patterns; maybe it was panspermia, the theory that materials from one world could find their way to influence creation on others. Maybe it was because some ancient race traveled around making things in their image. Whatever it was, it put the Delosian heart and lungs in just about the same general location as my own.

He dropped like a very heavy rock and the repulsor technology in his club bounced it once, then twice away from his body before settling down.

I stood up and looked at the blue four-armed hulk of a creature. He'd been sent to kill me.

I looked over to my pummeled mini-pod, "Damnit. Velma's going to be pissed. Clearly, Mouse doesn't want me continuing my investigation. But, why?"

It was time to go ask him that in person.

IV

CHAPTER FOUR

Load Playlist Track: Misfits, Some Kinda Hate

The blaster shots were likely to attract some unwanted attention from the locals. A small moon like this, with such a low population, wasn't likely to have much in the way of legitimate law enforcement. The other inhabitable moon for this planet ...? Maybe. But not Arcturis Minor.

Still, I didn't need any trouble with someone coming out and finding a body, and I sure as heck didn't need whatever passed for law enforcement here making my life more difficult than it just became.

After a quick visual scan of the area, I concluded that the motel didn't bother with security cameras on this part of the establishment. So, I pulled out a pair of handcuffs and latched him by two of his wrists around the back bumper of The Snowball and hopped in.

The Snowball struggled with the dense alien, but several hundred feet later, if he hadn't already been dead, he would have been. The now gravel strewn asshole likely had the ligaments in two of his arms pulled apart.

From a forensics scan kit, I performed a crime scene analysis on the body to locate any fingerprints or DNA I needed to clean. I then rolled his body downhill and tossed his club down a dip into nearby brambles. By the time he was found, *if ever*, I'd have my issues with Mouse sorted out.

"I won't be able to charge the kit to the client." I grumbled to myself. I was in a bad mood now. I hated when a job lead to violence or killing people. "I'm not a damned bounty hunter."

But the bills have been tight and I'm not sure which worried me more, the loss of cost of the scan kit's resources or the fact I just had to kill this mook.

I looked at the dents in my mini-pod and the busted rear window and frowned.

The Snowball could be fixed, but there's a principle of the thing. Even though I could, and would, charge my client for the price of the repairs...someone else was going to pay for damaging my ride. At the very least, I was going to get some answers as to why Mouse had put a hit on me. Maybe I'm a little petty, but what's mine is mine and, along with the danger to my life, I don't tolerate threats to myself, my people, or my property.

"Like sharks in the water." I muttered to myself. They say creatures on Earth called sharks used to home in on blood in the water. If I let one tough guy rough me up and get away with it, me whimpering home with my tail between my legs, soon I'd be watching over my shoulder at every two bit thug who thinks they can just scare off a P.I. with a show of muscle. I recalled what my father told me when I was young.

"When a bully shows up," he said, "you punch him in the nose and teach him a lesson. You might get your ass handed to you, but he'll think twice before starting something again."

A kilometer farther away, so I wouldn't be happened upon by accident with a potential body nearby, I tuned the Snowball's transceiver into the local subnet and contacted the *Legacy's Façade*. No matter where they were on the planet, as long as their ship's comms were online, they would detect a message coming out to them. If they weren't on planet anymore, which I knew they were, it wouldn't do me any good. I'd have to send them a ping on the HyperNet, and communications back and forth would depend on how far away in the galaxy they were.

"What do you want human?" boomed Tree, "The Odds require adequate rest to perform their nightly routine. They are scheduled for another two point three three...repeating...hours of rest."

"I need to talk to Captain Tora." I answered calmly to the screen on my wrist.

"The Captain is sleeping." Tree boomed again, "You are advised to contact her during daylight hours."

I swiped my free hand over the display on my wrist computer and made a throwing motion at my front window of Snowball. The image appeared there, much larger, and bringing Tree almost to true scale in size.

"Listen you white midget robot," I leaned into the image, in case I was full scale on that end as well,, "I just had a Delosian bouncer from the Mouse Club try and crack my head in, so I'm in a shit mood. You get her on the comms right now or I'm going to assume she had something to do with it and suddenly her location, and that of her outlaw friends, might find its way to the HyperNet. You won't have to worry about me dismantling your pasty plastic frame, because someone else will get around to it.'"

The little robot stepped backward with a an audible, and biologically unnecessary, gasp.

"Talk about life-realistic programming." I thought to myself, "That or he'd gone so long without experiential formatting that he's actually starting to display rudimentary sentience."

"I will get her right away, sir." He humbled his tone to the polite nature he displayed to Captain Tora.

A few minutes later a very disgruntled Captain Tora appeared, her hair was up in a towel and some form of green substance covered her face. She was also wrapped in a towel.

"What the fuck do you want Galwraith?" She glowered at me, "And what the fuck are you threatening us with going to the law for?"

"It's Galbraith." I clarified, "And your boss just tried to have me killed. So, I'd like to know why."

"My what?" she blinked, both eyes confused. "Who are you....*Mouse*? You mean that fat Delosian?"

"Yes." I replied, "He tried to have me..."

"He's not my boss, asshole." She pointed a finger at the screen while gripping her towel up with the other in a way that made her barely covered breasts rather distracting, "He's my fare."

"Your fare?" I tried to keep my eyes on hers, "You...so, he's not the ring leader of your operation?"

"Ha!" She laughed, adjusting the towel again, "I fly his stupid club around and he does whatever he wants when we get there. The band plays there for a few extra credits each planet, but they ride with me, not him. We find....side jobs...wherever he's raking in his unregistered, and untaxed, money. I don't ask about his side business – he doesn't ask about mine."

"You know why his bouncer would have come for me then?" I said, "What does he have to do with the missing girl?"

"Mouse doesn't have anything to do with anything that doesn't make Mouse profit." She answered, "The club's still in the same place. I'm not scheduled to pick him up for another six hours while they pack the place up."

"Any idea what profit he would have in offing me?" I followed up, "Or do I need to go ask him myself?"

"If the girl was actually looking for me or Eight after all," she amused, "then maybe she actually found us, but never got to our location. I can't think of any reason Mouse would know who she was or to consider interfering. Maybe you just pissed him off?"

"*I've never met him.*" I answered.

"Ok," she sighed, "fine. We'll find out together. But, if it isn't related to my business, you deal with him on your own."

"When can you make it out there?" I started bringing up a timer on the chronometer for my wrist computer. The display showed up on the window, as well as my wrist device.

"Give me thirty minutes to sort myself out and wake up the Odds." She answered, "Then, I'll just show up early for a pick up. Won't take me more than fifteen minutes to get out to him at that point."

"But," she added, "If he has legit beef with you, like I said, I'm not on your side. I'm only coming in case it has something to do with Conner's missing kid. I'm not getting involved in anything else. But Lin, well, I owe him enough to look into it."

Her face softened and her eyes went distant when she mentioned Ambassador and Totem Master Conner Blooming-Star, her former superior, by his nickname. They were clearly more than just coworkers. They were perhaps even more than just friends.

I broke the silence, "Just in case he's got anything else planned for me, I'm coming dressed up for the club. If it doesn't have anything to do with you, I hope you won't take offense if I interfere with your fare."

"Normally I would." She looked at me deadpan, "but you're looking for his kid and Mouse is a shit, even if he is a useful one. So, I'll make that call if it goes down that way."

She clicked off the comms on their subnet and I was left in the dim lighting of my wrist computer and the Snowball's displays.

Forty-five minutes until I was going to deal with the minor gangster who just tried to have me assassinated by repulsorclub. I ran the numbers on the distance over my land-nav computer and determined it was just less than a thirty-minute drive to The Mouse Club's location.

I got out and opened my slightly dented trunk. I moved my duffle bag out onto the ground and then lifted the cheap felt-covered floor panel that hid my more important gear.

Above, in the heavens, we'd slipped around to the dark side of the planet, which blotted out even the stars. I could see my breath in the rear lights of the mini-pod, which also illuminated the bush-filled field I'd parked in, away from the gravel roads that automated farming bots and potential pedestrians used to get between Arcturis Minor's many fields.

This smaller moon was the poorer moon. It was less populated and ignored. Perfect for the likes of Mouse to set up his roving club.

Those with the credits to pay for an illicit night out on another moon could get to The Mouse Club easy enough. Those looking to do business outside the eye of the local law could do the same. Locals from Arcturis Minor could find some temporary side money working the club, which only had The Mouse, his bouncer, and his robotic bartender as permanent employees.

Even local bands, when the Odds weren't playing, managed to get a venue out of it to be seen by the less rural types that visited the club. It provided an almost-hope to getting the hell out of a backwater nowhere.

A backwater nowhere that wasn't going to have much get in the way of me and Mouse for anything he might know about Neridah Blooming-Star's disappearance...not to mention answers about the attempt on my life and the damages to my ride.

Ten minutes later, I had my refractive plate vest under my hoodie, a pair of remote-detonated flash bombs set on Snowball's front seat, and my gun belt, my HUD goggles, and my bright red business fedora on.

The fedora was a restored antique from my great grandfather. Already a century out of style when he was wearing them, he believed that style never died.

And one thing this hat said was "style."

I slipped my HUD-linked heavy blaster into the holster of my gun belt.

One thing the gun, the flash bombs, and the hat definitely weren't going to say was "subtle."

"Fuck subtle." I muttered to my reflection before shutting Snowball's trunk and getting into the cab to zoom away into Arcturis Minor's increasingly cool night.

V

CHAPTER FIVE

Load Playlist Track: The Clash, Death or Glory

About a quarter mile out from the Mouse Club's location on the edge of a forest across the large planes, I skimmed by the small Artcuris Minor Starport and its little motel, I cut the running lights and slowed down so as not to hit any of the occasional rocks or deforested stumps I saw en route my first trip.

I could have jacked the repulsors up and hovered above them all, like I did the evening before, but the higher you go, the louder the repulsors.

I had said fuck it to subtle. I didn't say fuck it to surviving.

Since the Mouse Club was a space cargo pod, it wasn't graced with windows or view ports. I approached it in the silent black of the night from the side opposite the air lock that doubled as the club's entrance.

In the dark, the neon words "Mouse Club" were visible the entire way; neon blue Galactic Common Tongue alphabet and bright neon red in Earth English, which was common along the Rim of the Galaxy.

The Legacy's Façade, the Odds, and Captain Tora were nowhere in sight. Did she decide not to come and get involved after all? Did she warn them?

"Trap?" I muttered to myself as the distance slowly and quietly closed between my mini-pod and the brownish-tan cargo unit.

I steered myself around a particularly large rock sticking out the ground and caught a glimpse of the bartender robot standing just around the edge at the front of the pod in the glow of the lights. It was armed with some sort of rifle-sized object.

I stopped Snowball and flicked on my Head-Up-Display goggles. I switched it to low-light and got a better glimpse of the droid. It was about my height and about as thin. It was painted up like an old-earth butler. It was definitely holding a blaster rifle of some sort, maybe a rapid-fire model.

With the low-light I could make out the dim green light beam projecting from the front of its conical head which illuminated the grass and terrain at a forty-five degree angle ahead of the robot. To my luck, it was in exactly the opposite direction of the mini pod and myself.

Low-light mode also allowed me to make out the spot lights that were disabled on the corners of the club's exterior. They were probably motion sensitive and would trip off if I got any closer.

If I moved in, I would have to move in quick.

I looked up into the night sky, the gas giant's black shadow still above blocking out the starlight. No sign of the *Legacy's Façade*.

The chronometer read that the relative position of Jupiter, the Sun, and Arcturis Minor would soon cause something akin to a long, drawn out dawn. I couldn't stay hidden for more than a few more minutes; and not at all if that droid made any move towards my direction.

"Well," I switched off the low-light setting in prep for the flood lights, "trap or not...here I come."

I cued up some classical earth music on The Snowball's sound system.

I put my hand on the throttle and swiveled the mini-pod toward the droid with the foot controls and repeated the night's mantra.

"Fuck subtle."

I hummed the lyrics to myself as Joan Jett belted out of the speakers about her reputation with energetic drums and guitars as I drove the throttle forward.

Two meters and about sixty kilometers per hour later, the floods blasted on and my eyes lost sight of pretty much everything while they adapted.

My heart pumped with the beat of the music.

The droid managed to turn and raise the blaster rifle at me just in time. I heard, more than saw, the *thwap thwap thwap* of energized plasma slap against Snowball's front end. The shots drowned out the sound of the next line of the song.

The shots were immediately followed by a heavy thud as the droid rolled over the mini pod's front windshield and into the air behind me. By now I wasn't really listening to the lyrics as much as feeling the vibe of Joan Jett and the Blackhearts, an old-earth, classical punk band that recently got a Nouveau Matrian-Djugga remix in the *holonovelas* coming from Olympus Mons on Mars, the center of human cinema.

My speed had been at one hundred kilometers per hour, about sixty miles per hour, when I connected with the droid. While it was still airborne, I slowed down as quick as I could and spun the right side of the pod toward the air lock of the Mouse Club and tossed the remote flash bombs out the window.

I kept going for a few more meters before slamming the throttle into reverse enough to end my momentum, then as I jumped out, I flicked a switch on the blaster in my holster.

Out and ready, with the mini-pod between me and the airlock, the HUD goggles linked up with the heavy blaster. An aiming reticle appeared in the center of my vision and then moved in conjunction with the barrel of the gun.

The droid, clearly having an issue with its left arm and the servos in its right leg, clambered up and began to bring its rifle to bear.

"Oh, no you don't." I growled as the reticle made its way over the robot in command from my heavy blaster.

As a reddish outline appeared around the droid, I pulled the trigger once, then again, and one third time. Although the shots came out slower than the droid's rapid-fire rifle had managed, each consecutive shot rocked it back nearly a foot.

The first shot hit the droid square in the torso, slagging part of its butlerized outer shell and exposing its interior circuitry; which hadn't escaped unscathed. The second shot hit the bartender robot in its right shoulder, knocking out the rifles aim at me, and causing it to harmlessly fire a shot into the hull of the Mouse Club. My last shot caught the make-shift bodyguard of a droid in its right wrist, severing the hand holding the rifle.

I wish I had done it on purpose, but really I was aiming all the shots at the center mass of my target and the droid's knock back made me miss.

No one who might have seen that needed to know that though.

I strutted toward the airlock entrance with the heavy blaster pointed at the droid as it fell over on its back into the grass.

The pistol wheezed for a second as it cooled down. Heavy blasters are just modified and overpowered standard blasters. The trick is replacing the power back and bypassing the plasma energizers to accept the extra juice. It makes a blaster pistol as tough as a blaster rifle, but it slows down how fast the gun can fire, limits how many shots the plasma supply can output, and you can only get a few shots out before the heatsinks trip the safety for a very brief moment.

The gun was completely illegal in nearly every non-Rim system. I called it my Hot Rod, as I'd painted its typically gun metal black body with red and yellow racing flames backward from the barrel.

Fuck subtle.

I made my way to the airlock and pressed the actuator panel to open the seal. They hadn't locked it and the robot out on guard meant that this wasn't likely a trap.

So, where was the *Legacy's Façade*? I'd already gotten this ball rolling by zipping into this scene and shooting down the droid. So, I didn't have time to figure out what happened to them.

Before going into the club, I knelt down and picked up the unused remote flash bombs. I stepped into the airlock and pressed the next actuator panel and opened the second seal into the cargo-pod-turned-night-club.

Immediately, a blaster bolt hit the wall next to my head, forcing me to veer back into cover.

"It is very unfortunate you 'ave survived, detective." a deep voice bellowed over the sound system, it pronounced its r's thickly in Galactic Common Tongue, sounding like how an Armenian speaking Earth English would. Clearly, he didn't use it often enough, which wasn't unusual for Delosians. They were typically prideful about having to adapt to outsider tongues and insisted most people speak their language when doing business with them.

"I expected Mook to take care of you easily. Now you 'ave cost me a bouncer and I vill 'ave to train up. That is not very profitable."

I called out into the dimmed club, "Tell me why you sent him to kill me and I'll keep the recurring costs down for the night."

A red bolt of energized plasma screamed out of the darkness and hit the interior of the airlock walls.

"Vas a shame you had to involve the Odds." The voice said again over the speaker system, "I am hoping your death and sudden disappearance tonight does nawt hinder my business dealings vith them. Their transportation and music have been very profitable for me so far, and I still need them to transport me to our next show."

Another shot rung out to keep my head down. The angle was different that time. Mouse, no doubt my aggressor, had moved from one spot to another. He was probably making his way closer to get a cleaner shot, assuming for when I was dumb enough to stick my head out.

If I was going to keep him from killing me, I needed to deal with him before he got a good position on me. I reached into my pocket and grabbed the flash bombs and braced myself to move.

"Delivering the girl, Mouse?" I called out to him. He thought he had the upper hand on me. An ideal scenario to get him bragging. "Why else would you send Mook to kill me? We don't have other business I don't know about, do we?"

That's me, minor gang boss trying to take my head off with blaster, and I'm still working an interrogation.

"Ha!" He bellowed. I heard it over the sound system and in person. He was getting closer. "You tink I 'ave any business you vould be involved with? You are a little nothzing detective, from a little nothzing world. Blooming-Star should not hire second rate detectives to find people. Iz not profitable. You die wasting 'is money."

I tossed all the remote flash bombs into the club. They each landed in different locations and clattered along the metal flooring.

Two more shots rung out into the club followed by the wheeze of a heatsink cool down.

A heavy blaster pistol; something that heavy wouldn't be stopped entirely by the ablative vest I was wearing under my hoodie and jacket. I might survive a round to the chest, but I might be wishing I hadn't. I only had a second to act before he could fire again.

I tilted my head down so the brim of my fedora blocked out my vision as I pressed the red waiting light button glowing on my wrist computer's display.

A bright flare of light broke out inside the club and a bellowing yell screamed out over the sound system before whatever microphone Mouse had been using fell to the ground.

By the time the light had dissipated, no doubt leaving bright white splotches in the Delosian's vision, I was up and around the corner with my low-light filtered HUD goggles.

The gangster, shorter than I'd heard he was, and somehow fatter than I'd heard, had one of his four blue hands covering his eyes as two others flailed out blindly ahead of him. With his heavy blaster still aimed in the general direction of the entrance I had just slipped out of, he fired off three more shots as I stepped farther into the club.

He was dressed in what could best be described as a pair of large, expensive felt curtains with a matching waist wrap, all of which were held on by an enormous, gold-plated belt. Around his triple-chinned neck were clusters among clusters of jewelry, and on each of his stubby hands were a ring of some sort.

His enormous maw grimaced in discomfort and dismay as his gun failed to work on the next shot. It was too hot again, giving me my chance.

I put the reticle on the corpulent alien and put as much threat in my voice as possible; "Drop it, Mouse. Move wrong and I'll close your ledger permanently. No more profit for you."

His head turned to my direction as he took his hand off his eyes and tried to squint into the darkness. He dropped the gun.

"It seems you 'ave me at disadvantage." He said jovially, his bottom two arms opening palm up and out, resigned, "Clearly, ve can do business and resolve our differences, yes?"

Delosians, like the prideful reputations about their language, also had a reputation in the galaxy for being merchants, con men, and criminals. That may not be true on their home world and it might be a stereotype; but, so far, it's been true for the small handful of Delosians I'd met. Mouse was no exception.

But, today that was a good thing. His greed and desire to live were exactly what I would need to get the answers to my questions. Besides, I might get away with putting down one blue goon on a backwater moon. Taking out Mouse, however, might draw out more dangerous attention.

After all, I'm a private investigator. I'm no hired killer like some bounty hunter or hit man. I'm not being paid well enough to make a blood bath on the way to Blooming-Star's kid.

Or niece.

"Or whatever..." I finished that thought aloud, but Mouse misread my dismissive attitude to his pleading. His blue hue paled significantly as he felt a killing shot coming.

"Alright. Alright!" He spat out. He pressed his mass against the wall in a poor attempt to escape death. Those red felt window curtains of a robe actually tried to make him look thinner for a moment.

I really couldn't help myself at the sight and snorted a little laugh.

"Ok, fat man," I chuckled and leveled my heavy blaster square at his head in the most menacing bluff I could manage, "Give me the girl and I'll let you live."

Mouse's eyes went wide as he shuffled with surprising alacrity across the dance floor with his arms up. On the far end, which had all been secured for take-off, he pressed his hand on a two-dimensional signed portrait of Gizzy Galante, a galactic-wide famous soprano opera singer. When he took his hand off the portrait I caught a view of something on Gizzy's neck that I would have to bring up later, if I got the chance.

The portrait shifted a little and the wall opened to reveal a secret storage space. Inside the space were storage containers of various types, some shelves stacked with a variety of drinks, drugs, and weapons of a variety of contraband natures. There was also a simple chair from the club with a woman in it, gagged with her hands and feet crudely tied to the arms and legs.

The girl was definitely Neridah Blooming-Star. She looked just like her holo images, except she was dressed in night club clothing, her mascara had bled down her face with tears, but instead of the confident, official government identification photo of her, she was a picture of fear.

I wear a vintage fedora replica of an antique fashion style. I own a mini-pod that's somewhere between a parts project and a classic repulsor ride. I like classical music. I have flames on my blaster pistol. I also collect old stuff, junk really, from Earth's history. I've got pretty old-fashioned tastes, including on how you treat ladies. Maybe I'm a sexist.

But when I saw Neridah crying and looking at us in terror, some instinct in me dating back to pre-space travel humanity welled up. I went from amused at Mouse looking like he was going to piss himself to infuriated enough to consider following through with my bluff.

"Un...tie...her." I pressed the blaster against the back of his head, keeping myself aware of all four of his big meaty hands.

Mouse bent over and began undoing the restraints. He'd started to sweat in fear himself and he began to flatulent himself. He moved out of the way as best as he could when the girl pushed her way around him, fumbling with her gag's strap, and got behind me.

"Sit...down" I ordered Mouse, waving the gun toward the seat in the small storage room.

He barely fit in the seat, his rolls fell around the armrests, and the seat tilted back as he tucked his legs in to fit on it. He farted more and the stink was getting close to bad enough to make me gag.

I slapped the image of Gizzy Galante and the concealed door shut him in. I put a round from my heavy blaster pistol in the actuator panel the portrait concealed. It might have locked Mouse in, I wasn't really sure. But he stayed in there as I took Neridah by the hand and made my way out of the Mouse Club.

On the way to the air lock I introduced myself and said, "Your father sent me to find you and bring you home."

She tossed the rubber gag and its leather strap onto the floor, "N-n-no. I...I can't go home."

I stopped and turned to her, "What?"

"Thank you," she said shaking, "really. But...I can't go home."

I scooped up Mouse's heavy blaster from the floor and tucked it into my belt, after turning on the safety of course. It was a clunkier and bulkier piece than mine, built for his large, meaty Delosian hands.

"I'm sure he'll just be happy to have you home safe." I said. It wasn't the first time a runaway or someone I'd been sent to find was afraid to go back. "We should get going before Mouse gets out of there, or more of his goons show up."

She followed me, finding her courage, "No! I'm telling you I cannot go home. Not yet. I have to finish what I started."

The first airlock door closed behind us and I pressed the open button for the one that would lead out of the club.

"Why *did* you run off, anyway?" I said. It didn't really matter. The reward was the same either way. But I was curious: "Are you looking for where your real father was killed, or revenge, or what?"

"My real what?" she seemed thrown off by that.

"Your uncle." I clarified, "Your real father."

She blinked in shock like I'd slapped her in the face. The outside door opened and the early azure dawn light poured in the color of an atomic tangerine and it made her verdant green eyes take on an amber hue becoming a pair of jeweled islands in the sea of skin the color of red clay and earth, awash with her smeared mascara. The sheen of her raven black hair carried the sun like highlights made of campfires.

By the time I'd processed really seeing her in person, out of the dim lights of a club and not on the pale image of a holographic image, it finally occurred to me that she didn't know anything about her biological father's identity.

I would have chased the new line of questions that had come to mind with that realization, but I was too busy getting shot in the back from down the ramp.

I hit the ground hard, my breath knocked out of me from the charged slap of plasma. I lay there for what felt like an eternity, though it was probably just a matter of several seconds. My red fedora had fallen off my head and was lying on the ground in front of me.

My back screamed in pain as I looked up, blurry eyed, to a shadowy form coming up the ramp with the sun at its' back.

I couldn't make out his face, but I could make out the vaguely human shape and, with just enough light on it, the yellow number five across his chest.

"Sonofabitch." I grunted, realizing that Nephiri Tora and the Odds had, effectively and almost literally, stabbed me in the back. Red Shirt Number Five had me dead to rights and I was, by all rights, about to be dead.

VI

CHAPTER SIX

Load Playlist Track: Sex Pistols, God Save the Queen

Red Shirt Number Five was still dressed in his band garb. I couldn't clearly see his features in the flaming orange sunlight of the dawn behind him. The cresting sun of the star system had flipped the color on the back side of the gas giant and turned the already orangish-brown planet into a second dull sun that ate up half the sky.

He stood over me as a shadow from the neck to his head. His black cargo pants had tears in the knees and his combat boots were missing their ablative platings on one of the shins and over the toes.

I decided that would be a perfect place to put a hole in him. However, between the throbbing pain in my back and the swimming feeling over my head from the wind being knocked out of me, my right hand wouldn't obey and raise the heavy blaster toward him.

"Sorry, pal," the unremarkably bland drummer said as he lowered the gun at me, "but Mouse said this would get me a gig at the club, even if the band didn't keep me on."

I closed my eyes out of instinct, knowing it was coming. Not too courageous, I know. But really, do you want to see it coming?

The blaster shot was quieter than I expected. Neridah screamed in terror, and it was over. The weird thing was that the blaster shot didn't hurt; like, at all.

I opened my eyes and saw the flaming red light of the sun blazing through the growing shadow that was his chest. On the other side of the hole, just before the red shirt hit the ground, I could see The Trooper with a large rifle and scope pointed at our area from the airlock port of the distant *Legacy's Façade*.

Grunting, I rolled over onto my back and looked up to Neridah who was standing there still wide-eyed with both her hands over her mouth. That was probably the first time she'd ever seen someone killed.

"You alright?" I asked her from the deck of the airlock.

Shaking from shock she looked down at me and became even paler than she already was. I recognized the look and realized my jeopardous position just in time to painfully roll out of the way, barely grabbing my fedora as I went.

She fell to her hands and knees and wretched all over where I'd been laying. I would say that it was disgusting, but I hadn't gotten the smell of a sweaty, flatulent and corpulent Mouse out of my nostrils yet.

Small blessings, I guess.

I forced myself upright and waved an acknowledgement to Eight as the *Legacy's Façade* flew over and landed just outside the cargo pod. He raised his rifle, took a quick visual scan of the area, and then nodded.

He was adorned in a long, brown leather trench coat, not as long as mine, with a thick rifle pad on his right shoulder. Bits and pieces of old Colonial Trooper armor adorned on his legs, groin, and torso. Likely, he had some ablative armor under the jacket as well.

As the ship had settled into the field, Eight hopped out of the airlock, raised his rifle again, and made his way over to me while pivoting forty-five degrees to his right and checking for targets. Meanwhile, Kliff had appeared at the airlock entrance to the ship and was aiming a hip-fired blaster cannon, the kind normally mounted on armored vehicles, in the opposite forty five degree arc; covering Eight's back.

Vi'xiri, her red tones covered in a black body suit with some expensive and decorative ablative armor pieces covering only her vital organs, hopped out the door holding a pair of smaller blaster pistols, and then turned and faced underneath the ship to watch that direction. I could now see the large sheathed sword on her back.

When Eight reached me he didn't take his aim off his fire arc. He just called over to Neridah and I; "You two good?"

"What took you so long?" I growled, mostly out of pain rather than anger. I dusted off my fedora and brought it back onto my head with a wince as my back stung from the motion. Clearly, some of the tank top I wore under the ablative armor had gotten burned a little into my skin.

"This shit," he said as he kicked the side of his boot into Red Shirt, "disabled our thrusters. We could take off with repulsors, but we couldn't get here any faster than a repulsortruck. Still have to get them fixed."

"I'm guessing Tora decided to get involved after all." I muttered as I bent over to check on Neridah, who had finally stopped vomiting all over the steel flooring.

"She takes her ship seriously." He muttered, "Besides, this idiot didn't do a very good job of evading our security. We figured out who did it pretty quick and put two and two together."

"You ok, kid?" I asked Neridah.

She nodded and tried to catch her breath, "I'm fine. Fine."

"Ok," I said relieved, "Looks like we have this resolved. Let's get you home."

She shook her head standing up, "I told you. I can't go home. I have to finish what I started."

She was looking nervously at Eight. Was she there for some revenge after all?

I stood up.

"Ok," I said, "What did you come to actually do, then?"

"I came to get something from that ship." She pointed to the *Legacy's Façade*, which was now blocking out the sun.

Eight raised a scarred black eyebrow, relaxing some of the crags and wrinkles from around his reddish-brown good eye. The milky white eye continued to visually scan, disconcertingly yet neutral, its' brow remaining critically furrowed.

"What about Mouse?" I said, jamming a thumb back towards the interior of the pod.

The two eyes turned to me, "You didn't kill him?"

"I don't kill if I don't have to." I said and turned the thumb back to me, "Good guy...usually."

I wouldn't mention Mook in a ditch back near the motel though. I'm not *that* good a guy. You try and kill me, I kill you right back.

"We'll leave that up to the Captain." He answered, "Let's get out from this exposed position, at least."

"What are you worried about?" I said, looking around the large open field for potential enemies.

"Everything." He responded dead pan, not nearly the jovial attitude of the night before. But then, that made sense. This was a potential combat situation. He was in his element, what he was made for. The personality that had been virtually programmed into him had taken hold over the relaxed *staan'g* player that likely wouldn't return until he felt safe and secure.

Together, the three of us passed by Snowball. The sound system was blaring out another track from my classical punk playlist.

"*I've been blessed with the power to survive;*" Joey Ramone, singing from *I Believe in Miracles*, belted out "*After all these years I'm still alive. I'm out here kickin' with the band; Oh, I'm no longer a solitary man.*"

I clicked off the music with my wrist computer and helped lift Neridah to the ship's airlock door, where Kliff easily finished the job of assisting her through the door.

"Why didn't you just lower the ramp on the other side of the ship?" I said.

"Can't open the door for a firing position without the ramp already down." Eight answered, "Anyway, if we were going to end up hooking up to the club, I wanted to be by the entrance for a boarding assault."

"Good tactics." I said, comparing it to my own assault on the club. My plan was a close-in cheap attack from the back, his was a full on frontal assault. Shows the difference in our types of fighting; dirty dicks versus tactical soldiers.

The airlock was on the rear starboard-side of the ship, as opposed to the standard front portside entrance ramp. Really, it was only meant to get cargo pods docked into the ship. That placed the airlock directly near the galley where the crew had been drinking mere hours ago with, not much farther, the engine room at the rear of the ship.

From that direction, Nephiri Tora could be heard cursing in some blend of GCT and, I think, Neo-Nipponese. I've never solidly learned any languages outside of GCT other than some ancestral Scot's Gaelic and a little Icelandic my father made me learn. But, when it came to swearing, it was a minor hobby of mine to learn as many languages of pissed-off as I could. You never knew when you'd need it to start bar fights, which are a great distraction when pursuing someone.

It's not like I'm usually hired to find nice innocents like Neridah Blooming-Star.

"Captain." Reported Eight formally. He was still under the influences of his younger years, "We have the detective and Ms. Blooming-Star secured."

The sound of some metal object being put down was followed by the sigh of someone trying to compose themselves. A few seconds later, Captain Tora made her way out of the small engine crawl space. She was wearing the same outfit as the night before, but she had the jacket removed. Some oil had been smudged on her face.

Kliff helped Vi'xiri up into the airlock before sealing it.

A shaky Neridah stepped forward; her hand thrust out almost cartoonishly, and said, "Captain Nephiri Tora, I am Neridah Blooming-Star."

Captain Tora pulled a rag out of her pocket and wiped her hand before tenuously taking Neridah's. "It's nice to meet you. I knew your father."

Neridah looked confused at her for a moment and then back to me, "You said...before, my *real* father..."

"She doesn't know." I told Tora as they ungripped hands.

"Oh." Tora said chagrined and looked to Neridah, "I'm sorry. I didn't realize. I assumed you came looking for me because you found out about...your uncle; that he was really your father. This isn't how you should have found out."

Neridah looked to the floor distantly and then back up to Tora and me, "That explains a lot, actually."

Vi swaggered up beside me, the attention of her tendril points focused toward the young woman, "'ow so, sweet one?"

"The dreams." She said, "My uncle...was a Totem Master. That's supposed to be hereditary, but my...father...never demonstrated any ability. I had to get it from somewhere."

Kliff growled something as incoherent as everything else he said, but the Diva robot on his throat translated it, roughly, "My dear, are you saying you have the ability to speak to the Totems and spirits?"

She shrugged, "Of sorts. It started when I was a teen, but never really developed into anything until just recently, with dreams. From what I've read, it says that Totem Masters and Shamans can't all communicate with both totems and spirits. Usually it's one or the other, which is how they got categorized into the two terms. But some, like my uncle, could do both as they became stronger."

Kliff knelt down so he was the same height as Neridah and said something in Grothraki and the robot on his neck spoke monotone, demonstrating it was making his translation exact, "It is a rare blessing to be in the presence of one with The Gift. In the names of my Ancestors, I welcome you."

She blushed, "Thank you. But, I haven't been trained. I don't know the formalities or how to respond."

Kliff stood and spoke again, and Diva translated, less exactly, "You'll figure it out dear. Your kind do not live ordinary lives."

That was a truth, no matter how much you believe in supernatural and spiritual matters. Totem Master and Shamans were just two names of the myriad that could be used, depending on the religion or culture or species. But, ultimately, in Galactic Common Tongue, they boiled down to two types; those who claimed to speak to guides from beyond, and those who spoke to the dead.

Humans, prior to application of Alcubierre's mathematics and the eventual discovery of Hyperspace, had effectively grown out of a belief in Gods, the afterlife, and spirits. Sure, there were those who held to the ancient traditions. But, they didn't really command the control of our species the way they had for the centuries untold before.

Once we'd discovered the other planes of existence through the use of science, we seemingly returned to having access to, for lack of a better term, *a spiritual existence* that subsisted alongside our own. An existence that we could effect, and that could effect us in return.

Science and superstition started to shake hands with one another again. And with that relationship, returned the guides who had been beside us since the beginnings.

Ultimately, the more complex religions of the world, based on saviors and prophets and the like, had grown so wrapped up in themselves that their priests had long lost direct connection with their spiritual half. There were those who had found some way to connect through their faiths to...whatever it was that was out there...and translated it for the everyday sentient.

However, the more ancient traditions, the magical ones if you would, that lay in the First Peoples, had a better time of adapting to the reconnection with the rediscovered spiritual realms.

The First Peoples were born from what was left of the aboriginal cultures of Earth. The many "tribes" of the Earth, from all four corners, had been nearly wiped out by the progress and forward momentum of the more "civilized" cultures of the world, western and Asian alike.

The First Nations tribes of the northern Americas, the Aboriginal peoples of Australia, like the Gabi-Gabi, and the remnants of the Mayan peoples living secluded from the southern Americans, united with the remaining African tribes that still followed their Old Ways, and fought socially to protect their collective identity. Through the course of centuries, they found themselves blending together.

When Hyperspace opened up and the spirits became directly rele-

vant to society once again, some of the other older religions that had
begun to fade found new life; the druidic and Celtic faiths, and some of
the Old World religions of Europe and the Slavic peoples found themselves congruently uniting as well.

In the end, the aborigines and the older religions collectively became
The First Peoples; believers and followers of ancient gods and spirits
and totems. Not all of them were Medicine Men, Shamans, High
Priests, Witches, or Clevermen. But, it is from their numbers that the
majority of humanity's contribution to the galactic "Totem Masters"
and "Shamans" come from.

Neridah was the daughter of such a man. She wasn't raised by him
in his gifts, though she was raised by someone who luckily shared his
beliefs.

"So if you didn't know about your father," CaptainTora responded,
"why are you here?"

Eight spoke up, "Ma'am. She said she needed something off this
ship."

"Oh?" Captain Tora said, intrigued.

Neridah looked embarrassed, "This is going to sound crazy."

"It's been a day." I snarked, "Try us. Besides, the sooner you get this
resolved, the sooner I get you home and get paid by...well, I guess your
uncle."

"I had a dream." She said, "Five totem spirits came to me; Great
Bear, Lone Wolf, and Ghost Eagle of Earth, as well as the Gh'ar'tik of
Grathrak and the great Sand Snake of Tilaria. They showed me the five
of you and this ship. They showed me the ghost of my Uncle aboard this
ship, on this world."

"The five of them?" I said, confused, "There are only four band members."

"You mean Tommy?" Asked Vi'xiri about Red Shirt Number Five.

She shook her head and pointed to me, "No. Him. All of you. I need
your help."

"With what?" CaptainTora was pale, dreading something, "What did
they tell you?"

"I need you to stop it, whatever it is." She shook, as if remembering her dream vividly, "To stop so much death and horror."

"What?" I said, doubtful, "What death and horror?"

"It's happening just like he said it would." muttered CaptainTora horrified, but with realization in her eyes that betrayed she knew this was coming, "Gods! You're talking about a Second Betrayal."

"I'm talking about the end of natural life in the Galaxy." Neridah was almost crying again, "They say you're the only ones who can stop the Nether."

VII

⟨⟩⟨⟩

CHAPTER SEVEN

"You'll have to excuse me; I've got better things to do!" – Social Distortion, Far Behind

Everyone looked at the young, raven-haired diplomat in utter silence for a moment before the sound of the short, drill-sergeant-voiced droid broke the mood, bellowing; "Attention Odds! I have been instructed to remind you that it is time to pick up the Mouse Club and depart for our next destination! Grab your gear and get ready for take-off!"

Everyone jolted at the sound before Vi'xiri hissed almost musically at the little droid, all of her head tendrils up like the hackles of an animal, "Stupid robot! Shut up!"

Tree started with surprise, as if he wasn't accustomed to back talk, "Now listen here..."

Captain Tora cursed something to herself, "Right...Mouse. We'll need to dump him before we pick up the club and leave."

Kliff growled something and Diva replied monotone, "We are going to help her then? Good."

"Hold on." I put my hands up, "I didn't sign up for anything. I was hired to help find Miss Blooming-Star here. I found her. My job's done."

"He iz right." Vi's tendrils were investigating everyone at once as they came down from their defensive posture, "This is naught our fight. Ve are just smugglers and musicians."

"It's my fight." Tora spoke quietly, with conviction, "Always was going to be. And it's my ship. So, if you aren't coming, and I understand, this is your stop detective."

Kliff growled with approval and stood beside her. There was no point in the droid translating. Neridah looked to the two of them, hopeful.

Vi frowned as all the tendrils moved to Kliff and her voice was pouty and cute, "Really? Vhyyy? Ve don't know zthis girl. Ve don't even know vhat she vants us to do."

Eight primed and checked his blaster rifle, "She wants us to save the Galaxy. Just like a Totem Master to ask something so absurd."

"Absurd." I repeated, "That's a word for it."

Captain Tora, Kliff and Neridah were crestfallen.

"I'm in." Eight retorted with a wink to the young Earther, "I didn't know your father. But I did know my Shamaness. I owe her more than the little vengeance I gave in her name during the Betrayal."

Kliff growled approval and patted Eight on the shoulder as Vi looked back and forth between them dejected.

"Fine..." she sighed harmonically, "I guess if you're all going to be stupid enough to do this, I'll be stupid with you."

After a brief hug from the Grathrak and some mutters of approval from everyone, they all looked to me. Neridah's eyes were wide in hope and expectation. You could feel the innocence pouring out like some kid's film heroine.

I shook my head, "I'm a private eye. I'm not a hero, or a mercenary. I'm not out to save the universe. I'm out to pay my rent. And right now, that means going to your uncle and telling him I found you, that you're alive, and who you're with."

She dropped her head down and her shoulders slumped, "Please. I know it sounds crazy, but you have to be here. I 'saw' you in The Dreaming. They can't do it without you, and you can't do it without them."

"You all have your parts to play," she turned to everyone, "The Guides say each of us has a part in turning the Nether back and preventing them from consuming everything."

"Did they say what those roles were?" I asked her incredulously, "Come on. You have a dream and it told you the Expanse was going to be saved by a Smuggler Captain, a Private Dick, and a Djugga Band?"

"It's a Deep Voltch-Djugga band." Diva translated for Kliff, as if the clarification were all the credentials needed for Galaxy saving.

"Nothing clear." Neridah said, "After the vision of the ship and you all, the Totems sung me a song on the two voices of the Voltch'I. I'm not a singer, so the subtleties of the two tones are more complex than I can express. But, I do remember the words."

She closed her eyes and tried to hum the melody to herself. Vi'xiri closed her eyes and her tendrils began to lightly vibrate while examining the sound. At first it reminded me a little of *The Reaper* by Blue Oyster Cult, but she was either way out of key or added some notes that weren't supposed to be there.

> Queen Nefertiri moves a Wayward Sun
> And the Gladiator that always won
> Into the blackest chaotic night
> Will carry the serpent girl's song
> Find the Dagger of Augury
> To light the path ahead
> The Reluctant Seeker must chase
> The Last Trooper's fallen dead
> In Illuminated Path you'll see
> The Lost and Broken Man
> And return his spirit to rest
> Stemming the Hunger again.

"That's everything." Neridah blushed, "I'm sorry, it wasn't very good...and I don't know what it all means."

"I know the first line pretty well." CaptainTora sighed, "Queen Nefertiri was Conner's nickname for me. This ship was originally called *Wayward Son* when he used it for his diplomatic missions. It was his to use and take wherever he wanted. But as far as I was concerned, it wasn't the Expanse's ship. It was mine. I ran it like I owned it, and I gave a lot of guff to anyone who messed with it."

"You still do." Eight chimed in.

"Yeah, well..." Tora sat down at the table in the galley, "I was bossy and he knows my first name was Egyptian in origin. So, he called me Queen Nefertiri around his squad of Colonial Troopers. They even joked about it minutes before the Betrayal."

"You never really talk much about vat 'appened." Vi hummed to the Captain.

"Maybe later." She shook her head. "The rest of the first verse seems pretty obvious. We're a Wayward class freighter..."

"And Kliff here was the Gladiator, I presume," Diva chimed in, "Though from the skull plate, I'm sure the fact that he always won didn't come easily."

The big furry oaf shrugged and smiled with false humility and tapped his metal plate.

"Obviously," Vi writhed her tendrils and hypnotically swayed like a snake, "I am ze serpent girl, though I vouldn't say my singing was so great it vould save the galaxy...but it is quite good."

Diva, as if she had lips, made some sort of "p'ssssh" sound in disagreement; "You sing in dive bars, dear. If anything, I'd sing a song worth saving a galaxy for. I've performed in the greatest of galactic venues."

"Oh shut up, Diva." The Telarian hissed, "You vere just a microphone."

"Why I never..." the neck droid started to protest before Kliff smacked it and rolled his eyes.

"What about the rest?" Eight asked the group, "Obviously, I'm The Last Trooper. As far as I know, I'm the only one that didn't obey orders during The Betrayal."

"No idea." CaptainTora replied, "But, clearly what happened to you is important to all of this."

"And you seem to have expected it." I noted my observation of her earlier reactions, "What doyou know?"

"Why?" The Captain looked to me, "I thought you weren't here to save the Galaxy. You were just going to go back and collect your money to pay the rent."

She was right. Their fanciful mission wasn't my problem.

"I am." I attempted to appear unswayed, "I'm just curious. It's a mystery. They're what I do."

"It iz a fair question, Captain Tora." Vi used the momentum of my question, "I 'eard your fear vhen...vat's your name again, sweet'eart?"

"Neridah," the diplomat's daughter filled in.

"Vhen Neridah told 'er story." Vi continued, "But your feelings did naught say surprise."

"Hold on." I stepped away from the Tilarian, "Are you saying you can read people's minds?"

I faced a mind reader once, a trained former Psi-Ops Infiltrator for the Earther government. I was on a missing person's case. The psycho, or sociopath, or whatever he was, had been kidnapping young women. He used his mind-reading abilities to find their greatest fears and torment the women sexually with them. When I'd found the victim whose family sent me out to find her, I had fought him to protect her. He would finish my sentences when I tried to talk him down, and then could tell whenever I was about to shoot. He was slippery, and the most dangerous person I'd ever come up against.

Psychics creep me out now.

"Oh no!" Vi was obviously picking up my bad vibes, "I do naught read minds. Many species give off pheromones based on zeir feelings."

She lightly stroked one of her tendrils and looked at me seductively, "I detect zem through zese and I understand zem like a sound in music. I could 'ear your enjoyment while watching me dance. But I vasn't reading your mind... I don't 'ave to vith human men. Zey always tink ze same ting around me."

She winked and, well, knew she was right about my thoughts. I blushed a bit. But, at least she wasn't reading my mind.

"Uh...you were going to explain..." I tried to veer the conversation back to the Captain, "How you weren't surprised."

"Yeah," Captain Tora had been looking down into a drink she'd pulled from a rack at arm's reach of the table; the ones used to lock things in so they don't fall out during flight. She spoke reluctantly, "During the Betrayal, Conner told me to run and get away with the ship. He told me," she paused, "as he was being gunned down, that it wouldn't be the last time I saw him; that he would still need me again one day. For the Second Betrayal."

"Wow." Eight put the rifle in a rack against the wall, "He saw it coming."

Tora stayed silent.

"Okay..." This was all getting way too weird for me, "Well, I don't believe in Ghosts, or Totems, and I'm not here for this. I did my job, now I'm going to go get paid for it while I wait for my next one. Good luck." I grabbed Neridah's hand to lead her out with me.

"Wait!" She slipped from my grasp and stood between me and the hallway leading to the ship's exit ramp. "You're a private investigator, right?"

"Yes." I replied dubiously.

"You seek things!" She said desperately, "A-and you're reluctant!"

"Yeaaah..." I saw where this was going and didn't like it.

"So you're the reluctant seeker." She declared stepping closer to me, "Don't you see. You have to be part of this."

"Listen, kid," I gently reached for her hand, "I do seek things...for money. Not hopeless causes that involve fighting the Nether or any of their mutated people."

"S-so..." she looked down trying to think of something as I took my first step down the hall with her, "sooo...I'll hire you then!"

I stopped. A job? Well now. That was different. Still, this was all very crazy and we should have just left right then. But, my curiosity and the offer of pay had my attention.

"I still need to wrap up the job I'm on." I said, "I have rent due."

She looked up with those pleadingly innocent doe eyes again.

"But, if you did hire me..." I turned and leaned against the bulkhead carefully, my back burning with fire, reminding me what this job had already costed me, "What am I looking for?"

"Oh..." her shoulders slumped. "Well, I already know where that is."

"Where what is?" I said.

"The Dagger of Augury." She sighed.

"That's what was on the ship?" I laughed a little, feeling relieved I hadn't bought into some crazy adventure that was going to get me shot yet again, "Well, that was less than a minute. I'll call it a freebee and we can say I helped your prophecy, okay?"

"Except it isn't on the ship." Captain Tora interjected and stood up thoughtfully.

"What?" Neridah panicked, "It has to be. The Totems brought me here and sang the song about it."

"Nope." Tora shook her head and her long hair swayed like midnight, "But, what I do have on the ship is a copy of the diplomatic archives from Archimedes' Parliamentary Systems; all five-star systems. Totem Masters and Shamans were highly sought after diplomats by all the System Lords. If any of them had something called the Dagger of Augury, my computer systems might be able to tell us where it was at the time of the Betrayal."

"There you go," I pointed to the captain and looked at Neridah, "a couple extra seconds and still solved. Any more and I'd have to accept the deal and start charging you."

I got off the wall and waved to everyone, "It was nice getting shot around you all. Goodbye."

I made my way down the hallway, tired and sore, and wanting a real scotch. They could go find some mysterious dagger themselves.

I made Tree lower the ramp at the front of the ship, made my way back over to the entrance of the Mouse Club to my beat up mini-pod, and glowered at the damages.

"That's going to be expensive." I told myself. More expensive than the pay on this job was going to cover after I paid my rent...on top of my late rent from the previous month.

I glowered more. I would say I was downright brooding.

The engines on the *Legacy Façade* changed in pitch as the crew prepped to move the ship and collect the cargo pod turned night club.

"Don't be stupid." I told myself. "You were shot. You need to replace your vest first. And you deserve a break."

"Nope." I argued with myself, "We can't afford a new vest. I need the job. Besides…"

"No." I interrupted, "We don't believe in ghosts. We don't believe in totems. We don't believe in interplanetary galactic-ending space prophecies."

I glowered some more.

"Fuck." I keyed up my wrist computer and called the *Legacy's Façade* bridge.

Tora answered, "You forget something?"

"My rates are fifty credits an hour plus commission." I stated, "One week's retainer up front, not refundable."

I'd added the week's retainer to the cost to scare the girl and her Djugga band of heroes off. My normal retainer was two days, enough to find out if a case could be solved in the first place.

There was some discussion off screen and Neridah appeared on the screen, beaming, "Done! Send me your account details and I'll put the retainer in now."

She had the money. I muted the connection.

"Fuck." I repeated to myself.

"She has the money." I countered.

Hard to argue with that logic. I un-muted the line.

"Okay." I said, "But I need to send details to your fath-uncle, what-ever…about finding you. That way I can still get paid by him. And I don't work until your payment is in my account and I've paid off my late rent."

VIII

❧

CHAPTER EIGHT

Load Playlist Track: Joan Jett and the Blackhearts, I Love Rock 'N' Roll

Despite the existence of faster-than-light travel in the forms of warp and hyperspace, intersystem communication was actually fairly slow. You can't transmit data at warp speeds. It requires an Alcubierre drive to protect the energy signature from the laws of relativity. If you're going to do that, you need a ship to go around the Alcubierre drive.

In short, you still needed the post man. The Galactic Expanse had an answer for this; Messengers.

Messengers were certified by the Imperial Hegemony of the Expanse as almost incorruptible. If you gave the Messengers something to deliver, they would fight, to their very death, to protect the information.

In the old days, before Earth had made contact with the Hegemony, these superluminal postmen were responsible for carrying large data dumps from system to system. They delivered all navigational data regarding the warp from navigational buoy to navigational buoy, and all data and messaging from Earth outward to their colonies.

Likewise, any information and messages from the farthest reaches of the American Empire and the Eastern People's Republic, before they were united under the Hegemony, were brought back from their colony planets to the home world.

However, once the Hegemony found the existence of the rim-based Earth and its miniscule systems, the Messengers were instituted upon subversion to their appointed System Lord and the Parliament of the Benighted Final Spiral Arm.

The Benighted Final Spiral Arm was, one would think, a derogatory term for the Earther Systems. Some, like me, would say you were right.

But, conceptually, the term was referencing our relative ignorance of the galactic whole at the time and our recent emergence into the Hegemony; which was brought about by collusion that otherwise would have led to conquest by the System Lords. The concept was that we would eventually know enough about the workings of the galaxy, for humanity and its systems to elevate beyond the title of "benighted." After all, so had all the other "Spiral Arms" of the Galaxy that made up the rim around what is known as the "Core Systems" and the "Mid Systems."

But, that was over three hundred years ago. Humans, understandably, are getting a bit sick of waiting to be treated as equals by the galactic majority. It's part of the reason why, when we discovered the visceral music of the Voltch'I, we developed our own forms of Djugga and, ultimately, Deep Voltch-Djugga.

It's also why that relatively obscure planet, which we brought into the Benighted Final Spiral Arm, was such a hit with the entire Galaxy; Earth and our colonies were not the first system to be "benighted" by the Hegemony. But, it would, theoretically, be the last.

System Lords were not allowed to be citizens of the indigenous systems of which they ruled; which is how Archimedes the Third, the first System Lord from Earth, became the ruler of the Iblis Systems. The idea is that they would be more loyal to the Expanse than to the interests of their home systems.

The idea was also intended to bring a unity to the galaxy by sharing the ideas and leaderships of other star systems around the galaxy.

One method ensuring this galactic homogenization was to have the System Lords find those dedicated to the Galactic Ideal presented by the Hegemony, and their Pyqian advisors, and drive them to service in the Messengers. Messengers were trained to be ultimately loyal to communication between the System Lords and were considered devoid of political loyalties.

Every Expanse system had a centralized location that they could pass data to a Messenger and know that the network of messengers would ensure its direct delivery. To date, as far as the record showed galaxy-wide, the Messengers had about a ninety-six percent successful delivery rate.

It was a rate only thrown off by the arrival of the Nether, the spirit-bound mutants of the Iblis System and the unintentional Free Mutant Armada, and the subsequent war to suppress the Nether.

Captain Tora had agreed to transport me to Arcturis Major, the larger moon of this planet's system, to access the nearest Messenger Station. I had loaded Snowball into the middle of Mouse's Club, right onto the dance floor, for the journey. It looked ridiculously wrecked in the middle of a night club.

"I just finished getting you fixed again." I spoke what seemed to be a classic lament from working a job. I was always having to send Snowball in for repairs.

The smell of opiates and alien tobaccos were stale in the air now that the club was inactive. The smell of vomits and booze hadn't been cleaned up by the bartender robot before I'd shot it.

Sufficed to say, the club wasn't exactly the most pleasant environment before I had parked a beat up mini-pod in the middle of it.

Then there was the smell of Mouse leaking from behind the hidden compartment door. It reeked like the stench of rotten eggs and sweat that bordered on the unholy. You could smell it almost as far as the air lock doors that acted as the entrance to the club.

The Delosian had been trapped in the hidden storage compartment of the club for about three hours before we decided it was time to deal with him.

In the meantime, Tora had docked the *Legacy's Façade* with the *Mouse Club* cargo pod and run a diagnostic of the ship's system to ensure that Tommy the Red Shirt hadn't screwed up more than they'd known about.

Once the ship had been given a green light by Captain Tora and Tree, we all made our way to the dance floor to deal with the effervescent Mouse.

Vi'xiri wore a black form-fitting pair of black pants that stood out against her orange-red skin. A matching form-fitting tank top adorned, and lifted, her bosom to distracting levels.

The words "Twin Eclipse" were written in Galactic Common Tongue across her breasts. I'm sure the euphemism was completely unintentional. It was, after all, the name of a more mainstream Djugga band. That was why, right?

I tried not to think too directly on it. Not with my eyes anyway.

Her face, partially covered by a very thin veil draped from silver rings on her horns, didn't indicate that she'd noticed, but her onyx and silver adorned tendrils completely did. Upon each snake were a series of decorated ringlets. They kept their tips facing me as I worked to clear my head from the thoughts related to the eclipse her bosom could cause in the light of my life.

It was a little disturbing to be watched by someone who wasn't even looking at you; to be noticed by someone for how you felt without any indication that they had any reaction to those feelings. She just clearly acknowledged her awareness with disinterest.

But then, she'd been the object of sexual desire, and even slavery, for the majority of her life. She likely wouldn't be interested in base pheromone-harmonic reactions, except to manipulate them.

One new feature, previously hidden by the drapes of white fabric from her stage outfit, was a black, squid-like tattoo on her right shoulder. When I saw it, I knew it right away. That was the mark of the Free Mutant Armada; a fleet of ships of the former Iblis system that were transformed by the Nether, but somehow managed to break the psychospiritual controls of the other-realm beings and System Lord Archimedes. They had become slavers and pirates that harried the rim's entire expanse and were rumored to operate out of the ever moving Xanadu.

Kliff appeared relatively unchanged. His fur was the majority of his clothes and he wore a leather loin cloth in place of his kilt, more for the rest of the galaxy's sensibilities than his own; the Grothrark found any articles of clothing that didn't serve a functional purpose superfluous and prudish. They liked to "rock out" and "jam out", if you get my meaning.

Eight had shed his ablative armor pieces and even the trench coat. He was in nothing more than a pair of work out sweat pants and a long-sleeve black workout-shirt with the picture of a ripped golden humanoid lifting weights. He was barefoot, in place of the heavy ablative armor boots he'd been wearing earlier, and was silent in his gait, unlike the Telarian, who had slipped on a pair of knee-high, black and silver high-heeled boots with ornate silver buckles and straps.

Kliff's meaty pawed feet clicked a little as his obscured toe claws tapped the floor as he walked alongside the padded sound of everyone's footwear, Vi's heels as the exception.

The Captain was still wearing her orange spacer jacket and boots. She'd instructed Neridah to stay back on the ship proper. Clearly the ambassador's daughter, Page of the Expanse, was unsettled by violence. If it went that way, no one wanted her to have to see anything she wasn't ready for.

Collectively, we had all our blasters out. Well, everyone except Kliff. He had a Vibronic Axe, a two-handed shaft of a weapon with a metallic blade on one side that hummed with a power supply on the other to enhance its ability to slice through things.

They didn't do so great against ablative armor. But they didn't care about energy fields that stop lasers, or weaken blaster shots, and they sure did cut well through meat. A blaster shot, while it did sort of slightly explode the energy outward from the contact point, while blowing chunks of meat off someone, it also cauterized wounds usually due to the high energy and heat. A vibronic bladed weapon slices into, and then through soft tissue. A strong enough swing and you're missing limbs.

A Grothrark with a vibronic axe though? You'd have to be something really big to not be missing parts after it hit you.

I had ditched my leather trench coat into the passenger seat of Snowball. The duster-like jacket had a scorched hole the size of my fist in the middle of its back. I probably wouldn't fix it, but I didn't want to get rid of it right away in case I needed it later. The shirt I'd been wearing, however, had been completely ruined and I'd discarded the ablative armor vest I was wearing earlier.

Again, I didn't toss it out. It could still take a hit from the front and probably a light impact from the back. But, the structural integrity of the center of the back had been compromised and Vi'xiri had to peel it off some lightly burned skin when we took it off. She'd been kind enough to put some burn ointment on my back and make sure there wasn't any permanent damage back there.

"It is very red on your skin." She had mused before we'd come into the Mouse Club, "You look like you do not get much sunlight, Mister Galbraith."

I told her to call me Einar and had slipped back into my slightly scorched tank top. Before we made our way to letting Mouse out of his storage room, I took a moment to put my business hat back into the rear storage compartment of the mini-pod.

It took a little work to get the closet-sized hidden door open.

Delosians were like any other sapient humanoid species in the Expanse. Although they were generally larger than most humans, they still had their varieties of people. Some were fighters and tough guys, like the former Mook. Some were likely intellectuals and scientists. There had to be. Otherwise how would they have left their home world and been found by the Expanse?

Had I ever met one? No.

Then there were big and blustering types that ruled through fear and reputation. But, like most bullies, if you punch one in the nose, well...more like a short stubby pig snout really...then the water works come on and the tough guy breaks down and whines like a little bitch.

That was Mouse.

The big guy had been locked in a closet barely larger than a Delosian coffin, assuming such things exist, with the lights off. He'd been blinded by flash grenades. He'd been bested as he tried to be the tough guy and ended up shoved into that smuggling locker at gun point by a smaller guy.

That would be me.

When the door opened and the lights of the no-longer-dim club flooded in, he blinked his weird lizard-like eyes, both horizontal and vertical eyelids, and held his hands up to shield himself.

He caught a look at everyone pointing weapons at him and the seeping stink that had come from the compartment was joined by a fresh flatulent fear-fart from the tremendously obese alien.

I tend to be very descriptive, but honestly, there were no words for the horrific stench that waved out at us. My eyes had started to water, and my stomach actually turned a little.

Vi'xiri swore something less delicate sounding than her normal melodious voice and in her native language. I didn't need to translate the exact wording to get the gist of it. Neither did Captain Tora.

"Twin Suns!" she cursed as she covered her mouth with a leather gloved hand, "Amaterasu and Ra, you disgusting freak! Gods!"

"F-f-f-friends!" Mouse worked his way gingerly out of the compartment, all four of his large blue hands out submissively, "Clearly ve can overlook this misunderstanding."

"Misunderstanding?" I cussed, "You tried to have me killed and then tried to do it yourself."

"Vas only business, detective." He shrugged his upper and waist shoulders, "Nothing personal. You have von and I have lost. Is the vay of things. No need to kill old Mouse."

The Odds looked to Tora.

"We're not going to kill you." She waved her gun toward the air lock, "But this is your stop."

"But my club." He swung his hands around, "I paid for this. It is mine. You vould not leave me on this backwater planet. Is not good business. Is not profitable."

"...for you." Tora corrected him, "The business model has worked well enough so far, and, technically, I own the cargo pod. You just remodeled it."

Kliff growled and barked with the Diva robot roughly translating under its snobbish female voice, "Your investment in the night club is appreciated, Great Mouse. However, it seems our business is concluded and your life is the reward for your efforts after this faux pas."

Everyone turned and looked at Kliff who was looking down toward his own throat area confused before whispering something in "grrrs" and "garrghs" to himself.

"Oh very well," Diva would have rolled its photoreceptor if it were an eye and it switched monotone, "You screwed yourself, asshole. The club is ours and you are lucky we don't kill you, you fucking four-armed space slug."

Eight, Vi, and Captain Tora nodded approvingly and turned back to Mouse with their guns.

"Now," Tora said, "get off my boat."

Mouse was to the air lock and out of sight of our weapons when he growled and hollered a mixture of GCT and Delosian back to us.

"You *doughlosa* thieves!" he yelled on the way down the ramp, "You don't *greffin* steal from the Great Mouse, *kuskos*! You'll regret this!"

Tora shut the air lock door and flipped the bird to Mouse, assuming he could see through the transparent steel glass window in the door.

She turned to Tree who had been standing by in the background.

"Tree," she spoke authoritatively, "prepare for take off."

The little white robot saluted his captain and barked orders to the room; "All right Odds, to your stations! I want this boat off the ground in fifteen minutes!"

Vi rolled her eyes on the way back to the main part of the ship.

"Jesus 'uman Christ..." she muttered as Kliff followed along barking some sort of laugh. Eight mockingly saluted the little robot and then turned right at ninety-degrees in a military pivot and stomped along, marching behind them.

"Fuck," Tora said looking around the cargo pod, the rigged shoulders of her jacket seemed to slacken more than the fabric could have, "Now I have to run the club, too."

IX

CHAPTER NINE

Load Playlist Track: Guns N' Roses, Sweet Child O' Mine

The trip from Arcturis Minor to Arcturis Major took several hours. Unfortunately, traveling FTL through Hyperspace wasn't something you could easily turn on and off. Just a short hop would dump us far outside the star system at best. We had to travel in Real Space with all of its physics and lack of alacrity.

The two moons, by the time we'd left orbit, were on opposite sides of the gas giant below. From the cockpit of the *Legacy's Façade*, you could see the enormous gas-mining station hard at work. It was a sprawling megacity of a structure, with long metallic spires reaching out around the curvature of the planet, making the Manhattan-sized structure, like the legs of an adult crane fly, more than twice its' size in every direction.

I'd always been told adult crane flies were called mosquito eaters, but don't believe them. They don't help fight off mosquitoes at all. That was a waste of several credits to get some for my apartment on New Reykjavik. Also, they're terribly annoying and disturbing bugs.

Although it appeared to float on the orange clouds of the gas giant, the structure was actually a massive flying ship. It was greater in size than even the largest of the Expanse's warships. I didn't even know its

name, or if it had one. It was just "the mining platform" from the Arcturis Corporation, as far as I knew.

They didn't consider it a ship. Even though it had the power to keep
itself at the edge of the atmosphere, it lacked the power to actually
break orbit from Arcturis Prime itself. The structure, aside from some
corporate offices throughout the System, represented the entirety of the
company's holdings.

But, like New Reykjavik, it slowly worked its way across the surface
of its own ocean, this one made of clouds, performing its job below.

The sight of the giant machine made me miss my bed at home. Well,
that and having had been shot in the back and attacked by a Delosian
hitman. Near death and fatigue tends to do that.

But despite the sluggish speeds of Real Space, we approached the
larger, more populated moon of the Arcturis System.

"How much longer?" I asked Tora with the patience of a saint.

She was the only other person up on the bridge, if you didn't count
Tree manning the communications station.

"Not much longer," she said, rolling her eyes for now the second
time. "Another hour maybe. Just enough time for me to grab a shower
and some grub. You might as well get something to eat back in the galley. We have plenty of space rations."

I sneered at the words "space rations." Space rations were typical fare
on these types of ships. Cargo carriers, especially those with long hauls,
didn't have the luxury to carry fresh food on them. At best, they might
have frozen or refrigerated foods, which wasn't all that terrible com-
pared to living in any city. But, to ensure they had months of supplies
on hand in the event of some sort of damage to their FTL or Hyperspace drives, they kept space rations on board. It really was only good
enough to handle keeping you alive if one of the systems went down.
If both went down, and you were stuck in Real Space, you were dead
unless someone picked up your distress beacon while passing by in the
Warp.

After all, the distances between stars are staggeringly unimaginable
when thinking in Real Space terms. In the old days, when interstellar

travel started for humans, we had to use cryopods and sleep our way between systems. I think I remember learning in school that the first inhabitable system we traveled to, the TRAPPIST system, took about 30 years with the first Alcubierre drive. And it was one of the closest star systems in the galaxy, at only forty light years out.

By the time the first explorers, settlers really, arrived; better Alcubierre drives had been designed and the second batch of settlers were nearly caught up with them. They'd left only five years prior.

Hyperspace was discovered only twenty years after that. Then we exploded into the galaxy, exploring a dozen small nearby systems before the second generation of Trappist humans had lived their whole lives.

It was just about then, I think, that we discovered the Voltchi; and maybe a dozen years later that the Expanse discovered us.

And then the entire galaxy discovered Djugga. Earth doesn't get the credit for discovering it, but as the technologically more advanced species, Earth gets the credit for spreading it to the Expanse as we were absorbed into it by the Hegemony.

That only went to help the Deep Djugga enhance its' reputation as lower class and rebellious, thanks to it coming from the Benighted Last Spiral Arm.

As I made my way down to the galley for some unappetizing space rations, I heard the sound of that lower class, rebellious rhythm blasting down the halls through the airlock open to the, now former, Mouse Club. The galley thumped along with the beats and strings and growls with an alto edge.

Sitting there, deep in thought and on her own, was Neridah Blooming-Star. Vi had provided the young page with an outfit from her wardrobe and it was obvious the upper-class ambassador's daughter wasn't very comfortable in it. That, or she wasn't very comfortable in her own skin.

Quite a bit of which was showing.

The outfit the Tilarian had supplied her, as with all her outfits, revealed Neridah's dark-skinned midriff. It wasn't toned like Vi's, which had been dancing for the pleasure and eye-candy of crime lords and

Djugga fans since her teens. But, although not hard muscled, it wasn't unhealthy or particularly unfit. The soft exposed skin was largely what she was covering with her arms.

The arms were adorned to the wrists with billowing white sleeves that were slit from the cuff to the shoulders, held together at three points by golden buttons. They were fastened to the form fitting white top, accented with golden filigree-like thread, by buttons matching the ones on the sleeves.

Vi's breasts were larger than Neridah's, but somehow the performer had managed to tie the back of the top in a way that firmed up the material and kept it from looking slack on the girl.

To match the sleeves, Neridah was now wearing the sheer white skirt that Vi' had worn on stage the night before. It can only be hoped that the almost-visible white panties she was wearing underneath were hers.

Otherwise that would have been weird.

"Ah, detective." Neridah said as I walked in, trying to shrug off the obvious discomfort she had in the garments, "I've been looking through the ambassadorial records in the ship's database."

She nodded to the handheld terminal in her hand, which was synced to the *Legacy's Façade's* computer system.

I poured myself a cup of what might have passed as coffee, though the color was definitely not coffee. But the smell and effect were similar. Maybe it was a dark heavy tea. I wasn't sure.

"Did you find your Dagger of Augury?" I said with mixed feelings. If she found it, this job was already over, and I basically wasn't getting much pay. But, on the other hand, if what they were dealing with was true, they were going to need the dagger to supposedly face off against the chaotic monsters of some other-dimensional hellscape.

"No..." her visage became unsettled again, as it had been before.

So it wasn't the outfit that made her feel uncomfortable. I had mixed feelings again. The magical dagger of whatever-it-does wasn't in the ship's records. And whatever they were supposed to use it for in stopping a second Betrayal couldn't happen without it.

But hey, I was gonna get more pay. You have to find the silver lining in storm clouds, I guess.

"Ok." I walked over with my cup of Red Brew and sat across from her at the galley's table and motioned for her to hand me the tablet while I sipped the coffee-ish stuff with the other hand.

She did so, glumly.

To be a good private detective isn't, usually, about beating feet and hunting people down. It wasn't about dodging club-wielding Mooks or saving damsels in distress from interplanetary crime bosses.

Most of the time, the best detective work happened from your desk at the office with a computer system in front of you. Effectively, you had to be a galaxy-class library nerd.

Researching is what I did best.

The ambassadorial database from the ship was easily twenty years old, which fit with the war against Archimedes and pushing the Nether backward to the border systems of Iblis. The system they used for file structures were incredibly complex, but remained quite static after thousands of years of bureaucratic regulation from the Expanse.

That would mean very little about the gap in twenty years should have stood in my way.

"Ok," I punched in some search parameters for the name of the blade and got nothing, "so it isn't in there listed by its name. What else do we know about it?"

"Well..." she started to talk, but I silenced her with a raised hand after putting down the coffee. I hadn't taken my eyes off the tablet and the rhetorical question's answer was more a distraction than any help I predicted it would be.

I cross referenced all artifacts in the possession of Ambassador Conner Blooming-Star at the time of his death. Obviously, there was no reference to the Totem Master's death, because it happened when he and Captain Tora defected from the System Lords. So, I looked at the last entries regarding totem master artifacts.

Nothing there. Absolutely nothing.

I had never met a Totem Master or a Shaman personally, but I knew enough about them from popular media to know that almost no variety of their ilk was devoid of religious articles and artifacts of some sort; talismans, voodoo dolls, alien statues, holy tomes, bibles, torahs, Buddha statues, or any of countless other types depending on their ethnic origins.

Neridah could tell I was onto something. My secretary tells me I make "a face", that I've never gotten a straight on look at, when I've found a clue. It must be a pretty obvious tell because she'd clued into it.

"What is it?" she said excitedly.

"You know your father...er...uncle...well?" I said, "You know, Conner. Not the one who raised you?"

"Angus Blooming-Star will always be my dad." She straightened with prideful poise, "I don't know why Uncle Conner gave me up. But, whatever reason he had, good or bad, it was Angus that raised me. I'd been thinking about that since you told me."

"Ok," I nodded. I could respect that. My own bond with my biological father wasn't close. Parents are the ones who care for you and are there for you, even if they aren't your blood. "So, I'll just call him Conner to make life less confusing. You know him well?"

She shrugged, "He was there at Moots. I saw him then."

I tilted my head, confused. That was a word I didn't know well.

"Moots?" I said, "Is that like a holiday? Christmas, Easter, Freysblot?"

"Ah," she smiled, amused at my expense. It was cute really. She'd been so serious or scared or metaphysically deep that I hadn't seen that side closely yet. She had dimples, "No. A Moot is when a clan gathers to debate something important to them. You know the First Peoples is made up of many ethnicities?"

"Yes," I put the pad down and picked up the caffeinated-bean-of-red, "Pretty much all aboriginal peoples and the worshipers of the Old Religions, and even some of the newer ones like Christianity, uniting in one spiritual representation of humanity."

She nodded in approval, "Right. Well, I'm mostly aboriginal from the Australian continent in ancestry. But, my father and uncle both have British Islander first names because their mother was a Druidic Priestess from a line going back to the Awakening."

The Awakening is what the First Peoples called the reemergence of the spiritual world's significance with the discovery of Hyperspace and the parallel dimension's effects on our own, and vice versa. That's the point they can all point to the inclusion of humans in the galactic trend of what is known as Totem Masters and Shamans.

"Well," she continued, "My mother's clan has called a few moots that Conner and Angus both attended as they are technically clansmen despite our last name being based on Aboriginal beliefs. I get to go to the Moots as well and give input on matters of the clans."

"What were they discussing?" I said.

"Clan business." She said with finality. Clearly, clan business was not my business. "But, really, I have no idea. I was too young to participate at the time. There hasn't been one since I joined the Ambassadorial service."

"Did you have much exposure to Conner during that time?" I pressed, since the clan issues weren't the point.

"He always checked in with me." Neridah looked distant, remembering, "Made sure I was doing well in school and on track to the Ambassadorial Corps like father wanted. He'd usually bring me something small as a gift from whatever star system he'd been visiting last."

She looked sad and distant. He obviously did care about her, even if he wasn't there as a father figure. And he died in the Betrayal.

I decided to get the questions back on track so she didn't have to dwell on it.

"But he was a Totem Master." I continued, "Of the Druids or Aborigine?"

That snapped her back to the moment and she looked almost startled by the return, "Oh, um, both. Except he wasn't a Totem Master for us...er...the tribe. He was a Shaman, our Cleverman."

Whoa. A Totem Master and Shaman. That was supposed to be crazy rare. "You mean he could contact both the spirit guides from the Warp and he could commune with spirits of the dead?"

She nodded, "I guess so. I never really got to learn much about him regarding that. I was never there for him doing his work. He was always traveling."

"Did he have any artifacts of his own?" I said, "Anything he carried on him?"

"You mean the dagger?" she looked confused, "I couldn't find it in the system."

"That's just it." I turned the pad to her, "I couldn't find any in the system. Artifacts are powerful tools for those with the ability to use them. That is, at least, according to the Expanse. There are laws on their registration for anything more powerful than simple token representations."

She pulled the pad to her and double checked my work. As a diplomatic page she would have had the knowledge to peruse those particular systems almost as good as someone who's used to digging, like me.

"That can't be right." Her brow furrowed in frustration, "What does that mean?"

I took the pad back and began looking through the actual database, instead of the data stored on it. A few moments later, I found it. The gap in the data.

"Someone's deleted it." I beamed, proud of myself, "There was a section of data with a hidden header on *Registered Artifacts*...and, it's empty."

No. Not empty, replaced with useless data. I started tapping and swiping on the screen.

"What?" Neridah said and scooted around until she was sitting next to me. I didn't notice right away, enthralled as I was in the chase for information.

Then I noticed it. The sweet smell of jasmine from her hair. The warmth of a bare section of her arm against mine, which had previously been used to the cool air of the ship's interior. The touch of her hip against mine.

The excitement, welling up inside me, came at me like a wave of surprise and for a moment I rode it's inspiration to finish what I'd begun before having to scoot an inch away from her to compose myself.

You don't get attached to clients. It's not good for business.

"Um," I turned the pad to her and pointed to a section of screen. "There was some data placed here where someone snooping would eventually look. It's not the list of artifacts, it's an apparent jumble of numbers."

I swiped the screen to a different tab, showing star charts, "They're location coordinates."

I tapped on each sequence of numbers. The screen zoomed from the Expanse as a whole, to the Benighted Final Spiral Arm, to the Terran Systems, to the Sol System, to Earth, and finally down to the eastern seaboard of North America. A point on the northeastern of the primary landmass illuminated.

I noted the exact location in my wrist computer for later.

"I don't know what's there," I tapped the point, "But that's a message. Twenty years ago, before or about when Conner died, someone put this location in this database for someone else to find."

X

∞

CHAPTER TEN

Load Playlist Track: Drake, One Dance

We arrived at the Talal'k Spaceport on Arcturis Major not long after. I'd held off on sampling the "chicken noodle soup protein ration" bar, the only semi-appealing food selection on board the *Legacy's Façade* in the hopes of finding something more appetizing in one of the Starport's cantinas or cafes.

That's where the biggest differences, other than population, with the two moons of Arcturis lie; Arcturis Major had a legitimate spaceport. The one on Minor was basically just a landing field with an automated registration station for you to download the latest navigational charts, check for jobs, and post your availability for passengers or cargo.

Talal'k Spaceport was somewhat generic as far as Expanse Spaceports went, built and paid for with your income taxes. However, as the planet Minor and Major orbited were owned outright by the Arcturis Corporation, the "feel" of the only public spaceport in the system definitely had a very corporate feel.

Arcturis branding and propaganda, meant mostly for the loyalty of their workers, was everywhere. Although the corporation only created products based on the gasses of the host planet, they had an official store supplying every basic and entertainment product gas miners and their families could need.

Talal'k, the city itself, was a company town. It started off as a small-time mining settlement for those working up at the harvesting station. But, as with any population, those dedicated to servicing them migrated to the moon, or were eventually born locally.

And one thing that any service industry ultimately resulted in, unless the settlement was run by a hyper conservative group, like the NeoPuritanicals, were bars. And Bars provided access to possibly decent booze and, more important at the moment, proper food.

The *Legacy's Façade* needed to refuel, offload some of the more exotic contraband Mouse had been stashing in his club, and plan out what under-the-table angle they were going to plot for their next tour location. Planning to save the Galaxy didn't change the fact that Tora and her crew needed to earn credits to keep the fuel tanks full, the environmental systems charged, and their one defensive cannon armed.

I had told her about the coordinates on Earth and the crew agreed that the absence of the file was significant and that the clue was vital to chasing down the Dagger of Augury. However, a trip straight back to Earth would cost them most of a tank of fuel and there was very little likelihood of them being able to arrange a club venue in Sol Prime and hope to get away with it.

"We're going to have to play a few gigs on the way." Captain Tora had Tree run the numbers to her over an ear piece while we all wandered toward the *Talal'kantina*, "Probably three stops, some side business on the way, and then we can afford to go to Earth for a few days docking fees, refuel, and get back outward toward a smaller system."

Inside the cantina was a gaggle of beings from around the Expanse. Being a company town, they weren't the seedy or untrustworthy types you'd find in some starports. Most of them were contracted freighter crews, complete with company or ship uniforms. Others were general workers at the starport. In a way that made us stand out, despite the diversity of species present. You could feel it as the crowd got a little quieter and the feeling of being watched became palpable. We were the seedy, untrustworthy type now.

The cantina was about 300 square meters in size, pretty big for a bar, kinda small for a full on restaurant. The bar itself was at the center of the room, a rectangle bar front with hard angles all surrounding a centralized shelf system covered in bottles from a couple hundred different worlds. At a station on each side of the rectangle was a tap for pouring drinks, all hooked up to a network of kegs and containers inside the bar itself.

Overhead, modern popular music belted out with enough volume to obfuscate each table's conversation from the other. The Capital System's club music consisted of a thumping, digitized repetition almost instinctually uniform throughout the galaxy. It was catchy, short, simple and melodic with rhythms that were diluted enough to please the widest possible audience of Core World residents. It had no special name, like Rock and Roll, or Heavy Metal, or Djugga. Its galactic common tongue translation fit in pretty well with Earth's equivalent in English; "Pop music." Together with the murmur of a dozen tables and booths, and twice as many stools at the bar, you could hear everything, and yet nothing, of the room.

Unlike the scrapped bartender droid I'd destroyed outside the Mouse Club, the bartender here was an actual person. I wasn't sure what species, or even gender, of person it was, but it spoke clear GCT when taking orders for drinks. The being was the color of soot. Its bald head was a nose-less face with a bulbous cranium that had bulging veins riddled along the sides where there would have been ears on a human. The general body type was androgynous, but was adorned in a simple bipedal black jumpsuit that would have fit me; tall and wiry.

After settling into a booth, Kliff had to acquire a chair from a table and sit on the end, we all looked at copies of the menu projecting onto the table's surface, pressing the selections with our fingers so our order would go to the line cook located in some back room behind the bar. We also selected our drinks.

"I can't wait for three or four gigs. I'm on the clock and I'm not going to charge Neridah here my rate while I hitch hike with you back to Earth. My expenses cover getting me and my pod back with standard transport." I watched the Grey Bartender check his screen, look over to us, and then start prepping glasses.

"But..." Neridah pleaded, "You have to stick with us. The Totems had you all together. This isn't something only one of you can do."

I put my hand up and stopped her, "I'm not here for your prophecy, sister. I'm a private detective and you've hired me to do a job. I'm going to get my job done and collect my pay. And, I'll hopefully be done and waiting for you when you get to Earth. If that's not completing my part of both the bargain and your prophecy, I don't know what is."

She looked like she wanted to dispute it somehow, her lips pursed in on themselves. But, she had nothing. It was logical. I could possibly wrap up getting the Dagger of Augury and have it in their hands by the time the *Legacy's Façade* arrived at Earth, and she knew it.

"I think it's a good plan." Captain Tora said as a basket of appetizers were dropped off at the table by a green woman with completely black eyes, and dressed in a uniform with the pub's logo on it. Tora thanked her and tore into the small breadstick things with little red bugs crawling on it.

"What the hell are those?" I asked horrified, literally shifting in my seat a few inches.

"I call them Chili beetles." She said putting a mouthful of bread in and crunched the beetle husks with the softer bread, and mumbled, "Mther rrelly goot."

Kliff treated the bread like a lollipop and licked the bugs off and left the bread on the plate in front of him while Eight dove into the spicy smelling critters with almost wild abandon, hunched slightly over his portion and not looking up; like he was in some sort of hurry.

Vi sat back and waited for her own order.

"Not having any Vi?" I asked her, "Everyone else seems so...enthusiastic."

"Not me." Neridah muttered.

"Nor I," Vi seemed to hum, "I do naught eat anyzing living that isn't plant based, even bugs. Females of my species are typically vegetarian. I take it a little farther. We can technically eat meat, but ve only have the craving vhen pregnant with males. Our men are stronger and need more proteins than us. Eating them outside of child bearing tends to make us sick. Ve do naught process it vell."

"But why not the bugs?" Neridah asked her.

"Aside from moral reasons?" she sneered as she picked up a bread stick and placed it on my plate, "Really? Look at them? Crawling like that. You can have mine if you want."

Moral reasons? I shook my head and summoned up the courage and bit into the sweet fluffy bread and into the remarkably spicy beetles. They were strangely like chili peppers, hence Tora's name for them.

I forced the entire bread stick down and grabbed at my drink when the waitress dropped it off.

"Wow." I coughed, "Very hot."

Kliff growled amusedly and the Diva translated it as "Khaleef-graa says you wouldn't survive two meals on Grothrark."

I chuckled, "Probably not."

"Anyway," I said turning to Neridah, "I'll send the Message to your father, Angus, about what you're up to when I get to Earth. It'll get there faster from there than here anyway. Then, I'll pay my rent with your deposit. Then, while I'm waiting for his payment, I'll be working on your case."

"Do you want me to come with you?" she said, "It's not like I can play drums or anything."

There were chuckles across the table and she looked embarrassed.

"No." I said, she clearly didn't know the story of the drummers in the band. I decided to leave that to the Odds to explain the inside joke. "If you think I shouldn't leave the group because of some prophecy, how do you think your prophecy will do with you leaving the group? Besides, I work better alone."

We all ate in silence after our food showed up. Kliff was eating some large, living wormlike food, at least until he bit into it and it died. After that, he kept spooning some kind of sauce over it. Tora and I had ordered the same main course, a steak sandwich. I'm not sure what type of mammal the steak was made of, but it was red meat and delicious.

Vi and Neridah had ordered the same thing as well, a soup made from soy and the lactate of some sort of creature spiced with peppers, just not the crawling bug kind.

Eight continued his anxious eating right through the pork and beans, covered in ketchup. He didn't seem to relax until he was done eating. It was like he was racing us. But, he returned to his mellow and jovial self once finished.

I'd heard about that with soldiers. It had something to do with the need to be quick and on the move. Some said it was from the hurry and stress of eating while in basic training. I'd met a Colonial Trooper, not the manufactured human variety, back on Earth on leave.

She did the same thing and, like Eight, made sure she was always sitting facing the entrance of any public place we'd eaten together at. She'd hired me for a simple job.

Instead of a pure missing person's case, she just needed someone to hunt down old members of her unit that had left years prior. She wanted to look them up and relive some of the good old days from when the Sol Systems were embroiled in a smuggling and piracy epidemic that, likely, had ties back to Xanadu. They'd quelled the attacks on the shipping lanes, but it was its own miniature war.

I've been in my own scrapes over time and sometimes I have dreams about them. But soldiers, and the like, trained to face stress and anxiety from the beginning of their career?

Yeah, I couldn't do it. I don't want to spend the rest of my life rushing a meal and looking over my shoulder for an enemy that isn't there.

After I'd finished my meal, just a little bit after Eight, I washed my food down with some synthetic scotch on the rocks.

Standing up, I winked at Neridah, and said, "Ok, kid. This meal was on the clock. I won't send you a receipt since you're already here to cover it. I'll catch the lot of you back on Earth."

Tora air saluted with her sandwich.

"Be 'bout a week behind you, after stops." She said as she shoved the delectable meat and bread into her mouth. It'd obviously been a while since she'd been off ship's rations.

We all waved and I wandered my way out of the bar and away from the pop music and the Djugga band. I walked to the registration station, the one basic thing in common between the two moons of Arcturis' starports.

"Time to go home." I said to myself as I started checking for flights back to Earth.

XI

❧

CHAPTER ELEVEN

Load Playlist Track: Beats Antique, Looking For Something

Flying in a passenger ship across the vast expanse of stars, even on the economy class ticket I was going to expense to Neridah Blooming-Star, was orders of magnitude more luxurious and comfortable than my normal method of interplanetary travel. Typically, I'd be riding in Snowball in some cargo hold in an effort to both save some credits and to have the mini-pod with me for its flexibility of movement and utilitarian ability to carry more stuff with me.

But with the damage, I opted to leave Snowball with the *Legacy's Façade*. They'd be going to Earth soon enough anyway and I'd get it back. Besides, taking passenger transport would allow me more direct flights.

The cabins, if you could call them that, in steerage aboard the *Plentitude* were only three feet tall, horizontal sleeping spaces designed to fit at most a seven foot tall being. The bed was about the size of a twin mattress. Embedded in the walls was a small stowage compartment for a carryon bag.

The *Plentitude* was pretty large as far as passenger ships go. Practically a small city, the *Plentitude* was over 350 meters long from stem to stern with a passenger capacity of almost six thousand. Nearly half of that was in steerage, crammed together in the sleeping compartments.

The second third of the remaining passengers were business class, granted a small room with enough space for a private shower and a small desk beside an equally small bed. Some were larger rooms for couples traveling together.

The final third of the passenger population were in luxury-class staterooms. The jump between business and first class treatment represented a significant wealth gap. They had entire suites, with more than one bedroom, each with a queen-sized bed. They had small kitchenettes, which they rarely used. They tended to eat in the restaurants of the ship instead of the business class mess halls or the steerage's bulk galleys.

Steerage was relegated to a common eating area with food dispensers. At least the business class had freshly cooked cafeteria-style food.

The *Plentitude* wasn't uncommon for the style of large passenger ships throughout the Expanse. Sure, there were bigger and more luxurious cruise ships that took their time through their tour of the most aesthetically pleasing elements of the galaxy.

But, in terms of pure transportation, ships like this were the way to go. I wasn't complaining. Better than sleeping in the mini-pod – you'd think that would make me happy. My mini-pod doubled as my mobile office.

I felt a little naked without it. It made it hard to sleep, but sleep I did.

I was in that middle place, that veil between consciousness and imagination. That place Poe referred to in his poems about the Eidolon, named *NIGHT – a Thule*. Eidolons are ghosts or ideas of people. Thules are beyond the borders of the known world. Here I was in space and dreaming about the idea of a person, it fit.

But not just any person – I was dreaming of Neridah. She was there with me in the sleeping compartment, or some impossibly comfortable version of it. She lay there next to me, wearing that outfit Vi had dressed her up in. The weird lights of hyperspace played from behind me, swirling amber and purple in her eyes.

I brushed a length of impossibly smooth hair, not natural to her background, from her face with a gloved hand so I could look more at those stunning, swirling eyes. I watched as the lights of hyperspace danced and moved against shadows that swirled in reaction.

But something was wrong with one of her eyes – horribly wrong. Something writhed in the milky white of her inner left eye, like a black oozing worm trying to break into her iris.

"It's ok, Einar." She said smiling. "This is how it is supposed to be."

I startled awake and hit my head on the low ceiling of the compartment and banged around while I took control of the swirling feeling of being trapped.

The sleeping compartment could seal shut for both privacy and security. But, it could also cause a person with claustrophobia some serious discomfort. Even for me, who was used to sleeping in his mini-pod for a long series of flights, the space was like laying yourself out in a coffin.

That is, if the coffin had an individualized climate control and flat screen television in it with the latest downloads from the major news and entertainment Netlinks from throughout the expanse.

Either way, I was glad I got a window cabin. Laying there on my side, avoiding the tenderness in my back, I stared out at the psychedelic aurora-like colors of traveling at Warp through Hyperspace; Faster-than-Light through a parallel universe with less restrictive laws of relativity. Less than a hundred and fifty years ago and this would have been an impossibility of science fiction...fantasy even.

At least hard science-fiction had predicted the Alcubierre method as far back as the Nineteen Nineties.

But by now, the year Twenty-Two Forty-Five, by Earth's Calendar, we'd gone from a single planet without even an off-world colony in Sol Prime, to controlling three star systems in the Sol System. Some of them had multiple human colonies on them, and that ignores the few non-human worlds of the Sol System, like Voltch'I, that entered into the Expanse with us.

Between finding alien life on worlds we explored and being the primitives encountered by the Expanse, I'd say we got pretty lucky that no one tried conquering and wiping us out. It wasn't unheard of in the Expanse.

Not everyone who discovered how to travel the stars is nice.

Laying there, my thoughts were lost in the swirling nimbus of light. As much as I like old punk when I want to get my blood up, I tend to prefer more light and world gypsy-style music when relaxing.

I'd been listening to some tunes from the early twenty-first century. This time in what might be Hindi or Bengali, but the Net's file said it was Sankrit.

"*Hare Hare Ganges matev sri sankara Paravati pati mahatev sri sankara Jai Shiva om!*" the singer of the band called Sadhana sang what I think was a sutra to some kind of rain stick sound, chimes, and hand-played drums. It was soothing. I could have brought up the lyrics to know the words and how they translated into either Icelandic or GCT, but sometimes you just need to enjoy things for how they sounded.

This had been a simple job when it started out; find the girl, take her home. But, jobs were rarely as simple as all that. I should have expected a little more trouble.

Technically, I'd finished the job. The next morning, by New Reykjavik time, I'd be in Sol Prime's main orbiting starport, *Earthport Jennifer Sidey*, at Legrange Point Three. From there I could send Angus Blooming-Star my report and bill via the Expanse Messenger Station. So I was, technically, on a new job.

Still, what was I thinking? Some girl claims she could see extra-dimensional ghosts of animals from other worlds and says they told her a bunch of punk metal space gypsies and a private detective were going to save the Galaxy from the Nether? And I'm supposed to buy that?

And even if I did....was I crazy enough to actually try? The Nether? I'd never seen a Nether controlled mutant. The closest I'd ever come were those with free will. There were two types of free Mutants.

One type was someone who resisted the mind-controlling powers of the Nether; though a Shaman would tell you it was their spirit that was defeated and not their mind. Their body was still biologically twisted by the Nether, but they retained their original Free Will; as opposed to the warped version of their identity that was loyal to the Nether and, somehow, to System Lord Wilfred Archimedes the Third.

The second type were those who were born to a coupling between a Mutant and another sentient being. Sometimes that coupling was a relationship with the aforementioned free-willed Mutant. Sometimes it was the result of a less willing reproduction with what are called Nether Mutants, the evil mutants loyal to the Nether.

Only a full Nether can change you into a Mutant. But, that doesn't stop the twisted and evil versions of who people once were from trying to spread the Nether's existence.

Technically, a newborn of a Nether Mutant with a non-mutant might be instinctually loyal to the Nether. But, women impregnated by a Nether controlled Mutant rarely keep their children to find out. That is, if they ever got free from the Nether Mutant to do so.

I'd heard nightmares, from during the war, of entire colonies being overrun by Nether Mutants without access to a Nether creature. They'd slaughter all the males they didn't enslave to some labor purpose and take the women to help propagate their numbers.

But, maybe that was just horror stories to make us hate our enemies. Maybe some kind of propaganda. Or some kind of story to make kids stay in their beds. I dunno. For me, it was my mid-teens. For someone like Neridah it would have been a child, maybe pushing ten at most.

The thing with Mutants is that their twisted genetics could find a way to reproduce with any species. The Nether were designed to spread. Thankfully, a Mutant couldn't just turn anyone into a Mutant.

That'd be like some scary Zombie story.

Who would willingly go up against that kind of horror and evil?

"Not me, that's who." I spoke to my reflection in the window, "I'm just getting a Dagger. If it helps Miss Blooming-Star and the Odds to save the Galaxy, great. I'll feel proud of doing my part and be done with it."

But I wasn't going to go fight some unfathomable existential space horrors.

The vein on my neck was pulsing and I could feel the beginnings of a headache coming on. Thinking about space monsters and crazy prophecies was not in my best interest.

I was in a comfy cabin for a few days now. I had actually gotten a few decent night's sleep, when I wasn't waking myself up by rolling onto my back.

And, after being off world for a while, I was almost home.

My apartment wasn't much, but it was mine. And I had a cred stick in my pocket, the deposit from Neridah Blooming-Star, to pay my rent with. I even had enough to back pay my secretary Velma. My last pay check to her was the end of my money, which I gave her as I was leaving Earth, and I was already overdue by a week.

This trip home, I didn't have to sneak into New Reykjavik and avoid the office, as I'd had to do on an occasional job where she, mercifully, put up with my delays in payment. I'd go to the office before I went home. I could pay the rent from anywhere in the star system, anyway.

Once you were in a star system, you didn't have to worry about the problems with transmitting data or money within the system. Telecommunications in Normal Space were effectively instantaneous over the short distances of a star system thanks to quantum telecommunications. If only Einstein's "spooky action at a distance" didn't start to break down when you went light years out.

Technically, instantaneous communication across vast distances doesn't work. All you can tell is the state change of one point in relationship to the state change of an entangled object somewhere else. But, from those changes in state, you can interpret data out of it.

That's always how digital communications have effectively worked anyway. It's more complicated than the more ancient radio days, and seriously outside of my physics knowledge. They teach that stuff to high school kids these days, but when I was in school it was undergrad physics.

I never finished college. I'm smart and great at research. And I can do all the homework in the Galaxy to solve a case, if you pay me. If I'm paying you for me to do homework though, I find it hard to motivate myself to do the work. Besides, if it's high end physics I need to figure out, they have computers for that.

I'd deposit the money at the local bank at *Jennifer Side,y* and they'd quantum link up their status system-wide, and that status would sync up with the Messenger service, who carry and propagate these official system downloads to their destinations.

As a result, the farther out from the source of information; the more out of sync the Galaxy and the Expanse's records were with reality. This is why private investigators like me had jobs.

Sometimes, when research didn't work, you had to go and beat some feet on another world.

"Home." I muttered to myself as I carefully rolled onto my back. The skin ached, and probably would for a few more days, but I'd already had a few days to get used to it.

I placed my red fedora over my eyes, rather than closing the porthole shutters. The swirling lights of Hyperspace crept in under the brim of the hat and gently flashed through my closed eyelids.

The cabin was much less like a coffin when I could see the light. It was my fourth night on the ship and I'd basically avoided everyone except for those I passed on the way to the restroom, showers, or the shared galley for this section of *The Plentitude*.

The next day there'd be lots of people that I couldn't avoid.

XII

CHAPTER TWELVE

Load Playlist Track: Wu-Tang Clan (Prodigal Sunn), Slow Blues
"Welcome to *Earthport Jennifer Sidey*. Long may it serve the Empress."
A woman's voice spoke over the intercom in English as I crossed onto
the immense docking platform from the ship. She repeated the words
in Mandarin, German, and GCT. Finally, the voice said it again in High
Ara'lon, the official language of the Royal Expanse Hegemony. I didn't
know the language well myself, but every school kid was required to
learn the last part, "Long may it serve the Empress." I knew how to say it
in gender neutral, feminine, masculine, multi-gender, and the self-iden-
tifying phrases of the language.

Pretty much everybody did. That's how several millennia-old galactic spanning absolute sovereigns operate, I guess - loyalty through oaths
and pledges from birth until death.

All around me the thousands of passengers of the *Plentitude* were disembarking from the massive passenger ship and making their way into
the crowded Starport.

I had my headset in, wirelessly connected to my wrist computer. I
ignored the crowd around me and took in the space as I listened to the
sitar solo followed with the drums of Sel by Smadj.

The walls, floor and ceiling of the massive docking bay were all white, with the stained discoloring of age. The Earthport, as it was commonly called, was old – predating the merging of the Sol Systems with the Expanse. Very few people called it the *Jennifer Sidey*, though everyone recognized the name. The ancient Starport was named for a North American from the empire that had been called Canada before it was labeled The Canadian Zone by the System Parliament. Some sort of early astronaut from before we'd landed on Mars, whose engineering work in propulsion made the first Europa landing possible and gave Earth access to large bodies of water outside the home world.

Just like illudium as a fuel source, you don't get far into the cosmos without water. Her work helped change the game for humanity.

Back then, Earth wasn't a single government, but a gaggle of warring and rival nations.

At least we've managed to get that sorted. Sure, planets and entire systems will have disputes with one another. There might even be the occasional war somewhere in the Expanse, as some rebel system attempts to fight against the Hegemony or if they have some trouble with a neighbor. But, in terms of the classic wars of the pre-Expanse, we lived in relative peace.

Besides, the Betrayal was enough to get the whole galaxy back on board with one another – at least at first. That was back when I was a kid. So, while I remember how important it was to my parents and everyone around me, I didn't experience it the way an adult would. Nor the way someone who fought in it would.

I made my way over to the windows of the loading dock, where thousands of people were herded together waiting for authorization to board the *Plentitude*. The passengers for the next leg of the journey were destined for Tau Ceti's two colony worlds – a pair of planets with the gravity of Earth, barely in the habitable zones, requiring domed cities to maintain an atmosphere. However, they were great mining worlds that supplied natural resources to the Sol Systems.

They also had the best Astro Racing team in the Rim – at least according to fans; of which I was one.

Outside the windows, I looked back at the massive unpainted *Plentitude's* cylindrical body, with bulbous pods, almost organic looking, spread around its body and its round tipped nose. The large bulky engine section, the only straight edges on the ship, reach off into the distant, barely visible starlight. The light pollution of the sun off the Earthgate's far side almost masked the star.

The gigantic *Earthport* was a flying saucer-like disk, the kind people used to think aliens traveled in to abduct people – they were technically right by the way. But, that's another story. Off of the central large disk, which was close to three kilometers in diameter, were attached four similar, smaller disks. These were about a kilometer wide each – three of which had three docking ports for large vessels like the *Plentitude*. The last of the smaller disks were home to less significant vessels that could hop from system to system or within Sol Prime itself – ships ranging around the size of the *Legacy's Façade*r.

That's where I would be heading after a quick trip to the Messenger Station in the central disk – to look for a ride back to Earth.

The *Asiana* docking bay was awash with the smell of curries and stir fries – Asian and Indian foods mostly filled this section of the *Earthport's* food court. That'd traditionally been the case, since the old Indian Space Agency was responsible for constructing this docking disk.

Europa had been built by the Europeans, so most of the food there was likewise authentic – Germany, England, Italy, and France particularly. *Slavia* had been built by the New Russian Federation, which had just reformed after a coup against their oligarchy – the food there was mostly Slavic-Norse fusion. I was tempted to make my way in that direction and pick up a plate of Minkhe from their *Fiskmarkaðurinn* – their fish market serves as a buying spot for restaurants throughout Sol Prime. You aren't even allowed to fly to earth to buy seafood unless you're an Earth resident. It's a matter of health safety and port security.

But, I didn't have time for delicious smoked and dried whale, and get to my planned flight back to Earth – not if I wanted to stop at the

Messenger service on the way. If I missed my flight, I'd add an entire day to my trip with the slowness of Real Space.

I would have to beeline it to *The Hub*, the large central disk of the *Earthport*.

I caught a hyperloop vactrain from the station at the center of *Asiana*. If I hadn't, the walk would have been an all day affair. It cost me a couple of credits I would have to expend to Neridah, but twenty minutes after the transport tube took off, I was at the outer edges of an easily city-sized Starport.

Close to a half million people worked, operated, and lived at *Earthport Jennifer Sidey* – all of them lived in *The Hub*. The docking disks of *Asiana*, *Europa*, *Slavia*, and *New Cairo* were only for doing business or transient passenger hotels. All residents lived in *The Hub*. From there, the entire port system was managed, supported, and kept secure. Unauthorized personnel were not allowed into the docking disks from within *The Hub*.

"Ugh..." I groaned to myself. "I hate having to go through security between each of these friggin' disks."

But I would have to before heading to the *New Cairo* disk and catching a ferry to Earth.

The Hub itself had been constructed largely by the North American Alliance, with help from the Australian and African space programs – they lacked the honor of having their cultural name on the section, but it had the largest level of effort.

I turned off the music on my headset, which had progressed to *Chambermaid Swing* by Perov Stellar, an electro-swing composer that found worldwide fame in 2020 with the centennial anniversary of the Roaring Twenties.

"Hey!" I yelled in English. I waved to someone on the street outside the hyperloop station. A young fit Indian man on repulsor skates pulled up to me, pulling his hover rickshaw behind him.

He was a Sikh, an Indian of the Sikh religion. You could tell mostly by his turban, which was bright blue with some sort of white ornamental design on it. He also had a small dagger somehow tucked into a belt or strap of some kind. I recognized the look, but didn't know much about them.

All the time I'd spent traveling this corner of the Expanse on cases, I hadn't spent much time on the eastern side of the planet. I'd have to rectify that just as soon as a client could justify the travel expenses.

"Where to, sir?" he said to me in English with a British accent, which was less common off world than it used to be. This guy must have been a recent transplant to *The Hub* from Earth. That wasn't easy to do these day – they were pretty full up.

"The Messenger station." I instructed him, swiping my credit stick over my wrist computer, verifying the money, and then beaming the money to the guy's pay screen.

"Ah, very good, sir." He smiled and began skating off through a crowd of rickshaws and bicycles that somehow managed a dance of order in a sea of travel chaos throughout a city as busy as any urban sprawl on Earth.

Before long, we'd passed through crowded roads of pedestrians, bicyclists, and every form of manual conveyance imaginable from human and alien alike – there were no vehicles on the streets of *The Hub*. If I'd come to the *Earthport* on a cargo ship with Snowball, I would have had to fly it from docking disk to docking disk myself – something it could in no way have done in its' current condition.

The *Earthport* had just finished rotating so the sun had "set" below the radiation dome's horizon of the upper portion of the station. Below me, and inverted on *The Hub*, the day was just beginning for the other half of the population. They were living a mirrored-image life, with a nearly duplicate infrastructure to the side I was on. But, they made their half of the city their own. I've heard the rivalry between the Gravball clubs of each side was legendary; I noted I'd have to check out a game in person one season.

Luckily for me, the very center of *The Hub* was where the Space Traffic Control, the Starship Maintenance, and all vital Starport functions operated at. Not just the management of the station itself.

This was where the station's bureaucracy operated – and in the Expanse, the bureaucracy never sleeps. Messengers may come and go, but their offices are always open and ready to serve the collection and distribution of information for the good of the Hegemony, the System Lords, and the Parliaments.

I entered into the ten person operation. Messengers in a Messenger station were typically of two varieties; apprentice Messengers doing the dull and administrative tasks that no one else wanted to do, and the elder Messengers who were too old to make long journeys.

The Messenger who sat smiling at me as I came up to his window was an exception.

"Hey Casey!" I tipped my red hat at him.

Casey sat in his hover chair, both of his legs missing just above the knees. His left arm, or rather what was left of it, was covered by a strategically placed shawl with the logo of the Messenger service. His uniform, a regal looking blue suit, with gold trim, had a gold-and-silver lanyard attached to it with his biometric scanner in a pocket. The gold-and-silver lanyards were only given to Messengers who had earned their highest honors.

Typically, this indicated the act of dying in the line of duty. Few earned it alive.

He beamed, "Well if it isn't the intrepid space sleuth, himself. You got anything going out?"

We fist bumped one another. I always made it a habit to hit up Casey Langley if he was on shift and I had time when passing through *The Hub*.

"Sure do." I confirmed, rummaging into my bag. "Can you ring up my account from the HyperNet and stream them over to my wrist comp?"

With half a million people living in the station, another twelve billion living between Earth and all the Sol Prime colonies, you'd think the central hub of communications aboard the port city would be very busy. Thankfully, most people just transmitted their information through the HyperNet to the Messengers and paid their fee online. So, most users of the Messenger stations were transients like myself – those who were just passing through and needed access to a HyperNet terminal to set the communications up.

The rest were people delivering small packages by hand. Sending a package by Messenger was remarkably expensive because of the dedication toward delivery. That's why most people gave their packages to major shipping companies at their "postal stations" – where they were gathered up, put in shipping containers like the Mouse Club was supposed to be, and hauled out to corporate distribution centers.

But, I was a particularly odd case. Out of my back pack, I pulled a sealed paper envelope with the address and Messenger account number of my client - Honorable Angus Blooming-Star, Ambassador, Sol System, Olympus Mons, Mars.

"Man!" Casey shook his head bemusedly. "I don't think I'll ever get over that. You are the only person I know who still sends actual letters, you know that?"

I shrugged. "It's like I keep telling you, Case – a handwritten letter is all but fool proof in its security."

"Come on." the veteran Messenger looked offended, "You know once a message is in our system, we don't snoop."

"That doesn't mean someone else won't." I balked, "I'm a P.I. My clients' discretion is as paramount to me as making your deliveries are to you."

"We have the tightest information security this side of the Pyqians, Einar." Casey got a little serious. It was an old debate. But, he lightened up as he took the envelope in his hand, "But, I gotta say. There's just something about the idea of actually delivering a letter. I wish I could do it, myself."

"Missing the action?" I said, leaning in on the counter and swiping my payment into the system.

"Well, yeah." He said, "But really, it's the stories the others tell me about the looks on people's faces when they get actual fucking mail."

I raised my eyebrows.

"Sorry." He side-eyed the other messengers, "That was unprofessional."

We both laughed as he checked my messages and got ready to beam them over to me.

"Wow." Casey said taken aback at the screen.

My computer beeped as I received my mail from the central core of the Messenger system – Late Notice on the Mail. HyperNet account due notice. About a dozen junk messages from advertisers. Nothing weird. Beside, he just said he wasn't allowed to read my mail.

"What?" I tried to peak over the counter.

"You have..." he looked up to me in awe, "...a letter."

"What?!" I must have made the face my clients make to the other Messengers. "Here?"

He beamed. "You just made my day, Galbraith."

Casey hovered his chair out of the room and was gone for close to five minutes. My time was running out. If I didn't get going, I wouldn't make it in time for my flight to Earth. I was going to lose over twenty-four hours over a five minute mail delivery?

I checked my downloaded messages while Casey was out of the room. Three messages, all from my Mother. I didn't need to listen to them. I rarely did. They were almost all the same lines of conversation; Why am I not married yet? She wanted to tell me the latest gossip from back home. Or, I really should give up this phase I call being a detective and to come back home.

I flicked the first message on, having not heard my mother's voice in a while. "Einar, I was speaking with Helen Jonsdittir. Her father Jon and her brother Olaf Jonsson left her at the Market while they were busy at the pub. Did you know that she's back from University and that she still isn't married? I know you two were close in secondary school. You should come home and check in on her."

I flicked the message off and didn't bother with the other two from my mother. Not until I had nothing better to do, at least.

Casey appeared a moment later and I found I was balancing back and forth between both feet like a toddler who had to pee.

"Here you go." He reached out and handed me a scroll with small, gold colored caps on each end and a wax seal keeping it closed – real expensive stuff. "What's it say?!"

He watched in wonder like a kid waiting for a Christmas present. I don't think he'd ever seen someone open mail in person.

"I wish I could tell you, Case." I said stuffing the message into my bag, "But I'm going to miss my flight if I don't hurry."

As I reached the door to the Messenger station I turned back, "Drinks next trip through?"

"You say that every time." He waved at me dismissively.

I paid the rickshaw guy enough to hurry and had to hold onto the little hover cart to keep from being tossed out as he made some risky turns and quick stops. I didn't have time to read the letter on the way to my flight.

I'd have more than a day on the flight to Earth to read the letter.

"Assuming this guy doesn't kill me on the way to my flight." I muttered to myself, looking down to the taxi token on the inside wall of the cart.

"Your name is Ram Bandage Singh?" I said, "That's kinda bad ass."

He came to a stop at a red light for a breather. He'd run the last two. "No, it is not pronounced Ram, it is pronounced Rhom. And it is not Bandage, it is pronounced Bond-a-hey."

"Hey, I pronounced Singh right at least, right?" We both chuckled a moment as the light turned green and the Sikh man hurried back to his duty of hauling me to my flight. They should have just put the power supply for the Hyperdrive engines on this guy's feet.

Before long I was hustling and bustling through the security check point with just enough time to ride the hyperloop to my landing bay and catch my flight aboard a small passenger transport barely the size of the *Legacy's Façade*.

My carry on was taken at the check-in by an attractive flight attendant as they were out of room above the seating. Despite offering to keep the bag on my lap, she insisted that it be checked in main storage to save overhead space.

The passenger seating was even more economy than the sleeping coffin on the *Plentitude*. I was sitting, but only in name; my feet on the floor kept me from sliding out of the chair and the seat ahead of me was so close that I had to keep my head pinned to the headrest behind me so I could clearly see the display mounted there showing the latest Earth weather and news – economic unrest in Seattle again, a mega typhoon potentially forming near the Hawaiian Remnants, and the completion of the final tethers on the Lunar space elevator.

The double shoulder-harness kept me in place on the seat and I remembered why I really preferred traveling in my mini-pod. As cramped as it was, I couldn't imagine anyone choosing to be bondage strapped into a chair with about five-hundred other victims for a twenty-hour trip traveling at the edge of Real Space speeds.

XIII

⁂

CHAPTER THIRTEEN

Load Playlist Track: Kaleo, Vor í Vaglaskógi

The passenger ship broke into Earth's atmosphere just as the sun was coming up off the eastern coast of the African continent along the equator. The equator was the only part of the atmosphere that was stable year round, the temperature fairly constant.

We were coming in from the east, with the sun behind us. As such, I never got a good view of the coastal nation of Guinea, or what was left of it from the flooding; nor that of Gabon, which had finally begun to flourish with the increased water and their desalination plants. The small African nation supplied almost a quarter of the salt to the planet. It was their only real export now.

Of course, most of the rest of the world's salt came from the city I tried to see out the window, but couldn't quite yet. It was home to a hundred different races, mostly off-worlders and alien immigrants doing the jobs that Terrans didn't want to do – processing salt in the desalination furnaces, managing the waste clean up of hundreds of years of waste and pollution by an uncaring humanity, and harvesting the multitude of aquacultural and maricultural projects.

New Reykajavik supplied the majority of Sol Prime's fish, crustaceans, seaweed, and mollusks. Some were grown in fish and algae farms located within the city itself. The rest were harvested and processed from throughout the Atlantic Ocean along the 'Atlantic Basin Route.'

The city I called home was a giant machine, similar in concept to the Arcturis' mining platform, but with a massive population that made it more an organic creature than some robotic spaceship. It didn't fly. It was too heavy to float, though significant improvements had been made over the decades to improve its buoyancy to take the weight off its legs.

That's right! My city has legs. It walks the entire circumference of the Atlantic Basin about once every three years in a counter-clockwise fashion– from the coast of Iceland, where it first launched, westward to the southern tip of Greenland, down the eastern coast of the American Continents. It made a point of timing the trip to miss hurricane season.

From the tip of South America, the massive creature of a city tip-toed, barely touching the bottom of the ocean, down along the re-sorts of the Antarctic continent before heading back up along the African continent. Off the coast of Morocco, home of Earth's third largest planet-side immigration processing station, non-resident aliens (humans and otherwise) traded off for their tours of duty in the plants.

Then, after a short jaunt in and out of the Mediterranean, New Reykjavik made its way up along the Spanish coast, the remnants of the long ago flooded British Isles (to include the Highlands of Scotland) and to the end of the circuit.

Arching my neck into the personal space of a sleeping Mereleen, I managed to finally see it just as the sun overtook us and reached the spires up in the sky.

Home.

With the gurgling snores of the amphibious, black spotted, green and rubber-skinned Merelene in my ear, I watched as the gold and silver solar windows of sky scrapers, housing the best offices in the small city-state, caught the rays of the morning sun to help supplement the fusion reactor powering the city. From the top of a chimney-like black tube, purified water steam pumped into the sky above the city from the cooling process of the reactor.

I know, I know, water steam from a fusion reactor is weird. Everyone knows the output is harmless helium. But, that helium is very useful in cooling hydrogen-3 manufacturing, where purified water from the desalination plants is merged with the extra carbon in our atmosphere in a steam-process I don't completely understand. But, the outcome is we can make hydrogen-3 fuel cells to power systems in space, outside of a livable atmosphere. All that, and we get to clean up the excess carbon dioxide that helped lead to our fledgling greenhouse effect.

Had we not learned the processes, we would have just abandoned Earth and let it go the direction of Venus. We'd probably still be out there in the Expanse on a dozen worlds and colonies without Earth, and also not be the center of the Benighted Final Spiral Arm of the Expanse.

New Reykajavik is slowly saving the world. It's hard work. But my city is a city for hard workers.

The Merelene shifted uncomfortably, smacked its mouth, and made a half-muffled croak as I leaned in a little farther. I never got tired of the view.

The ship passed through the valley of spiral buildings and disappeared into the shadows behind the gleaming light. Behind the dawn flashing back against the glass walls of the skyscrapers lay the shadows of a less glamorous city.

Earth was a poor capital world in respects to the rest of the capitals of the Expanse. New Reykajvik, like all industrial cities, attracted the poorer, harder, workers and immigrants willing to put labor on their shoulders. So, the quality of life among all but the elite was less than that of the rest of the world.

That showed in the dingy streets and littered thoroughfares which returned a small portion of waste back into the oceans with the winds of each strong storm. It showed with the graffiti from angry workers who came for the opportunity, found it, and discovered the overseers of the city and the corporation's unappreciativeness of their efforts.

It showed in the gangs that sprouted up among the youth of the workers, in the limited educations of people with less opportunity that were, as if by design, kept from finding more opportunity through learning.

Like most intensely urban centers, there were more people than vehicles to move them – most relied on public transports – the elevators that reached a mile long from the sky-bound spire down to the sub-aquatic dwellings, the hyperloops that ran in concentric rings around the interior of the city, and the maglev trains that moved in and out from the edges to the city center like spokes on a wheel above ground.

Most people who owned a repulsor vehicle, like me, found them practically useless in the city itself. I kept mine because I needed it on business as I traveled. It was useful on the sea to get to land if we were close enough and the waves weren't too intense. Repulsortech kept you aloft above solid matter – less so with water, but still some. If a strong wave happened below you though, you might find yourself propelled into the sky and the repulsors wouldn't push as solidly against water on the way down to keep you from plunging under.

Snowball is sealed enough to handle space, but once under water, the repulsors wouldn't do me much good with 'the ground' in every direction. I wouldn't be able to pull back out and my thrusters would get extinguished.

Most of the time I left it in a parking garage at a significant price that I rolled into my daily expenses. It was the only bill I kept consistently paid on time, for two reasons – spaces were rare and if I lost it I might not get it back, and if I failed to pay my rent on my office-apartment, I could always live in the mini-pod.

The passenger transport stopped mid-flight and hovered over the medium Starport landing zone. The vertical descent brought the ship down through one of several open entrances into the core of the city, equidistantly placed around a central control tower

Inside the opening were three levels of outcroppings, about a dozen each, capable of supporting crafts like the one I was on. Most were full and would only be touched down long enough to drop off passengers, load up others, possibly change crew, and go through a flight check while refueling.

It's a transportation hub model that had been working well since flight became ubiquitous on Earth; even longer throughout the rest of the Expanse.

By the time we touched down, I had stopped peeking out the window over the Merelene. The ship made a significant bounce as the shock absorbers in the landing gear adjusted for the weight of the ship. I immediately slipped out of my harness to make a break from the seat when the froglike alien snapped awake in surprise from the landing. Its glossy black eyes blinked at me as I slipped past the person sitting between me and the aisle.

"Oh!" it said in a croaking voice that did well enough at speaking GCT. "I didn't mean to doze off! I hope I wasn't snoring."

"You were fine!" I said to him as I bolted down the aisle. I didn't get far before the light authorizing disembarking came on. I found myself stuck in a crowd of people making their way to their overhead luggage about six rows toward the exit.

Since they'd checked my carry-on, the other passengers were the only thing I had to wait on. So, with many an "excuse me" and a "sorry" and a few "can I get through, please"; I managed to save myself several minutes to getting off the ship.

I'd been off world for a while and I looked forward to the familiar hum of the ship's momentum, get my stuff, and make my way to my office. I had missed my city and I wanted to be in it.

The flight attendants managed an insincere "uh-bye. Enjoy your stay. Buh-bye. Thanks for flying with..." as I made my way past them onto the landing platform. I was the last one off the ship, so my carry-on was the first one waiting for us as I came out of the transport.

I scooped it up and hoofed it down past the luggage trucks that were going to carry everyone else's checked luggage back to the baggage claim. There were two rows of yellow lights meant to keep you on the path back to the terminal and out of the dangers of getting too close to the platform's edge.

I politely sped my way between them as I pressed a series of holographic buttons on my wrist computer without even looking. A few moments and the familiar beeping of a connection being made followed by a familiar voice greeting me with her normal charm.

"Damnit, Einar!" Velma said sternly, "It's been over a week since you checked in. You better have gotten paid!"

I smiled at the sound of her voice. Another holographic button push and a two-dimensional image of her appeared floating over my wrist, which I grabbed with my free hand and threw out in front of me. The wrist projector was smart enough to keep her now three-dimensional head and bust stable in front of me as I talked to her "eye to eye."

"Yes!" I chortled, "I did, in fact, get paid."

"So you finished the job?" My secretary had shoulder-length, neon pink hair that was feathered shorter in the front to frame her smooth pale face. The bangs seemed wild and stopped before they reached her equally pink eyes, almost obscuring her pink perfect eyebrows. The black eyeliner of her eyelashes spread as the look of surprise from her widening eyes and her pink lipsticked mouth curled on one side. "So, that means I also got paid?"

I laughed with acknowledgement. "Yes. You also got paid."

"Foxy!" she cheered the slang for 'cool' or 'awesome.' "I've been drumming up some more possible gigs while you were away. Ones I can actually help on."

Velma's primary employment with me was as an administrative assistant. That's the level of pay I could afford, so that was the kind of work I tended to give her. But, in the years she's worked for me, she'd managed to take some classes and afford to get her private investigator's license. I never officially put her on a case with me, and that wasn't financially likely this time either.

"Sorry, Vel." I shrugged, "I've already taken on another case. Technically, it's part two of the last case – except this time the client was the girl I'd gone looking for."

"Neridah Blooming-Star?" she confirmed from her notes, "What's she paying?"

"Just the standard rate." I declared to her disappointment, "I can't afford to bring you on at your full skills."

"You know what, Galbraith." She frowned at me, "I half think you just don't want me to get enough done to be able to make being an investigator my full-time gig and get my own work."

"That's not it, Vel." I pleaded, "The money just isn't there. Although, I would be lost without you at any level."

"Yeah..." she side-eyed me as she turned to glance at something off to the side, "...you just keep buttering me up like that. I'd rather have the credits though. When will you be in the office?"

"Headed there now." I said, "About to get to the hyperloop and ride in from the Starport."

"Hyperloop?" her face got more serious, "What did you do to the pod this time!"

"Um..." I pushed a button on the computer that made the image look distorted, a small program I'd added, "...I'm almost all the way inside and must be getting to a dead zone. I'll see you soon!"

I pressed the disconnect button and winced. "At least I expensed it...?"

XIV

CHAPTER FOURTEEN

Load Playlist Track: Ramones, Blitzkreig Bop

The hyperloop from the Starport into the city proper was brief, with just enough time to get up to speed before slowing down. The 'Loops of New Reykajavik were a very old design, from when the city was first being constructed. They weren't as clunky and inefficient as the Elon Musk era hyperloops, nor as prone to break down. But, they weren't the more modern style used in the more recently settled cities of the Sol Systems and the rest of the Benighted.

The seats on the carriage pod were old and worn, many of the seats frayed where actual fabric covered old cushions. The walls were cleaned regularly, but just as regularly vandalized by disgruntled off-worlders whose hopes had not met the city's promise; graffiti made of simple paints dotted the walls in a few different languages, genitals of humans and aliens alike had been scratched into the walls, and one much more disturbing mark was present – the laser burned mark of the Ne'wreyks covered the exit from the carriage.

The Ne'wreyks were an Earther Supremacist gang, with ties to the local labor unions. New Reykjavik did not require you to be a member of a union to work in the city. It certainly helped with finding any skilled labor jobs. However, many aliens didn't participate in the unions because they were willing to take less for their work than most humans.

So, whenever there were about to be labor disputes between the union bosses and the suits that ran the city, you'd start seeing threatening marks from the Ne'wreyks. It was as much a warning to the bosses as it was to the "scabs" not to take union jobs during an upcoming strike.

And by warning, I mean it was a threat that alien "scabs" were going to get trouble from Ne'wreyks loyal to the mostly human unions. The last time there was a labor dispute worthy of Ne'wreyk activity, the city actually stopped walking, unessential functions were turned off, and curfews had to be instated for alien protection by the city.

It almost resulted in the walking island-state from getting so far out of cycle that the massive hurricanes resulting from the world's endangered climate becoming a threat.

I hadn't made any serious note of it until then, but there were a considerably smaller number of people on the Loop than normal. I probably wouldn't have paid much attention to it, as I usually fly The Snowball from the Starport to the parking area. But seeing the mark had made me think.

The carriage was comfortable capable of holding a hundred or a hundred and fifty average sized humanoids. But that day, in the beginning of a business day, there were less than fifty. I'm sure with the sheer number of beings that had been on my flight in, and the many other flights in, that the bulk of the passengers simply were a few rides behind me getting their luggage; or they were taking different Loops to other parts of New Reykajavik.

But this number was still small. The humans didn't seem too concerned by it, but they were distanced from the aliens aboard. As with all cities folk flock to their own. So, it isn't weird to see humans sticking together on alien worlds or various aliens sticking to their own species on ours.

This time the different groups of aliens were sticking together entirely. There was a clear delineation between human and nonhuman present. Safety in numbers.

Did it get that bad in just a week and a half since I'd been gone?

The Loop took less than 10 minutes to reach the destination at the far end of the city from the Starport. There was an audible 'swoosh' as the vacuum of the tube outside the carriage was replaced with stabilized air and then a second, less pronounced, 'swoosh' and 'ding' as the doors to the carriage opened into the small terminal for my quarter of the Upper City.

It was my quarter, but not my half of the city. The upper city was typically where the humans lived. But, to keep my rent cheep, I lived where there wasn't much sunshine and even less view. I lived in the Undercity, known by its residents as the "Low Down."

I exited from the hyperloop terminal, the outer most ring in the system into the bright warm sunlight of the equatorial atlantic ocean. Tilting my fedora so the brim blocked the bright gold reflections of the solar collecting tower windows, I looked around me to the sprawl of the ring neighborhoods.

The ground levels of the buildings were not shiny, chrome, and golden like above. At eye level the buildings were easily obscured by the shadows of the monolithic high rises. The foundational structures of the buildings were grey painted metal, the same as the platform itself that also acted as the roadways, alleys and sidewalks of the city below the glistening demesnes of the corporations and landlords above.

The city's population was lacking its usual degree of hustle and bustle. Not so much a ghost town as if the city was currently the victim of a sick-in. But, even with the reduction of workers rushing to their jobs, it was still busy. Not every job in the city was a skilled labor – many were businessmen, professionals, management, or small shop owners and their employees.

People needed to eat, tensions or no. So everyone who wasn't prepping to go on strike or planning to break a line if one formed was out and on the move still.

I crossed the road to open air stairway down to the levels below, making my way by the many pedestrials, rickshaws, bicycles, and the occasional specially licensed repulsor vehicles. Down the metal stairs, with their ridged crisscrossing grips, I saw another burned in Ne'wreyk mark.

"That's bold." I muttered to myself. A pair of angry Naucistatians click and clacked to one another with their mandibles while looking at the mark with white stalks tipped with ebony eyes. Their normally orange exoskeleton shells were flared red and the two large pincer claw arms coming off each of their backs were snapping open and shut while their more humanoid chitonous arms wildly swished their fine hairy feelers which doubled as fingers. With their temperament, whoever made the mark was in danger if they were found out. Naucistatians were very territorial, like many of the Low Down.

I'm not saying speciesism was big problem in New Reykjavik, but like I said, folk tend to flock to their own kind. A sense of familiarity, unity, and commonality is what makes up a society the most easily. So, the human majority tended to live in Upper City. The outsiders, the aliens, tended to live in the Low Down and even then tended to split into neighborhoods by species.

Me, I was the outsider down there. But, I'd been operating out of the Low Down long enough, and helped out just enough of its residents, that I'd begun to get accepted down there. The rent was cheep enough to support myself and I was able to find a slightly larger place that I could run as an office out it.

The Low Down had its own streets and allies. They were a mirror of the city above. While the lower border that was the surface streets of the Upper City's glimmering towers was no pristine, graffiti-free paradise, it was a stark reflection of the Low Down.

Each street was in the same place and with the same layout. But, with no sunlight even reaching there, it was illuminated by a florescent flickering luminescence from panels along a sky made of the steel belly of the Upper city streets above. Support beams, struts, cables and water and waste tubes cross crossed and lined the sky like the wires of a giant circuitboard. The Low Down was the guts of the city.

Unlike the two sides of *Earthport Jennifer Sidey* the bottom side of the city didn't share a gravity that allowed a true mirror with the surface above. New Reykjavik didn't need artificial gravity because it still had the good old fashioned gravity of the Earth itself. As such, instead of a sky that reflected the one of the surface, each few stories of the Low Down was simply the next copy of the surface downward. Each of the levels, with its own shops, apartments, and services, was another copy of the one above it; eith the total diameter of city on each segment smaller than the one above.

The Naucistatians and Merelenes referred to this as the "Belly of the Beast." Exterior work on New Reykjavik's underwater segments, particularly the lower water pressure areas of the upper hull was usually the maintenance work of the two amphibious races. They treated the city as a great mother beast, almost revering it. As such they were very protective of the work that kept the city afloat and, despite the union's desire to control all labor in the city, it was the one area even the "Ne'Wrecs" didn't interfere with.

I guess even racism has a pragmatic side. Sinking and dying makes the attitude "aliens out, Earthers in" hard to keep pushing too far. I think though, this just fueled the bigots bitterness about their dependence on the two alien races.

Two of the Low Down's levels down, or about six stories underwater, occasional pools of water could be found. Naucistatians, Merelenes, or other humanoids in diving gear could be seen getting in or out of the pools, usually carrying some kind of tools. The pools were the entrances to a tube system that led farther down in the Low Down or out to the exterior of the city. The atmosphere on that level was sealed to keep the water from flooding in, allowing easy access for workers to the Belly.

There were several more levels below that, each less and less habitable and more and more the operation of the city's environmental systems and the mechanisms for the propulsion legs of New Reykjavik. I hadn't been down there much as humans were less and less welcome and my apartment was on the level with the first pools you encountered. I'd heard there were more access pools in the lowest of levels.

I loved my city, but it was big and I still hadn't been all over it. Who really ever gets to know every street of their city?

I made my way through a segment of the level that was made up largely of shops, selling daily conveniences, or groceries for the most common species living on the level, or parts for maintaining your apartments or small hydroponics greenhouses. Since vehicles were forbidden in the Low Down entirely, foot traffic was heavier down there. Humans may have been the majority species of the city, but they weren't the majority of the total population.

And that majority lived in the Low Down. This larger foot traffic meant that the streets in that section were less streets than pathways through additional shopping, like one giant underground bazaar.

Maybe that's why it took me so long to notice them following me. A group of hooded figures, in generic grey and brown robes or overcoats milled through the morning shoppers and kept a perpetually even distance from me. I only caught them because I was taking in my city after a long break and paying more attention around me. I had turned and saw one of them make the mistake of forcing themselves to turn to look busy at a shop when they had been clearly walking the same path as me.

After testing my suspicions with a few stops at a couple of shops before continuing on my path I was certain; they were on my tail.

I still had to pay the rent. But, I doubted it was my landlord Girchanizoth. He was shady, but there was no way he'd send thugs to collect – I wasn't THAT late. Could it be someone connected to Mouse? A little revenge? Someone bitter about an old case?

I decided I wasn't going to get beat up to find out.

I doubted they knew these streets the way I did. The walked like humans and not like the locals aliens. I knew nearly all the humans that lived in this section of the Low Down. These were outsiders.

I had a chance! The Bento booth on the corner was run by a Japanese descended Near Human, a catchphrase for the human-like species close enough they can breed with us, I'd helped once. I slipped inside the shed that had been welded to the exterior of a support beam.

"Hiya Nagako-san!" I said pulling the red curtains that came down to waist height. The morning's customers looked up from their stools at the bar, most of them eating some sort of Japanese-style fish meal you'd conceivably expect to see at lunch or dinner. But, considering the diets of the aliens of this level, variety of fish was more important than variety of food in general. "Mind if I hop over your bar and slip out the back?"

The elderly Japanese woman blinked her pink eyes, the only feature of her alien heritage, in surprise. "Dou natte iruno, Einar-san?!"

I paused for a moment; taken aback by the Japanese instead of the GCT I was accustomed to. "Um..."

"What's going on?" she repeated for me, her accent thick and representative of her generation. As recently as my grandparents, GCT was not ubiquitous with Terrans, especially Earthbound ones. I spoke it and Icelandic equally, but there were teens in my old homeland for whom our old 'national language' was their second language, instead of their first.

I pointed a thumb backward, "Being followed." I then pointed to the side door on the other side of the bar with an expectant face.

"Hi!" she nodded an affirmation and lifted the barrier between the front of the shop and the back.

We gave each other a short bow at one another as I made my way into the three foot wide kitchen space behind the bar. Nagako handed one of her ready-to-go bento boxes as I passed her.

"Thanks Nagako-san." I winked to the old woman, eliciting a blush, and slipped out the little door into an alleyway. By the time they'd likely noticed I wasn't coming out of "Nagako's Bento Barn", I was down the alleyway and to the next street and at the entrance to my apartment building.

XV

CHAPTER FIFTEEN

Load Playlist Track: The Runaways, Cherry Bomb

In my hurry to get out of sight and into my building, I didn't take a close look at it. I didn't need to. I'd been living it my apartment and using it as my office for close to five years now, ever since I'd made enough on my own cases with old agency to start up an independent operation.

But, if I had I would have seen the same thing I did every day. The "building" was a slate grey paint structure built onto the sides the typical steel and titanium column that supported the levels above. The buildings of this giant strut were rounded on the front as they curved around the body of the pillar.

The body of the buildings' structure bled out over the painted roadway and looked like it had grown directly over the catwalks, beams, and struts of the levels' roof. The third story of the buildings were secured to the top and the bottom levels of the buildings were welded to the streets.

While most of the city was designed uniform level to level in the Low Down, and generally reflected the ground level city above, the growing population of the undercity meant that some sections of the city had to be expanded upon. Since the streets, originally designed to allow vehicles, were for pedestrian traffic only in the current day and age, most of those streets weren't as necessary.

So, just like the bazaar I'd just ditched my tails in, buildings began to buldge and mutate out into the open spaces. Sometimes it was done with the blessings of the city planners, like my building. In the deepest places of the Low Down, as square footage got increasingly more rare (and thus more expensive), inhabitants of the Low Down began squatting in the more industrial areas, constructing their homes upon the superstructure of the very machines that made the city move along its circuitous route along the rim of the Atlantic Ocean.

Down there, crime was higher, and people of all species were poorer. Of course, it was the source of most of the Ne'Wrec's propaganda about Alien "infestation" in "their" city.

At the door of my building I punched in my code on my wrist computer and it transmitted an encrypted signal only a building resident's mobile devices should have. A red photoreceptor opened in the frame of the door and a feminine human-ish robot voice spoke a command.

"Please look at the scanner for facial recognition, Mister Galbraith."

I looked at the red eye and heard the magnetic lock on the heavy duty door *click-clack* and I made my way into the bottom floors foyer. It was simple, dirty, and slate gray everywhere except the floor.

Girchanizoth, the landlord whose father had funded building *The Main Strut Apartments*, had allowed the old Merelene matriarch on the first floor to have some of her grand-tads to line the floor in shiny multicolored shells from their home world.

The shells were from some small crustacean that were a delicacy on their world and which Girchanizoth's family made for the local population at the Main Strut Pub adjacent to the apartments. The landlord and his extended family lived in the two floors above the restaurant in relative luxury with the two apartments per floor of the three-story apartment building I lived in.

In the foyer there was an apartment door on each side, both Merelenes if I remembered right. I opted out of taking the lift up to the third floor, assuming it was working that month. The landlord was good at keeping things up and maintained but keeping the lift running wasn't cheap. I never knew if it was working though, because I never bothered with it. I liked using the stairs for the exercise. I already spent too much time either sitting in the mini-pod or in low or no gravity situations. So, for short distances up and down stairs, I preferred doing things the old-fashioned way.

Up the stairs I went to the second floor, much less decorated than the first floor foyer, though one of the occupants had a Downside Sprockets Gravball flag hanging on their front door.

"Is it Gravball season already?" I muttered to myself as I worked my way up the last flight of stairs to the third floor.

There were two doors on that floor at the top of the stairs. To the left was the same boring slate grey, with the number "6" on it. I'd never met my neighbor before. I don't think he's home very much, which was probably for the best. I tended to play my music pretty loud and I never got a knock on the door from him.

The floor below? That's another story. But they never had the guts to come up and do anything about it. Just a few bangs on the floor and I'd usually turn it down a notch for a few songs.

The door on the right was mine. I'd gotten permission from "Girch", back when I was regular on my rent payments, to paint the door with a mural of a classic old style wooden door with frosted glass and the block letters, in GCT, saying "Einar Galbraith, Private Detective" and my Comms number.

It was business hours, which meant that the door was unlocked.

Before I even registered the visuals of being home, I was awash in the language of my people. Not nearly as loud as I tended to play it, music was waving in through the open door from my play list – *Let's Dance by the Ramones*.

"Hey baby, if you're all alone. Baby, you'll let me walk you home." I mouthed the words under my breath as I stepped in.

My office was the front entrance of the apartment. It was made up of the small meter and a half by meter and a half foyer with some hooks for coats and hats, which is right where the fedora immediately ended up. It also flowed in two directions from there. Straight ahead was blocked by a piece of furniture in what was supposed to be my living room. The idea was to funnel people coming in the front door into what was supposed to be my dining room.

The dining room had been converted into the actual front office for my detective agency. It had an old wooden desk I'd collected on an early case, before I'd even started my own agency. On the shelves were mementos from private investigators of pre-Warp earth, real and fictitious. In the later case, there were also copies of books starring my childhood heroes written by the legends – Warschawski, Chandler, and Doyle particularly.

The walls were decorated with old-style two-dimensional printed photographs. Physical print photography was a hobby of mine, which was useful when trying to catch a good shot of some subject cheating on his wife or when you're trying to collect some evidence of alien sex trafficking for the Olympus Mons Police Department.

Sure, anyone can take a photo these days with a smart lens and a mobile device. But, the art of skilled photography let you catch details the camera doesn't know to auto focus on. And nothings more discrete for showing your client what you found out than handing it to them in an envelope.

No one's digital security or hired hackers can catch what you shot that way. They'd have to physically hunt you down to find out what you had on you.

Speaking of which, I needed to warn Velma I was being tailed.

She wasn't at the wooden desk, which I'd reserved for her to act initially as a receptionist at. I called her my "secretary", which she called "sexist", but its what the brass plaque I found had written on it. It was there on the desk, part of the ambiance. Otherwise, the desk was covered in her stuff. Her palm computer, a higher powered version of my more convenient wrist machine, had shut down from lack of activity. Her coffee cup, which I had given her on a long dead American corporate holiday said "#1 Secretary" in English, was still steaming with the peppermint tea she loved so much.

It must have been more than just steaming fresh since I could smell it from the entrance to the apartment.

"Val?" I called out to the attached kitchen off of the secretary's office, which also doubled as the only way into my actual apartment. Or rather into the livingroom I'd converted into my personal office. My very small bedroom and a bathroom were off that room.

But I didn't get that far as my secretary poked her cotton candy colored coiffe through the brown and beige wooden beads dangling down and acting as a faux barrier between rooms.

"Boss!" she beamed her rose colored eyes and pearly white teeth framed in the same shade at me. "What took you so long?"

"We might have trouble." I warned her as I broke into my backpack to excavate my blasters from their lock boxes, a required travel precaution by most passenger transports.

She stepped out, tossing a white drying rag back into the kitchen. She was wearing a pair of blue denim-like jeans with no right leg. It exposed the alabaster skin of her leg, but the style offset the purple and black shrug that only went to below her right elbow, but which had no left sleeve, revealing her clearly mechanical cybernetic metallic arm.

It glowed at the joints with some completely cosmetic lights, which she could change to match her outfit or turn off entirely. The glowing lights from the arm reflected a little from the grey and purple bodysuit she wore underneath the shrug. It was made of a plastic-like fabric that automatically sealed to form fit her body. The material was popular with mammalian humans in the Low Down for their usefulness with SCUBA diving.

She'd lost the arm after being kidnapped as a teen. It'd been my first solo case, for her great-auntie, Misses Nagako Tachibana. Unlike Nagako-san, her Near Human lineage was purely alien.

'Near Human' was a generic term for any of a dozen species or so throughout the Expanse, to include even the Royalty of the Hegemony, which were so close to human that they could actually interbreed. Unlike Vi'Xiri and other Telarian women, which were close enough to share reproductive processes, true Near Humans like Velma's species could make babies.

That was the case with Vel's great-aunt's mother and a sushi chef out of Tokyo. It's a very romantic story to hear about over a breakfast bento box like the one she'd handed me. If you ever get a chance, you should totally go hear her tell you about it.

Nagako had hired me to find her kidnapped great-niece out of desperation. She'd found me listed on the city directory near the top of Private Detectives. My name, Einar, comes up near the top because a roman "E" is the first letter in the alphabet of the Hegemony.

So, by chance, I got the case and I spent a month chasing down her kidnappers to Mars. They'd taken a lot of "earth girls", humans mostly, to sell into the sex trade there. But at the illegal auction where they'd sold her off, which I had almost made it into in time to see her up for sale, she'd been sold to an Argorg.

Argorg were a reclusive species that didn't normally leave their homeworld on Orh'neon. They were a typically pessimistic and xenophobic race of siphonophores that used robotic probes to explore and interact with the other races of the galaxy.

I didn't know anything about the species before my encounter trying to save her from it. I'd shown up expecting some alien Terra-phile trying to rape her. But what I found was that she'd been dumped into the Argorg's mobile habitat, a fish tank on repulsors and with a translator droid mounted on the outside.

The jellyfish-looking slime of an alien had wrapped itself around her arm and was quickly digesting her arm as her screams began drowning her. I'd smashed the tank and the entire colony of hive minded organisms that made up the whole dispersed to stay in whatever water they could survive in.

I don't know if any of the alien survived Velma's rescue, but after I got her medical attention the local police detective informed me they'd been tracking the Agorg. It had been banished from Orh'neon because it had gone mad on its' Agorgian Wine, an intoxicant produced from their own droppings. Apparently insane Agorgs begin feeding on others of its species and once forced off world it started looking for alternative sentient species.

Orh'neon needs a death penalty is all I have to say about that banishment.

Velma went to her desk and opened the drawer and pulled out her hold out blaster. At about the same time I managed to get mine loaded with a freshly charged plasma cell.

"So, what are we doing?" She said, nervous. "Set up an ambush or something?"

I poked my head into the small galley kitchen, greeted by the smell of dish cleaner. Normally, the kitchen was more of a science experiment than this, but Velma had kept it clean and relatively unused. It had all the standard things you'd find in an apartment galley kitchen: refrigerator, oven, range top, food printer loaded with all of the proteins and carb flavors of the rainbow.

But one thing my kitchen had that most didn't was a DNA sampler and chemical sniffer with access to an online, subscription only, database listing the DNAs of criminals wanted by the Hegemony, which usually didn't help finding people for a little detective like me in the edge of the galaxy, and a connection the Royal Science Administration for the chemicals. That last part was more often useful than the first.

Unfortunately, like my rent, I was late on paying my subscription.

"No databases for me right now." I told myself. "After this job I'll get them up and running again...take on some more forensic focused cases."

"You're staying up here." I told her. "Don't look at me like that. You've never been in a firefight. Keep the door locked. I'm going to slip out the back and see if I can get a look at them."

There was no real 'back' to slip out of, technically. The buildings were fused to the giant strut holding up that section of the level above. So, I made my way down the stairs to the first floor of the building and opened a maintenance hatch to the strut that allowed access for the city's repair teams.

City planning actually doing its' job there. I doubt the lower levels of the Low Down would have given me this option to get around.

XVI

∞

CHAPTER SIXTEEN

Load Playlist Track: Social Distortion, Far Behind

The maintenance hatch allowed me to move between the buildings fused to the support strut. In terms of building security, it was a tremendous flaw which could be exploited by any would be thief.

The only saving grace is that to get into the hatches located inside each building, you'd have to have access to the building. Theoretically, that would limit access to the city maintenance teams, the landlords of the buildings, and the residents of them as well.

In reality, anyone could get through if they planned it out a little.

Maybe I wasn't a good person for having considered that exploit as a way to rob people. I wasn't a thief, but it was in my nature to mistrust things and to look at the angles someone could hurt me. Paranoid? Maybe.

But, that type of thinking also allowed me, in my opinion at least, to be a decent detective. It allowed me to consider how actual criminals or ne'er-do-wells thought.

The tunnel was dark, thin, and short. I had to crouch to move along it, almost sideways. I made my way with the light from the wrist computer. Water and electrical pipes lined the walls and ceiling. Heat radiated off of some and I made it a point not to touch that side of the walls.

After a short distance, I came to the hatch of the neighboring building and popped it open from the inside.

A rush of cold air waved over me and against the almost steaming heat of the maintenance tunnel.

The Main Strut Restaurant's freezer was just as dark as the tunnel, but I cross it to find the light. A quick flick and I could see the aluminum storage racks with aluminum tubs of ingredients and frozen fish and crustaceans.

I popped the lever inside the freezer and just as the cold of the freezer had waved against me, I was assaulted by the heat of the Main Strut's kitchen. Hot, cold, and then hot again. It was like a tide of temperatures.

This wave, however, came with the delicious smells of fried batter and fish.

Nearby a Merelene with a white apron blinked its black eyes at me surprised from his dishwashing station and croaked something at me in his native tongue.

"Sorry." I raised my hands after closing the freezer door. "Um, just inspecting that it works."

That was a lame excuse. But, usually, those were good enough if you just got out of a situation quickly.

I made my way through the kitchen, the cooks and staff paying me only the slightest attention. They were focused on getting their plates out on time and with a fast turn around.

I was through the pair of double doors, which swung either way, and into the main room of the kitchen before I made too much of a ruckus – but, not in time to keep the Restaurants owner, and my landlord, from seeing me in his restaurant.

"Galbraith!" I heard Girchanizoth's voice before I saw him. "Where the hell is-s-s my rent?!"

"Fuck..." I stopped where I standing, put on a fake smile, and turned to face my landlord. "Heya Girch! I just came to tell you I have your money."

Girch crossed his crimson scaled arms over his bare pale scaled chest and rested them on his beer keg of a gut. His head tilted to the side so one of his eyes could independently focus on me while his other checked to see if anyone in the restaurant was in need of assistance. I could tell he was angry based on the ridges of his snout curling down a little to squint the eye at me. He switched sides of his angular head and reversed the curled ridge to that side while he checked the other side of the room.

"S-s-so.." he tapped a raptor-like claw on the floor with his bare foot. "Where is-s-s it then?"

I padded my inside breast pocket on the trench coat, "Right here. But, I've got some business out front I need to take care of real quick – time critical stuff. I'll come back in and pay you in a minute."

The Tetrapilian switched sides of his head again, dubious; but, his four fingered hands relaxed and he uncrossed his arms to adjust the half apron over his baggy wrap pants. "I want that money today or I'm tacking on a late fee. I'm tired of you Terrans-s-s and your entitled attitudes-s-s thinking you can be late with your business-s-s."

I looked wounded and shrugged my shoulders. "Girch. I'm hurt. You've fully immigrated. You and me we're both Terran, man. We gotta get along."

"Fuck off, Einar." He flipped his two middle fingers at me. "Get me my money and get out. I have customers-s-s to deal with."

"You're a champ, Girch." I winked at him before I turned to walk out and called back, "Be back in a bit!"

He hissed something behind me as I reached the door, cautiously checking up and down the street before slipping into the morning crowd. I immediately and innocuously made my way across the street to look back at the apartment building. My face was exposed and I wished I'd had my hat to cover it with a little while I leaned against the wall looking for who was following me.

But, the hat was bright red and they'd already seen it. In the drab colors of the Low Down, surrounded by a multitude of Aliens in which I already stuck out, I didn't need to either draw attention to myself by color or familiarity. So, I made my way to behind one of the large metal light posts. It, like so much of the Low Down, was low on the priority of repairs. This one was flickering on and off and seeing me clearly would have been a bit of a challenge.

On the other hand, the lights in front of the apartments were still working ok. Girch was a miser and brusk, but he was no slum lord. He maintained his property and sources of income like a professional. Even when I was behind on my rent, he'd repair problems I complained about it – for the next guy if Girch ended up kicking me out, which is more than many could say about other, sleazier, landlords in this part of town.

After a few more minutes, I spotted one of them. The three hooded figures hadn't made an approach on the apartment complex itself. They had this one scoping out the building from the next building over, opposite direction of the restaurant.. Thanks to his drab and neutral colors, he didn't stand out at first. I was lucky to have gotten across the street from the restaurant unseen.

If I had gone the other way down the maintenance tunnel for the strut, I would have come out right on top of him. He was staying concealed from my building by the archway leading to the adjacent building's front door.

This guy was a scout, likely there to report to his other two friends when I was on the move. If they were smart they had someone down the street in both directions ready to pick up my trail as I passed them, so I wouldn't notice the tail as easily this time.

But, it was my turn to get up on them and get some answers. I didn't know who these guys were or why they were after me, but it was time to find out.

I stayed across the street and kept out of sight as best as I could. Once I was behind him by a building or two, I made my way across the street and worked my way back toward my apartment, approaching him from behind.

As I reached the building's edge, half its length from him in the archway, I reached into my jacket pulled out my heavy blaster. It was likely overkill and, if I shot this guy and wasn't defending myself, it was a quick way to a jail cell for the rest of my life. But, guns were a great social lubricant for breaking the ice when asking someone questions about why they were following you.

He didn't see me coming. But, just before I got to him I saw him tense up. He somehow knew I was there.

"Don't move." I said authoritatively as I jammed my gun against the back of his head before he could turn around. A few pedestrians gasped and backed away. It wasn't exactly the most subtle display, but if I hadn't hurried I'd have lost the drop on him. "Get your hands where I can see them. No tricks."

The being raised his robed hands until the fabric slipped off revealing very high tech cybernetic hands, really expensive stuff. The only thing that would have made it better was if it had been covered with syntheskin to prevent you from telling it was mechanical. Usually, when you didn't cover up those expensive polymers and the exposed articulated artificial tendons, it was because you want to show off your technology. That was typical of high end gangsters and low lifes alike. The difference was usually just the quality of the cybernetics. But, in both cases, you usually saw the technology chromed out or stylized.

For all of its high tech quality, it was plain. The polymers weren't modified for tactical purposes like you'd expect from a mercenary or a hit man. The tech was simple, pragmatic, and in replacement of limbs for prosthetic purposes. But the top of the line nature still represented serious money or access.

"Mister Galbraith, wait." The lookout said in a synthesized voice. It wasn't some robotic voice, mind you. More like someone speaking with a normal human voice, except out a high quality speaker – the normal sound you can still tell isn't "real."

"Why are you following me?" I demanded, pressing the barrel harder against the back of his skull. "What do you want? Like I said, no tricks."

His hands turned palm up, almost apologetically. "I am sorry, Mister Galbraith. It is too late for that."

"What do you mea..." I didn't get to finish the last word as blinding pain lashed out at the back of my head. Whatever hit me got me hard enough I couldn't really process yet that I'd been struck as my vision flashed into a bright light. I recall hitting the ground and the city swimming around me.

"Sonofa..." I raised my blaster vaguely in the direction of the guy I'd previously gotten the drop on, but it was useless. Someone pulled the gun out of my hand effortless. I don't think my hand was under my control well enough to resist. I probably couldn't even have pulled the trigger anyway.

I had considered that if they were smart they'd have been waiting down the street in both directions ready to follow me based on this guy's signals. But, I was wrong. They were definitely smart, but I hadn't been. He wasn't the look out – he was the decoy.

"...bitch." I managed to finish my curse some time later. I wasn't sure how long it had been between starting cussing and saying the last bit. I just knew the floor was against my face. It was the cold metal of the street and I was laying there drooling.

"It's not on him." Another speaker-voice, a woman's I think, spoke. "He could have dropped it in his apartment."

"Bring him along, before the police show up." A third voice, this one familiar and not synthesized, commanded. "Get his wrist device. We'll use it to get in and search his place."

The world started spinning more, I was slipping out of consciousness again. I remembered being annoyed as my booted feet bounced over and over as I was dragged up some stairs – pretty sure they were the stairs of my building. Really, Girch needed to get along with fixing the lift.

They were taking me to my apartment. I started to stir as I realized they were going to bust in on Velma. She was in danger! I shifted my weight to escape, but all I did was make the world spin again. This time it went black and I was somehow conscious of being unconscious.

XVII

CHAPTER SEVENTEEN

Load Playlist Track: Blue Oyster Cult, Veteran of the Psychic Wars

"Unconsciousness is a state which occurs when the ability to maintain an awareness of self and environment is lost. It involves a complete or near-complete lack of responsiveness to people and other environmental stimuli." Someone was reading something to me. I blinked my eyes open to look at who was talking. "Clearly, the fact you think you're aware of being unconscious, means that you are not."

To my surprise, I was back in the *Legacy's Façade*. I'd been propped up on a seat in the galley. It was cleaner than when I'd left and the logo of the Expanse was painted cleanly on the wall.

I could smell coffee brewing. Actual coffee, not one of the knock off stimulants found throughout the galaxy that served the same purpose. It was real, honest to Earth, coffee.

The man in front of me looked familiar, but I couldn't quite place him yet. He was sitting in the chair opposite of me at the table. He had a data pad in his hand, the same model Neridah and I had looked through to find the location of the Dagger of Augury on Earth. His clothes were the official robes of an Ambassador of the Expanse. I'd seen them before when I was hired by Angus Blooming-Star.

In fact, he looked an awful lot like Ambassador Blooming-Star. Except instead of the red hair and beard, his hair was darker and he looked a lot younger.

"I'm not younger." He answered my thoughts. "This is just how I looked when I died."

I snapped myself more alert. *Died.*

Bohemian Rhapsody played in the distance, somewhere in the cargo pod that was the old Mouse Club. "Is this the real life...." Freddie Mercury sang.

"I'm not dead am I?" I realized the back of my head didn't hurt from the hit on the street. "Are you saying I'm dead?"

"No." he smiled, "And thank the spirits. You still have work to do."

"You're Conner Blooming-Star." I said as his face finally clicked in my memory. "What is this some kind of messed up dream?"

"In a way." He answered. "Somehow you found yourself in a state of consciousness that outsiders, like you, would call unconsciousness. Something deeper than sleep where we could reach you."

"We?" I said.

I was answered by the growl of a large wolf I had somehow not noticed laying down at my feet. I'd only ever seen a wolf on holovids. They were all but extinct, only alive in one preserve – in the Yellowstone-Sol System Park on the North American continent. The white furred beast looked up at me with all-to-knowing blue eyes.

"Yes," Conner answered me, "Brother Lone Wolf found you adrift. He'd been keeping an eye on you since you'd left the others."

"The Odds." I began to feel like I was starting to understand things more intuitively. "The other totems Neridah told us about. They're back with her and the Odds."

"Ah, yes." Conner stood up, putting down the data pad. "The great Sand Snake of Tilaria was correct. You do have potential. She could smell it on you when you were near the dancing girl."

"Huh?" Ok. Maybe I wasn't starting to understand things more intuitively as well as I thought.

Conner pointed to the data pad. "I see that you found the discrepancy in the records. That was smart."

"How?" I was getting more confused. "You're dead. Where am I?"

"It's hard to explain if you haven't had any training." His mustache hairs began to slowly curl, as did his hair. "And we don't have much time. You're slipping out of the Dreaming."

"The..." I tried to focus, but it was getting harder. The colors of the room had begun to get more muted. "...Dreaming? What are you talking about?"

"We don't have time for that." He put a finger to his lips in a silencing motion. "Just listen while you can. Everything in the world has some sort of gravity. Even if sensors cannot detect them, it's there. Everything exists between places. But great things, important things, have more reality outside of the waking world."

"Uhuh..." I began to slump down off the chair.

"Quiet." He spoke sternly to me. "Now that you've found your way here, you can do it again. And it will be easier to come to you as well. You know where it is. I'll help you fulfill your role in all of this. We'll meet ag..."

His words trailed off as the light went out. The cold of the floor returned to my cheek and the pain slowly throbbed its way back into my skull. I'm not sure how I lay there before I finally opened my eyes again and forced myself to roll over on my back.

I was on the floor in the middle of my office in the apartment – what should have been any other tenants' living room.

"Galbraith, I s-s-s-said wake up." Girchanizoth was standing over me. He'd lost the apron and replaced it with a tool belt, which was typical of when he was working on the apartments. In the background my antique mid-twenty-first century reproduction record player was stuck skipping over and over the line from Bohemian Rhapsody and Girch was holding two cups of coffee in his hands.

"Aw, man." I muttered as I looked at my wrecked apartment. They'd gone through everything. "They scratched my vinyl."

"Is that what you call that racket?" Girch said handing me a coffee. "I didn't know how to turn it off."

I sat up and accepted the coffee. "What happened?"

"You never paid me your rent." He hissed bluntly. "S-s-s-so, I came looking. One of your downstairs neighbors complained about the sound of a fight as I came up the stairs. I found you in here like this. I saw you starting to wake up, so I figured you'd want the coffee."

"I don't care what anyone says about you, Girch." I sipped at the magical brew. "You're a saint. I take everything I ever said back."

He hissed dismissively and then enjoyed some of the other cup of my coffee. That stuff was expensive. Don't let anyone tell me I'm not hospitable, I guess.

"You said there was a fight?" I more thought out loud than actually asked him. "Crap. Do you know what happened to Velma?"

"Not my problem." He said. "She doesn't live here and she doesn't owe me rent. You do."

I reached over to call her and see if she made it out before the thugs made it upstairs. My wrist computer wasn't there. "Shit!"

I found it a moment later. But, you know that feeling you get when you're missing your communications device? That dropping feeling like everything was falling apart around you? Psychologists say we're effectively addicted to devices these days, as a species. Yeah. That's pretty much right. In the short gap between realizing it wasn't on my wrist and finding it laying in the mess of a room near me, I felt almost sincere panic.

I powered it up and rang up Velma's communications number. It went straight to voice mail.

"Fuck." I stood up too quickly and stumbled. Girch held me up and steadied me. Somehow, maybe it was the fact he worked all day in a restaurant, he managed to keep either of us from spilling any of the sacred Java.

"S-s-s-sounds like you've got some problems." He eased me into my desk chair. "You should really take care of that head and figure out where your pink human is-s-s."

"Thanks, Girch." I nodded in agreement, putting a hand to the back of my head.

"As-s-s s-s-s-oon as-s-s you pay your rent." His raptor claw tapped the floor.

"Jezzus, Girch. You know what? Fine."

I reached into my pocket and pulled out my cred stick. "You ready?"

He hissed an affirmative as he pulled his device out of a tool belt pocket. I typed in an amount into a banking application on my wrist computer, swiped the stick over it, and watched the numerals on the stick change.

Girch pulled out a cred stick of his own and swiped it over his device, waiting a moment for the numerals to shift, an eye on the stick and another eye on me – which is just creepy by the way – and finally nodded. "Good. Onc-c-c-e you get this-s-s cleaned up, let me know if anything is-s-s broken and I'll come s-s-sort it out."

"You're a real human being, Girch." I said as he made his way out of my office, stepping over the bookshelf that had been previously blocking the main foyer from the living room.

He flipped two central scaly fingers at me as he walked out.

Once Girch was out the apartment, I checked my assets – Heavy blaster? Gone, nothing but an empty shoulder harness. Hold out blaster? Check. They'd definitely searched me. I was pretty sure they'd mentioned not having "it" on me. But, they didn't concern themselves with otherwise robbing me. Either they took my heavy blaster with them or it just got dumped where they'd put me down.

I tried Velma again on the off chance she'd gotten away from them.

"*beep beep* Hi!" Her voicemail kicked in, "you've reached Vel'shan Ma, Assistant Private Investigator with the Galbraith detective agency. I'm likely on a case right now and can't talk. Please leave a vidmail and I'll reach back out to you as soon as possible. *beep beep*"

I hadn't listened to the message past the "hi" the first time. When did she start calling herself my assistant private investigator instead of my administrative assistant? She did have her license, but I haven't let her take a case yet. But then, I haven't been back in the office much. Was she taking cases on the sly and I hadn't noticed? Not just found some "new" cases to have me help her with?

"Shit Velma." I muttered to myself, "What have you been getting yourself in to?"

I looked at the mess around me and realized I had another missing person's case on my hands. "Time to start detecting, I guess. And fast."

When I was back in the office, I usually talked to Velma about the case. Mostly this was to help me think...and to keep me from looking crazy when I talk to myself out loud. But, Velma wasn't there.

"Crazy it is." I grumbled.

"Yep." I answered myself.

"Ok, they were stalking me to get something off me." I started my thoughts out loud. "That means they expected I'd have whatever it was on me or near me. They must have been scoping out my part of town to catch sight of me to tail me. Odds are they knew I was off world, so they might even have been waiting for me to fly in from my case."

"Seems reasonable." I concurred. "But, how would they know which flight you came in on? That's watching a whole lot of the Starport."

I put a finger on my chin and paused my search of the room as I considered that. "More than likely, they waited at the hyperloop terminal. That's the only way into the zone from the Starport. That leaves a lot less to have to watch."

I nodded as I lifted the book case back up over the hallway entrance and looked at the mess on the floor.

"Yeah." I agreed with myself, again. "So they tail me from the hyperloop terminal. And, when I broke their tail they knew they'd been made. So, instead of trying again, knowing I'd take the threat serious enough to look into, they laid a trap."

"And you walked right into it."

"Shut up."

I snorted derisively at myself. "Ok. So, what do we know about them?"

"Expensive cybernetics on at least one of them." I followed the train of thought as I finished the last of the coffee and tip toed over the mess of my livingroom/office into the kitchen. "Voxcoders on two of them."

Voxcoders were a type of cybernetic that was used in place of vocal cords to simulate voice. Usually, they were used by people who had esophageal cancer. But, anyone who could afford the quality workings seen in that guy's cybernetic arm could have easily chosen to have a new esophagus and the skin around it medically printed from his DNA.

"So that means they chose to deliberately not get organics." I mused as I looked around the dining room I'd converted into Velma's front desk. I started looking for what was missing from there, since I couldn't identify anything of importance missing from my livingroom. "Who would do that?"

"Certain gangsters?" I asked myself.

"No. Not showy enough for a gangster."

"But certainly a sign of toughness. Kind of like scars."

"Nah. Too elegant for that without the bling."

They'd thought I had whatever they were looking for on me. I started chasing that train of thought while continuing my self-debate over the clues about their identity. I began back-tracing my steps in the apartment from when I made it there.

"Mercenaries maybe?" There were mercenary teams out there, supposedly, that used cybernetics to enhance themselves and make them more effective combatants. And they wouldn't want to stand out too much.

"Nahhhhh." I shut that line down. "Even a mercenary covering themselves with tech that expensive could afford to be superhuman and still try and look, well, actually human. Bad ass, money making, adventure capitalists want to buy things with that money. And half of those things involved impressing someone, usually girls...or whatever they're sexual preference was."

I hadn't gotten past Velma's desk when I came in warning her I was followed. So, it wouldn't have been in the rest of the apartment. Whatever they were looking for was either in the room or in the foyer...

"My backpack." I'd put it down under the coat rack, right below my hat. "Maybe I did really have whatever it was on me."

So, they weren't gangsters. They weren't mercenaries. They had access to the highest tech possible to replace the human body.

"They were polite."

"Bullshit! They hit you in the head from behind."

"Yes. But the first guy called me 'Mister Galbraith.' There was no 'Hey asshole', like you'd expect from the other two."

These were people of standing. People who had money, but didn't care about appearances, and didn't care about even looking flesh and blood.

"Pyqeans?" I asked myself. "Do Pyqeans rob people? They almost all work for the Hegemony..."

Then it hit me. The Pyqean Machines were almost like an order of monks. They were people, of every imaginable species, that sought to attain a higher state of being free of the flesh. The first Pyqeans were actually of a race called Pyqeans – a humanoid species, like most of the Galaxy. But, they were one of the first species to travel out into the galaxy. The Hegemony, the foundation of the Expanse, already existed throughout a small segment of the Galaxy.

But, that was thousands of years ago, long before the even the first of the Spiral Arms had been explored from the Core of the Galaxy, where the Hegemony called home from their Galactic Arcology – a capital "world" constructed, like a Dyson Sphere, around one of their suns.

The Pyqeans, prior to encountering the Hegemony, had not discovered Warp or Hyperspace on their own. Bound by the limits of Real Space, the Pyqeans realized they would never, as individuals, explore the Galaxy beyond their own star system; no matter how fast they could get below light speed. So, they discovered the Singularity, as it was theorized on Earth – a state where the mind, the very essence of a being, was transferred to a machine.

They eventually did discovered the Hegemony, the Warp, and Hyperspace. But, they were...beings...of incredible life spans. As machines, they could theoretically live forever. That comes with a lot of wisdom and detachment from, lacking a better word, their humanity.

The Hegemony, a gaggle of early empires, kingdoms, and democracies that had discovered one another shared their technology with the Pyqeans. The Pyqeans, in turn, shared their knowledge, wisdom, and their service.

If the Hegemony Royalty were the kings and queens of the Galaxy; The Pyqeans were their court wizards. Armed with the technology of the Hegemony, the Pyqeans evolved to newer and newer heights, drawing in followers from throughout the Expanse over the millennia. They were all, almost to a one, in the service of the Expanse at some level – acting as advisors to the Empress, to the System Lords, to key Parliamentary members...

And it hit me. I'd recognized the voice of the third man.

At the same time, I realized what was missing from my backpack.

"That son of a bitch took the scroll." I cursed to myself. I was supposed to read it on the flight in from the *Earthport* at the Lagrange Point. But, they'd stowed my bag and I'd let it slip.

I slipped the shoulder holster off. It wouldn't do me any good. But, I still had the holdout blaster. I grabbed my fedora off the floor where it'd been knocked down and readied it on my head, even over the sore spot on the back of my head.

Then, I started to make my way to the seat of the local Terran Ambassadorial offices. It was time I had a talk with Angus Blooming-Star.

XVIII

CHAPTER EIGHTEEN

Load Playlist Track: Dead Kennedys, Halloween

Ambassador Blooming-Star's offices weren't located on New Reykjavik. He operated from the Solar System capital, which was also the Sol Systems Parliamentary headquarters. The naming was a bit redundant and confusing.

I never liked that the Hegemony named the entire collective of star systems for the Sol Systems after our Sol System. The entire Benighted Final Spiral Arm of the Galaxy was made up of a few System Lords, each with a collection of star systems under them.

Earth was the home of the Sol System, also known as the Solar System. The Solar System was the capital of the Sol System, the collection of star systems and all space between them under the control of the Sol System Lord, Sch'Gwenish.

Sch'Gwenish, like all System Lords, was from an alien from outside of the system he'd been put in charge of by the Hegemony. The idea was that this would ensure the homogenization of the plethora of Systems within the Expanse by forcing a "melting pot" of ideas and cultures. Some humans were System Lords outside of the Sol System for the same reason. The secondary effect was ensuring that the ruler of a

System was loyal to the Hegemony and not the interests of the System they were assigned to.

Theoretically, that should have prevented the events of the Betrayal. System Lord Archimedes was a human from Earth. His Colonial Troopers were an aberration to the normal process – with conscription or voluntary enlistment coming from the local population. But, he got away with it because the local primary species, the Gresanorn, were a pacifist species that hated war, but also saw themselves as a superior species to non-photosynthetic species. So, they were more than happy to have their System defended and secured by disposable beings like humans.

After all, if someone had to fight and die to protect them, it might as well be short-lived lowly humans – and artificial ones at that. They were only in the Hegemony because their homeworld, Kzideon, had been discovered by non-Expanse aliens that were stopped by the System Lords from conquering the planet for their natural resources. After that, the Hegemony offered to extend that protection permanently, in exchange for trade agreements for the same resources. As long as Archimedes stayed out of their local affairs, they hadn't bothered interfering with how he ran the rest of the System.

Lord Sch'Gwensh, on the other hand, ran the Sol Systems, and even headed the System Lords Council for the Benighted Final Spiral Arm, very intimately. The old slug was a Sozarian, one of the handfuls of non-humanoid species in the Galaxy. He was old, by even the best human standards, and had the support of the Totem Masters and Shamans of the various Benighted Systems because of his ties to those of his own species.

Sozarians were a race of intelligent mollusks. One of their evolutionary traits, from back when they were just little snails living inside of shells, was that when threatened they could enter a state of suspended animation that, from the outside, looked like they'd died.

Apparently, some ancient predators on their world only wanted their slugs wiggling.

What that did for them these days though was that even the least spiritual of the Sozarians could slip into that state willingly as a meditation, finding some kind of guidance "from beyond."

Lord Sch'Gwensh was no wormy priest. If anything, he was the slimiest politician, literally and metaphorically, in the outer rim. But, he'd wormed his way into the good graces of the religious leaders of a dozen worlds because of supposed insights from his meditations – not that he needed to get along with anyone. System Lords were like the nobles of old on Earth. They were appointed for life and their children, or spawn in his case, inherited their titles.

That was one really interesting thing about living under an active monarchy like the Galactic Expanse. The Hegemony, which ruled the Expanse, after assigning those deemed worthy to rule a collection of Systems, accepted every species into the nobility and all of them had some chance, theoretically, of ascending to the seat of the Emperor or Empress of the Expanse.

So, though he couldn't have any children with any of the humanoid majority species of the Galaxy, Lord Sch'Gwensh could technically find the right marriage to the right heir and work his family's way up to ruling the known galaxy.

I shivered at that thought. I don't like to think of myself as a speciesist, but I don't like the thought of a giant slimy space slug ruling all of humanoid kind.

But, neither Lord Sch'Gwensh nor Ambassador Blooming-Star had offices in my city. The ambassadorial corps did, however, have offices here. And, if Angus Blooming-Star was that third guy who mugged me for that scroll, then he'd likely have been operating out of those offices as a cover for his presence there.

It was the first step in tracking him, and Velma, down at the moment. I was going to take what I could get.

Through the crowded thoroughfare of the Low Down, navigating the bazaar by Velma's auntie Nagako's bento bar, up the stairs into the first under level of the city, and into the bright light of the surface of the Upper City, I walked with deliberate intent of violence. Someone had come into my city, down into my neighborhood, busted their way into my home...into my office...and robbed me. Worse yet, they put someone who I'd saved the life of in danger – someone important to me and my business.

Worse yet, it seemed the one responsible was a client. Not just that, but a client that was a representative of the Galactic Expanse – the faceless "they" who ruled over all of us. We lived in a democracy but, at the end of the day, everyone knew that democracy only went so far under the rule of a monarchy like the Hegemony. A lot of people didn't like that.

I was somewhat anti-establishment as it was, the Hegemony aside. Maybe that's why I identified with the music I did. Or, maybe the music I identified with made me anti-establishment. I'm no anarchist, but I'm not a company man either. I'm no Statist and I'm no monarchist. Sure, they're romantic and all, but they were "them" and I was the "us" us that makes up everyone else.

And as an Ambassador, he's one of "them" and "they" just robbed me and took one of mine.

That wasn't going to stand.

That fire burned deep inside me the whole way to the surface. It burned as I made my way to the hyperloop station I road to the junction station that would lead me from the outer rings of the city deeper into the city's core, where the government operated New Reykjavik.

By the time I was on the meg-level train that traveled in and out of the core like a spoke on a giant wheel, surrounded by innocent people oblivious to the wrongs and slights against me, the fire turned into more of an angry simmer. I was still pacing back and forth on the mostly empty train, everyone had traveled inward that morning for their corporate wage slave jobs or to push buttons for the governments all – city, planetary, or System.

They were the victims of the morning commute, the experiments in the rat race we call life, chasing their cheese to the center of the maze. They were as far from free from that city as you could get for half a day at a time. Only in the end would they escape outward to the 'burbs of the Upper City or, for the poorer lot, down into the depths of the

Low Down – to be locked up in the Oubliette the city species majority would prefer they stayed forgotten in. A social prison of the like the Ne'wreyks saw themselves as the wardens up – keeping the amphibians and lizard people and the crustaceans in their place.

Three stops in and I'd stopped pacing. I started to remind myself that whatever Angus Blooming-Star had done, he wasn't probably acting on behalf of the Expanse. This wasn't some statist attempt to hold down the common working class private dick. Whatever his agenda, even if he was abusing his office to pull it off with some Pyqean employees, he would have just sent some kind of government henchmen to take care of me solo if it was a vast government conspiracy.

Two stops later and I was sitting in a seat, holding onto one of the poles on the maglev. I'd started to come down off the adrenaline and along with a clearer head, I was getting a sick stomach. I wasn't bad in a fight, but I wasn't really a violent person.

But I'd gotten shot in the back trying to find his daughter for him, his niece really. On this job for her, I'd been mugged by him and robbed of a parchment. A parchment sent by who?

"Ok." I muttered to myself trying to fight off the queezy feeling of being post fight-or-flight. "Good, you're asking questions. You're past realizing who attacked you and you're thinking like a detective...again. So, why would a client you completed a job for come after you?"

I decided not to answer myself out loud that time. There were people on the train and I didn't want to come off as crazy or anything. I mean, really, who talks to themselves and actually answers? Right?

He'd lied to me about his relationship with Neridah. But then, he'd lied to her for her entire life about it. So, as far as he was concerned, he probably really was her father – biologically or not. She'd gone missing and he wanted her found.

Or had she really gone missing? Maybe he didn't want her found because he was worried about her. She was a fledgling Totem-Master, her real father's daughter in that respect. As far as I knew, Angus didn't display either Conner's or Neridah's talents.

She was on a quest, at least in her head, put on her by the spirits. She was on a quest to stop a second Betrayal. That was huge! Something on the scale of the Betrayal would require an infrastructure put in place to pull off – an infrastructure in the service of the Nether, but which took a System Lord and a somnambulant public oblivious and uncaring to the acts of their leadership.

Was I wrong? Was this some level of government conspiracy after all? Was Angus Blooming-Star behind some plan to serve the Nether on the scale of Lord Archimedes's Betrayal? Was he, at least, a major lieutenant in a plot?

"That's crazy!" I finally couldn't stop myself from arguing aloud, "Even if he was, what's with the Pyqeans? They don't even function on a spiritual level. They're immune to the corruption of the Nether. Archimedes had all of his Pyqeans killed because of it. More of them died than Totem Masters."

Well, I returned to my inside voice, they didn't actually "die." They were reloaded from their back ups on Pyqea. But, since they didn't have their latest save data, they didn't have any memory of the last actions around them before they died. They were effectively 'sentient' program copies of their old 'real' selves.

By the time the mag-lev reached the stop for the Nýtt Óðinsvé hotel in the Down Town area of the Upper City, I decided it didn't matter if it was a government conspiracy or the act of some Ambassador with some undecipherable personal agenda. I wasn't going to get into a Solar Embassy with a holdout blaster blazing, especially without a plan.

I would have to figure out what he was up to as I went. But, I had to stop and figure out what I was going to do to save my Secretary and retrieve that scroll. I didn't care what was written on it. The fact he was going to take it from me made it something I wanted.

No one bullies a Galbraith. I was Icelander by birth, but I was of a people born from the Highlands of Scotland, which survived the rising waters of the Atlantic – the Earth itself didn't bully us.

They'd left me alive and relatively unhurt. I was hopeful they were unlikely to hurt or kill Velma. Whatever Ambassador Blooming-Star was after, it didn't plan for covering up bodies and a string of murders.

That would give me a little time to think this out. My head was raging and keeping me from thinking straight, though my indignation wasn't helping.

It was still morning and I was a cup of Joe in thanks to Girchanizoth. A second cup and some pain killers would be a good start to dealing with this and getting my head around what to do.

In the mag-lev station was one of the common examples of aliens living in the Upper City – a convenience store. I made my way into the small shop run by some short reptilian humanoid whose species I didn't recognize. The short blue lizard-like being pursed his puffy teal...were those lips?...at me, before greeting me in GCT.

"Hallowed Bleshingsh, Shyr." It nodded at me as it flapped its' little wings that kept it hovering a few inches above the check out counter. Its' feet had three toes and reminded me more of some sort of tree frog than a lizard.

It watched me as I pressed the button for a Mocha Latte at the dispenser and pressed another button for a scone at the 3D printer food station. I wanted to be plotting and scheming my mission to save Velma, but he was eying me with those black balls for eyes and it was unsettling.

After the printer finished my scone, vanilla flavored bread with a chocolate glazed topping and crunchy bits inside with the flavor of al-monds, I swiped my credit chip over my wrist computer and then my wrist comp over the check out station. The flying reptilian bowed his head at me and smacked his...whatever those were...as I left to return to my thoughts as I rode the escalators to the platform below.

The surface level of the inner city was a stark contrast to the dirtier and less kept exterior rim of the town. Here there was no graffiti and the unwritten dress code of the workers and inhabitants were clearly broken down pretty clearly – "cube worker", "uniformed maintenance", "up scale service industry", "lawyer or bureaucrat", "law enforcement", or the like. Nowhere were seen any of the seemingly random clothing styles, low end at that, of the Low Down at all and not much even of the Upper City rim that hadn't commuted in.

They'd made a mistake by mugging me and leaving me alive. They probably didn't think I'd realize who attacked me. But, even if they had, they made the serious mistake of giving me time to come up with a plan.

I wasn't a guns blazing soldier like Eight of the Odds. I could hold my own, don't get me wrong. But, I was a detective and I functioned on details and getting what I wanted to know through a mix of sneaky espionage, calculated manipulation, and often bluffing intimidation and coercion. Usually I didn't have the budget for it, mind you, but I was also known to use bribery.

I'd gotten paid by Angus. He'd gotten the message that I'd completed the job. I didn't see anything wrong with returning some of his money to his employees to get what I needed.

Don't get me wrong, bribing a government official or a security guard was risky at best. Not only was it a very criminal act, it wasn't guaranteed to work.

But the service staff at the back entrance to a building? Well, that was something else.

I'd been to the Embassy before. It's where I took the conference call from Ambassador Blooming-Star when he reached out to me for the job. I knew the general layout of the building from my first visit.

All I had to do was get from the back entrance to somewhere familiar and then I'd be in a better position to find my man...and my secretary.

I'd be winging it to pull this off, but it was the only way I was getting in with my holdout blaster – and I wasn't going to go in without it.

A few blocks from the mag-lev station, I'd made it to the Embassy's supply dock at the back of the building. I was in an alleyway across from the loading dock, where there were no guards on duty – just a couple of security cameras, indicated by the small black orbs with their little red light glowing inside.

Outside, smoking, was part of the staff. That's the good thing about most government buildings, most public buildings on Earth actually – you weren't allowed to smoke inside. No matter what people tried, over the course of hundreds of years, you couldn't break people of their collective vices. The best you could hope for was to redirect what those vices were.

Smoking, tobacco from earth or otherwise, in some form of another was one of those millennia old institutions that humans just couldn't shake. I activated the camera on my wrist computer and snapped a few moments of video of the guy and then slipped back into the alleyway out of sight of any nosey security guys looking through the cameras.

I brought up a 3D hologram of the employee, wearing what looked like a cook's whites, and zoomed in on him. There it was! He was wearing a name tag - *Victor*.

A few minutes later and I was using a search on the Dark Net through some encryption to keep the city network security from detecting me accessing it. It didn't take me long to find the Terran Anarchism Movement's listing of the New Reykjavik Solar Embassy and the "traitors" who worked there. The TAM felt that anyone who supported the Galactic Expanse, or any subsidiary government within it, were enemies of the Free People of Earth.

They were nuts. I understood them a little, but that probably just meant I was a little nuts too.

Still, the name Victor Herrera came up when I looked through the list. That was all I needed to set my plan in motion. Well, that and the fact it was almost lunch time.

I closed down the holo-vid of my poor sap, Victor Herrera, and proceeded to dial up my secret weapon – *Hot'landic Pizza Delivery*. I entered my order and my special delivery instructions.

Then, I just had to wait.

XIX

CHAPTER NINETEEN

Load Playlist Track: The Clash, London Calling

Hot'landic Pizza Delivery was an oddity in the modern era of 3D printed foods, vacuum sealed protein space rations, instant-this, and instant-that. They were a good old fashioned pizza parlour, with four locations throughout New Reykjavik, with delivery anywhere in the city in under thirty minutes or your credits back. Their first shop, opened when the mobile city was still in early construction, was the first restaurant in New Reykjavik. Unlike the other locations, it had an actual dine-in option with seating for about forty beings.

The restaurant's name was a portmanteau of the worlds Hot and Icelandic. While Pizza definitively had its origins in Italy, the popularity of the bread and tomato paste flat pies permeated nearly every culture on Earth. So, just as New York had its' famous flats and Chicago had its' deep dish, so did New Reykjavik have its' own unique style of pizza joint. Hot'landic Pizza, named for the restaurant, was a fusion of pizza and Icelandic dishes.

The dough is made using *skyr* instead of water, giving it a mild, almost yogurt like, tang. But, it's also popular to order *flatkaka* bread as a crust. Iceland is known for its dairy products, so cheese toppings on the pizza are imported from the Homeland exclusively. In terms of toppings, you can usually order all the traditional stuff – pepperoni, pineapple, sausages of a dozen cultures, and the like. But, for a real Icelandic edge, I like to order some *Hangikjöt*, *Þorramatur*, or Angelica. It's rare to get, but if I've got a chest cold and just want the pizza as comfort food, I'd order it with some heavily spiced Iceland moss. My grandmother used to use it in home remedies, but you want to spice it; it's not that tasty on its own. Occasionally, especially if I've been drinking, I'd order it with a side of *Klenät* – a delicious fried pastry that'd suck up the booze.

Pizza delivery used to be a very common thing, even when *Hot'landic Pizza* started their operation on the fledgling New Reykjavik. But these days, with the easy access to near instant meals at home, having anything hand made was considered a luxury – even if delivered.

That's what I was counting on.

Mr. Herrera was dressed like a cook. Since he was working in the Embassy, he was one of two things, either just a cook or a chef. His frock wasn't red, so it meant he wasn't a sous-chef. He was either some line cook in the embassy's cafeteria or he was a someone even more significant in the kitchen than just some number two.

Either way, he was someone who worked around food and would more than likely appreciate the hard work that goes into making what Hot'landic delivers to your door.

So, he wasn't going to dismiss it out of hand.

I waited impatiently for what felt like forever before my stakeout of the embassy was interrupted by the "ding" of receiving voicemail on my wrist computer. I pulled a pair of wireless ear buds out of my pocket and slipped them into my ears and hit play.

It was a data burst, several messages all at once, with dates spread over a few days – and all from the same sender address.

"Einar." The first message played. "This is Nephiri Tora. Neridah asked me to give a progress report on our journey to Earth. We've set down in the Caleron system. It's my first time running the Mouse Club, but we brought in a decent haul. More than I was expecting, actually –

makes me wonder if that Delosian son of a bitch was shorting us our cut. Anyway, if we can keep this income going, we might be able to pick up the pace getting to you. If you get this before we do, send a comms through the network and let us know how the search is going."

So, she'd decided to keep the name "Mouse Club." Makes sense, really. The sign is written in electric lighting on the side of the cargo pod and it probably had some name recognition. It might even be possible that most people didn't even know who Mouse, the owner, was.

By the time the delivery showed up, at fifteen minutes, I decided to listen to the rest of the data burst when I was free.

Victor Herrera had long finished his smoke break. I hadn't expected him to float out there sucking down cancer sticks that long. I just needed him because he had a name tag I could research and, better yet, because he was someone who had a connection to food.

The delivery kid on the repulsor scooter, one of the few allowed-for vehicles in the city, pulled up to the back of the Embassy, just like I'd instructed. A security guard was quick to intercept him and demand what he was doing back there.

I slipped across the street, stuffing my red fedora under the blazer I'd donned in the absence of my ruined trench coat – red tends to stand out. I kept as out of sight as possible while I watched the guard call in on the radio after checking the kid's delivery slip.

Yep, the guard acknowledged that Victor did in fact work at the embassy. Yep, Victor was on duty. Yep, Victor was on his way down to check out what was going on.

The kid, as planned, stayed the focus of the guard's attention, as I slipped all the way up to back entrance, flipping up my collar to hide as much of my face as possible while avoided looking in the direction of the most obvious points for cameras.

When Victor stepped out the door, I let him pass and put my foot in the doorway behind him. After he was passed, I opened it and slipped into the Embassy.

I looked back just in time for him to look surprised as he looked in the Pizza Box longingly. If a delivery had made its way to an embassy that wasn't food, an employee would have alerted security and raised the alarm.

But food? Especially good food? No. It was getting in and no one was going to complain if it had been paid for in advance.

So, the pizza and I both got in without claxons and armed security swarming out of every crack and doorway.

I slipped on my red fedora again. Although it makes an impression, it wouldn't register as out of place on the inside of the Embassy. After all, if you're inside the Embassy, you're probably supposed to be there – and who would sneak around inside an embassy with a bright red hat on? Down through the service hallways, past the kitchens, and out into the main hall behind the front door's security, I made my way deep into the heart of the halls of our Parliamentary embassy.

From there, I knew enough of the layout to start a search. I started with where I'd been before. I caught a lift to up to the same floor I had the conference call with Ambassador Blooming-Star the first time. I re-called that it was selected because it belonged to the primary adminis-trator of that particular embassy.

Since it wasn't the planetary Embassy, it served primarily as an ad-ministration of passports for those traveling throughout the Galaxy. I'd gotten my passport here before starting my job for the Ambassador. They'd done a rush job on the travel data, so I could get right to work.

Normally, you don't need papers to move around within your own star system, or, in most cases, within the demesne of your System Lord. There were exceptions under the more rigid System Lords or where so-cial unrest was growing. Such restrictions were also common in more corrupt Systems, where the Parliament was more for show than actu-ally responsible for the rule of law. These more tyrannical system lords were frowned upon. Under the Hallmarked Charter of the Hegemony, each System was to be a democracy with certain laws and rights as-signed to all beings regardless of their planet of origin, their biology, or their technological development. But, with literally thousands of Sys-tem Lords, ruling some times a dozen or more star systems, each with varying political allegiances and designs on growing their fiefdoms and the power of their Houses and Families, the idea of free democracies were hard to enforce.

In the old days, before mankind had spread into the stars, ambassadors and Embassies were a means for the multitude of nations of the Earth to talk to one another and manage the business of diplomacy in a world that only had the alternative of war. In the Expanse, a single Galactic rule, Ambassadors and Embassies represented the System Lords and the Parliaments they presided over. They were used to carry official communiqués between the System Lords or to the Royalty of the Hegemony in the Central Worlds.

The lift opened to the administration level, where the common joe like me wouldn't be a bother. I walked by a Terran Colonial Trooper that had been set up there, more ceremonial than not. He wasn't there to look for badges, though perhaps he should have been. I didn't have anything to indicate that I belonged.

He was a clean cut looking young man, perhaps in his early twenties. Based on his age, he'd likely already served in the Terran Colonial Troopers for as many as four years already. The fact he'd gotten an Embassy gig that young implied he was either connected or very good at what he did.

I decided I didn't want to risk anything but good will from him.

I tipped my hat to him and made eye contact with that confidence that said we both knew each other, the kind of nod a veteran gives to another – like the hand wave outward a repulsor biker gives to another on the mainland. The instinct when you get that is to make that eye contact back and give a nod.

That kept his eyes off anything except me and my remarkable hat. He'd remember me, and truth be told, if things got ugly, he'd probably be the closest to me to put me down when I tried to rescue Velma. But, at the moment, he felt like I belonged there because I walked like I did.

Two doors down and I slipped into the conference room I'd used the first trip. They'd had a terminal interface there that they connected the call to the main embassy through. It was still there, like I hoped.

"Now let's hope that it isn't that hard to get into." I basically prayed aloud. This deep into the building, more secret things happened. It could have meant more security. But, it also meant that no one expected anyone to try accessing it in person.

I pulled the sleeve up off my wrist computer and tugged a small nub from the corner. A thin ribbon of cable pulled out with it. "A system this important isn't going to have lax wireless security. But...."

The terminal was built into the table, so that the entire table could act as a three dimensional projection – a giant version of my wrist computer. I popped the jack into an interface port on the terminal.

"...for a direct connection, lets see if they have a good I.T. guy."

They were still using an operating system a couple versions back. That was good for me. I'd learned how to hack that one. Much newer and I might have been able to break in, but it'd take me easily twice as long. I worried that Velma didn't have that kind of time.

After a few inputs I managed to access the retina passkey. I put my eye to my own wrist computer, which was now acting as an authorizing machine, instead of the one for the table.

The computer's AI came online with a feminine voice, speaking in an extremely proper and posh sounding High Ara'lon. I recognized the greeting and the declaration of the sovereigns' reign. I was prompted to choose a preferred language. I chose GCT.

"Hello, Ambassador Smith. Welcome New Reykjavik Embassy. You may call me Alita. How can I help you?"

"Hello Alita." I beamed, proud of myself. "I am looking for Ambassador Angus Blooming-Star. Can you tell me where in the building he is?"

"The Ambassador is currently located in storage closet six on the third floor." The AI answered me.

"That is an odd location for an Ambassador." I muttered more to myself than the system, but like any attentive system, she decided to answer the rhetorical statement anyway.

"Should I send security to check on his well being?" the system said, bringing up a prompt for an alert button I could press in the air in front of me. I could probably answer verbally as well.

"Not yet." I answered and thought to myself. "I'll check first and make sure he's safe. Can you transfer the security prompt to my personal computer and leave a network connection open for me while I do?"

The AI seemingly chirped pleased to receive a command and having obeyed it.

I switched tabs on the holographic screen and dialed up a second pizza delivery before I slipped out the hall.

I was on the third floor already, so my guess as to its' importance was a good one. I made my way out of the room and started walking the hall again, away from the Colonial Trooper. Each of the doors had a small metal plate on the wall indicating its location. It was printed in High Ara'lon and Galactic Common Tongue, embossed so someone blind could feel the letters in both languages.

I turned a corner, following the pattern of nameplates. I'd already passed three storage closets, with numbers increasing toward six. I was going the right way.

This corner of the Embassy was all but abandoned. Whatever he was doing in Closet six, Ambassador Blooming-Star didn't want anyone hearing or seeing it.

"Tell me where he hid it!" A man was speaking gruffly to someone on the opposite side of a wall I was at in the hallway. Ahead was a corner, so I guessed Storage Closet six was right around there as well. I stopped and crouched to pull my holdout blaster from its ankle holder.

"Ambassador." A synthesized voice advised him. "I do not believe she knows where Mister Galbraith hid the Dagger. This is a futile interrogation."

"Indeed." A second voice, distinct, but still synthesized, agreed. "I suspect we intercepted the detective too soon. His letter and request for remuneration indicated that he was on retainer to your daughter, having completed your assignment. You may have been incorrect to assume that he already possessed the Artifact."

"No!" there was a distinct slap of flesh on flesh and a muffled cry of a woman. "He must have hidden it after he saw my warning to him. He could have left it on the Earthport."

There was a second slap, which felt like a sick slap against my insides when Velma whimpered from the hit. "Did he leave it on the Earthport?!"

Anger welled up inside me. It was all I could do not to turn the corner and put down both Pyqeans and the Ambassador right there. But what didn't make sense was that he had stolen a warning to me from himself. Why was he trying to steal the Dagger of Augury from me – from his daughter effectively? And why would the Pyqeans, the Hegemony's advisors, be helping him?

He slapped her again and I grit my teeth. I could kill all three of them, but then I'd have a dead ambassador, two dead Pyqeans, and a blaster pistol in the heart of an Embassy. It'd be a death sentence. I needed to get Velma and get out without being seen.

Better to use the plan I'd gone down the hall with.

I stepped into the nearest office and left the door slightly ajar, blaster pistol ready – just in case.

"Alita." I whispered to my wrist computer. "Are you there?"

"Yes, Ambassador Smith." The voice whispered conspiratorially, emulating my tone. It was a well designed Pyqean AI – almost as realistic as a real Pyqean. "Have you confirmed the Ambassador's safety or shall I give the alarm?"

"Alarm, please." I answered. "There are two men posing as Pyqeans and they have the Ambassador at gun point."

"Oh my!" the little voice whispered.

"Alert! Alert! Alert!" Alita's voice called out through the buildings' intercom. "Intruders in the Embassy. Alert! Alert! Alert! Security to Level three. Ambassador under duress. Intruders are armed. Alert! Alert! Alert! Intruders are posing as Pyqean Advisors! Alert! Alert! Alert!..."

The alarm repeated as flashing lights at each of the buildings' interior corners began to strobe red and white.

"What the hell?!" Blooming-Star yelled.

"The Investigator." The first Pyqean answered. "He must be on the premises."

"He has set the security against us." Captain Obvious Pyqean number two answered. "We must clear ourselves with security before they discover our captive."

"You fool!" The Ambassador barked at him, "They might just shoot you down as a threat."

"We are Pyqean." His thug answered with a matter of fact tone. "If that happens, we will transmit to our backup in the Embassy and then again back for new bodies on Pyqea. We do not die."

"But you'll be gone for weeks while you travel back here with new host shells. We don't have that kind of time." The Ambassador began cussing in some language I didn't know. It sounded like it might be Gaelic.

"We have been discovered by the detective." The first Pyqean answered. "Revealing to security, even in death, that we are Pyqean will show the alarm to be false. This will allow you to maintain your secrecy while you seek the Dagger and fulfill our agreement."

Agreement? So, they were working with the Ambassador for a purpose. But, what could you offer the Pyqeans to make them break their vows to the Empire. That was supposed to be almost impossible.

"It is the most logical solution, Ambassador." The second robotic man assured the Ambassador. "I suspect there is only a fifty percent chance both of these shells will be damaged irreparably. Come with us and you can explain afterward and divert attention from the girl."

"Damned right." He cussed again and slammed a door shut. "And after that we'll sick security on finding Galbraith. Now that he's invading an Embassy, I can use it to legally interrogate him and find where he hid the Dagger."

"We should not have left him in his apartment." A Pyqean countered him as they left.

"His assistance distraction was effective." The other Pyqean defended the Ambassador as they walked by the room. "She deduced we were searching the apartment for something. By attacking us and stealing something from it, she succeeded in the subterfuge that she had acquired what we sought. By the time we had acquired her and learned she had tricked us, it was too late to go back unnoticed."

The sound of the claxons and Alita's "Alert! Alert! Alert" drowned out the rest of their discussion as they made their way toward the lift.

I slipped out of the officer and opened the storage closet. Velma was already half out of her bonds.

"That was quick." She smiled neon pink smeared lips at me. The smudged lipstick stood out starkly on her almost porcelain flesh, as did the red mark on her cheek where she'd been slapped more than once. "I didn't think you'd be so close or I'd have let you save me from being tied up by bad guys."

"So you remembered that trick I showed you then." I said pointing to her robotic arm, which was clearly displaced.

"Yeah." Velma said popping it back into place. "I don't know how you can do that with your flesh and blood. It's gotta hurt."

I winced with the thought, "Its not something I like to do, yeah. But, it's a good thing you can dislodge yours for maintenance."

"So, what's going on boss?" She peaked down the hall. "What's a Dagger of Augury and why is this guy looking for it?"

"Any idea what he's looking for it?" I asked her as I helped her up off the chair.

"Nope." She pointed to the office across the hall. "But I suspect it has something to do with what's written in that letter they stole. He seemed really concerned about if you'd managed to read it or not."

I walked across, opened the door to the small office they'd set aside for the Ambassador and grabbed the scroll tube off the desk. "We'll read it later. First, let's get out of here."

"Any plan for that?" she asked, following me down the hall, continuing to follow the interior of the building's edge, opposite of the direction as the Pyqeans and Blooming-Star, but ultimately destined to head back to the same point.

As we neared the lift area from the opposite direction I'd gone in, we heard the sound of a standard issued military blaster pistol go off.

It was slightly heavier than most blaster pistols, but not rigged like a Heavy Blaster pistol. Two shots fired and a cluster of Embassy personnel from the floor that hadn't made it past security screamed and hurried through a door labeled as the stairs.

"Stand down Trooper!" yelled the Ambassador, "Stand down."

"Now, hurry!" I pushed Velma ahead of me as I pulled my hat off and tucked it under my blazer, my holdout blaster inside it. Together we rushed forward into the small crowd behind the Trooper who was fixated at two heavily damaged Pyqeans, their full robotic forms visible – expensive, otherwise unassuming, ultra high tech machine recreations of humanoid forms.

Each was laying on the floor with a slagged hole in their chest with precise hits from the Trooper. He was there because he was good, not because he was connected.

"Get on the ground!" the Trooper was yelling back at the Ambassador. "Hands up where I can see them. Where are your credentials, sir?!"

"In my robes." The man said. He looked like a dark haired version of his brother, but without any beard and a little more heavyset with age. "I have to warn you. This wasn't what you think. We're still under attack, son."

He was looking through the crowd instead of at the Trooper – looking for me. Shit.

Then, like a mist over my mind, I thought I saw Conner shimmer into existence beside Angus and whisper something. Angus' eyes glossed for a second and went back to the Trooper, "We have to stop them, son. They're coming. They're coming...the nether."

"What?" the Trooper paused at that. "What did you say, sir?"

The Ambassador shook his head and looked angry again. "What are you talking about boy?!"

I slipped down the stairs behind Velma along with the fleeing crowd. They poured through the front doors of past another dozen Colonial Troopers checking identifications with scanners before letting them through the front doors.

Which is why we were going back down through the service hallway past the kitchens.

As we reached the back door I peaked out the security peephole. Yep, fifteen minutes again. I popped the door open quietly and kept Velma with me as we worked our way out of the loading entrance around the two Colonial Troopers that had the poor delivery kid jacked up on the ground. We broke for the shadows of the alley before I slipped my hat back on and holstered my holdout.

"Going to explain what's going on Einar?" Velma almost bounced along beside me. "How big a case is this?"

"I dunno, kid." I handed her a handkerchief for the smudged lipstick. "Big. Really big."

"What's the matter, boss?" She stopped me. "You look like you saw a ghost. You're whiter than me."

"Yeah." I looked at the ground thoughtfully. "Ghosts."

I took her arm and headed straight to the Spaceport. "We need to get to the mainland, now. To North America."

"Are you going to explain things, Einar?" She pulled away from me, the adrenaline of our escape must have been wearing off – she was starting to get the shakes and her porcelain complexion started to look a little green. Clearly this wasn't one of our normal cases and adventures.

"Yeah." I looked around to make sure we hadn't been followed. "But let's do it on the way, okay?"

I pulled her along again and we hurried to get off New Reykjavik and away from Ambassador Blooming-Star.

XX

༒

CHAPTER TWENTY

Load Playlist Track: Violent Femms, Add It Up

We grabbed a last-minute flight aboard a Leo. Leo's were Low Earth Orbit craft that hopped from continent to continent. There were easily a dozen styles of Leos that operated from New Reykjavik to North America.

This particular Leo was flying us to Philadelphia, Pennsylvania – North America's largest northeastern Starport. It was a nice Starport with docks into the Atlantic Ocean capable of interlocking with the outermost edges of New Reykjavik whenever it stopped there while in the Sea of Jersey. Usually, the city was parked there for part of summer and I'd tour around what was left of old New England before the flooding. Meanwhile, the work and clean up crews would start their latest salvages of the old cities in the area.

But, our sudden trip from the Earth's equator was going to land us there in the winter. This last minute trip, which was more expensive than I like, was going to have an added expense of some new winter gear for both myself and Velma. I couldn't justify either of those expenses to Neridah.

We were both alive and safe, though. I guess I couldn't put too high a price tag on that.

"Okay," Velma said impatiently. "We're safely on our way. Will you tell me where we're going?"

I looked around me, checking over my shoulder in the flight compartment. It wasn't a sealed room, more a partition with two seats facing two other seats with a thin wall between the compartment and the next. Each compartment had an emergency blast door that would lower in the event of explosive decompression. The individual hull modules were tough enough to handle a large number of reentry scenarios in the event the explosive decompression happened in low earth orbit.

The stats on survival were estimated to be about fifty percent in the worst case scenarios, according to an article I read while investigating a robbery of a Leo where the culprit jettisoned his compartment to escape. It was considered the most ambitious mid-flight escape since D.B. Cooper.

I never solved that one. It was a case open to anyone for the reward of a percentage of the stolen credits. No one had solved it yet.

With the blast canopy up, Velma and I could be overheard by someone who was deliberately eavesdropping.

"We're going to some wilderness northwest of the Philly metroplex." I whispered to her. "It's the location of something called the Dagger of Augury. It's what I was hired by Neridah Blooming-Star to find."

"That's what the Ambassador was grilling me about." Velma leaned into me and kept her voice low. "They were trying to figure out if you had it yet. He wanted to know if you'd read the warning in the note and if it stopped you from finding it."

"Damnit." I muttered. "I wish I'd read that on the way from the *Earthport*. By the time I'd landed on Earth I'd forgotten I even had it."

"Well let's at least see what it says." She patted it a few times into an open hand with her other.

I nodded and she broke the seal on the scroll work. "Expensive paper."

Opened, you could see that the owner actually hand wrote the note.

It wasn't as neat a hand writing as I had expected to see. But, who really uses actual handwriting these days instead of a computer input?

"Mister Galbraith," Velma read the letter, rolling the scroll slowly more open with her robotic right hand as her flesh hand pulled the end upward. "I write this in haste. I don't know how long I can resist its Will. The Whispers are helping me. I have to warn you and get this to you by Messenger before I stop myself. If I send it by paper, I can't rescind the message and I'm sending it on official Ambassadorial scroll and with official seal to protect it from any eyes but yours. No one may open it but the intended or a member of the Hegemony. This is how we keep some communications offline in government. I'll trust you not to share that..."

I put my hand on Velma's bionic hand to stop her from unrolling. "You're working with me. That knowledge is client privilege ok?"

"Are you nuts?!" She sat up in surprise, "That bastard tried to kill us."

I shook my head. "No. If he wanted us dead, we would have been. I don't think he's completely in control of himself."

"What do you mean?" Her face looked incredulous.

Did I tell her about my messed up dream of Angus Blooming-Star and his totem wolf? Did I tell her I saw him again whispering in his brother's ear?

"Whispering?" I thought to myself out loud. "He said 'The Whispers are helping me.'"

"No way." I argued to myself, knowing what I was thinking.

"Boss." Velma interrupted. "You're doing that thing again."

I snapped out of it and looked to her. "You're a near human, Vel. Do your people's fall in with the Totem Masters and Shamans and their powers?"

"Pfft." She let loose a small raspberry and raised an eyebrow defiantly. "Excuse ME, Mister. I am NOT 'near human.' YOU are 'near Milanoa.'"

I rolled my eyes. I knew she was just giving me guff. It wasn't the first time she clarified the distinction to mess with me. "Semantics. Anyway – yes or no?"

She shrugged. "Not me much. But, yeah. We have our Shamans and something like what they call Totem Masters. Even Honorable Oba Nagako-Sama follows a fusion of Milanoa Spiritualism and Shinto worship of the Kami. Why?"

"It's possible," I couldn't believe I was saying this. "That the Ambassador is being influenced by some being or person spiritually. The Whispering he's talking about, I believe, to be his dead brother the former Totem Master and Ambassador Conner Blooming-Star."

"Based on what evidence?!" She went from incredulous to a look that all but screamed "bullshit" at me. She may have been working as my secretary, but she was training to be like the man who saved her from that water tank. She believed in the real world and in evidence. Detective work had a strong element of physical evidence and a grounding in what happened in the world around us. It wasn't too unlike being a scientist.

But, Expanse science was on the side of the Totem Masters officially, even if the average citizen couldn't feel, see, or prove what the Totem Masters could do. There was, however, a considerable amount of evidence that they produced results when they got involved in things beyond being simple spiritual advisors.

I'd have to give it deeper thoughts.

"I saw things." I told her. "I don't know what I saw or what it means. But, I saw things. My point is that the Ambassador may have been legit when he wrote this note to us – and, more importantly, I was still employed by him when he wrote it."

"So, 'client privilege.'" She responded. "What kind of things?"

"Later." I told her, "It's an hour tops from take off to disembarking. Let's finish reading this thing."

"Right." She rolled the scroll back to where we left off. I glanced out the window to gauge how much time we had left before we set down. The craft's acceleration and deceleration were designed to help produce some of the artificial gravity. That helped keep the energy costs, and our flight costs, down. The curve of the Earth was rotating as we switched from "going up" to getting ready to go back down. "...with the common public. It's not a total secret, but we must protect the security of the Expanse where we can. That's why I write you. I was under Its influence when I hired you to find Neridah. It was a trick to get you with her. She'd begun to have visions, like her Uncle. She had told me she was dreaming of the Dagger of Augury, an item in my brother's possession. They want it from her. It's a key to their freedom and to resume their march upon the Galaxy. I encouraged her to seek it. I want to explain more, but I feel my will weakening. I must hurry. If she finds it, I will try and take it from her. If I do, I will give it to Lord Wilfred Archimedes, the Betrayer. You must not let that happen. They have already started to slip out of their prison. One has me. You must stop it. The..."

She paused as the writing became almost incoherent, "I can't read this part. It's very sloppy. Um...oh Goddess. Does that say "the Nether?"

"Yeah." I confirmed. "That's who I've been hired to help stop."

"Let me get this straight." Velma said a little too loudly as she rolled up the parchment. I put a finger to my lips and she lowered her voice again. "You were hired by an Ambassador working to recover an Artifact he's going to use to help the Nether start attacking the Galaxy?"

"No." I corrected her. "I was hired by an Ambassador to find his missing daughter so she could have me present faster and speed up her prophetic quest to find the Artifact in the hopes of stopping a second Betrayal....so he could probably steal it from us and then use it to help the Nether start attacking the Galaxy."

"AND YOU'RE STILL ON THE CASE?!" She yelled at me in horror.

"SHHH!" I meekly waved to everyone to indicate everything was ok. "Quiet..."

"Seriously?" My secretary hissed at me. "That guy beat you up and robbed you and when I tried to get away they kidnapped me to find out what I knew. This isn't good, Einar. Why are you still on this case?"

"Two very good reasons," I lied, because right then they didn't feel like very good reasons, "First – she could afford to pay me and with the retainer I could afford to pay you. Second – she said she had a vision and that I was destined to help her, along with the Odds."

"The who?" She said.

"No, the Odds." I quipped, "The Who are a different band entirely."

"What?!"

I rolled my eyes realizing yet another twentieth century historical earth reference had slipped and gone over her head. "The Odds. They're a Deep Voltch-Djugga band made up of smugglers and mercenaries. They're the rest of the prophesized heroes she says are destined to help her stop a second Betrayal."

"And you believed her?" She was clearly having trouble with all of this. So, was I. But, I saw Angus whispering in Conner's ear.

"I believe she has the credits." I reassured her. "And I believe I was getting jumped and searched for the Dagger even if I hadn't taken the case. That makes this case more personal. I'm involved either way...might as well get paid for it."

"We're involved either way." She countered. "I'm on the run with you from the Expanse Ambassador of the Sol Parliament and a pair of Pyqeans. I get a cut."

"Yeah, that's weird." I muttered as a stray thought triggered.

"Why is it weird I get paid?" She nudged me. "Come on boss. I'm doing more than answering the phone this time."

"Oh yeah." I nodded in agreement. "No, I meant the Pyqeans. What the hell are Pyqeans even doing involved with this?"

"Well they're advisors to the government, right?" Velma was onto my train of thought.

"Yeah, but..." I thought about the letter. "Could they be working for the Nether?"

"No!" I answered myself, cutting off Velma's unspoken response. "They can't be corrupted by the Nether. Everyone says that the Nether corrupt your spirit, not just your body."

"Right." She managed to edge into my self-dialog. "And anything I've read about Totem Masters and Shamans say that Pyqeans don't have spirits...or bodies for that matter. They're just data copies of their living selves."

"Yeah," I agreed. "But, they do grow and develop like any living being. They learn."

"Have you ever dealt with Pyqeans before?" Velma said.

I shook my head. "Nope. I really don't know much about them. These gigs for the Blooming-Stars are the first time I've dealt with anything bigger than Sol law enforcement."

"I thought that was weird, yeah." She crossed her arms pensively.

"What?" She had that look that she was onto something.

"You've done some interesting cases." She said. "But you've never done any jobs that should have drawn the attention of the Sol Ambassador for the Parliament."

"I helped shut down the humanoid trafficking ring that kidnapped you." I retorted. "That involved interplanetary law enforcement and a missing girl...you. It's not that far a jump."

"Nope." Velma shook her head, waving her bright pink hair defiantly. "Not that big a jump, but also not that big a headline on Earth. Sure, it made news on Mars – where the ring was located..."

"...but not on Earth." I finished the though as I remembered back to the case. "And its not like your Auntie paid me particularly well. So, it wouldn't have even made a blip to the tax man, let alone the Ambassador."

"So, why you?"

"Neridah knew she was looking for the Odds, the Captain of the *Legacy's Façade*, and me." I surmised. "Maybe the Ambassador knew that...put me on the case to get me to her sooner."

"Yeah," she agreed with a nod. "But why didn't Miss Blooming-Star look for you on Earth, where you were...instead of with...the Odds?"

"Yeah, the Odds." I tapped a finger on my chin thoughtfully. "Not sure really. That's something I'll have to ask her when she gets here in a couple of days."

"She's coming here?"

I explained the events of the case and the adventures on Arcturis Minor. We hadn't had time for me to debrief her on the case notes before we were assaulted by the Pyqeans and the Ambassador. This conversation normally happened over some coffee in the front office as she made notes for future reference.

"So," She summarized the details from memory. She was smart. "A Grathrak, a Telarian, a Cloned Colonial Trooper, and a Smuggler are somehow supposed to help you and this proto-Totem Master to girl stop the Nether from pulling off a second Betrayal. And we have her uncle, who she thought was her father, who hired you to find her, chasing us to steal a magical dagger that she needs to stop them. But, he wants the magic knife to give to The Betrayer and make let loose the Nether on the Galaxy, dooming all living kind to a second war with them?"

"Basically, yeah."

"Goddess, Einar." She looked out the window as the heat shields started to glow orange against her white skin. "If we're doing this, I want half. This isn't secretary work."

"Nope." I winked at her as she looked back to me. "This is apprentice detective work. You can have thirty percent, after expenses."

She narrowed her eyes at me, before her wicked and playful young smile erupted back on her face, "That makes me officially an apprentice then! No more answering calls like a secretary?"

"Maybe." I muttered before I waved a finger at her. "But that means you do what you're told on a case. And...you still make the coffee."

A mock salute from her sealed the deal. "Yes, boss."

She beamed and flipped on the complementary virtual reality goggles that came with the flight and slipped into watching one of the latest holo-films to grace your in flight experience.

Finally settled and with her on board, I decided to check the rest of the data bursts from Tora's communications burst.

"Einar." Purred the voice of Vi'xiri the Vixen. "You 'ave been gone for only two days and already I feel am not getting the attention I deserve on stage. Our little friend looks too delicious dancing on stage with us. You will have to find her dagger soon or she's going to make me a jealous girl. It's a lucky thing for me that while she is pretty, she does not know how to dance."

"Hey!" a shocked voice, Neridah's, shouted from the background. "Vi! Who are you messaging?"

"No one, pet." Vixiri called out to the background. "I 'ave attached some images from last night's show. See our little shaman looking almost as good as me."

Sure enough, Vi'xiri had included some three dimensional holo images of the band playing in the Mouse Club. Vi was more filled out, like a woman, than Neridah. But the young ambassadorial paige had more of a girl-next-door look to her. Toss that into a skimpy dancing girl outfit to primal Djugga music and I can see how the crowd could notice.

"Who's that?" Velma asked me, peaking out from under her goggles dubiously.

"Our client." I answered and switched it off. She eyeballed me and looked to the wrist computer and back once. I don't know what I did to upset her, but she narrowed those pink eyes at me for a moment then disappeared back into her holovids.

"Attention guests." The flight attendant came over the intercom. "We are 15 minutes from landing. Please put your seats in the upright position and ensure your shoulder and waist belts are firmly in place. Prepare for landing."

"Oh, boss." Velma slipped the goggles off and turned to me as she buckled in. "You still didn't tell me where we're going?"

"To get the Dagger, obviously." I answered her. "From a place some people think is a doorway to Hell."

"What?!"

I smiled the whole way through the landing, listening to "what does that mean?" a few more times. I'd explain on the next leg where we were headed.

XXI

⟨◈⟩

CHAPTER TWENTY-ONE

Load Playlist Track: Willy Moon, Railroad Track

A long time ago, not long after the first man left the Earth's surface and tipped humanity's toes into space, the world was very different. Global warming, climate change, or any of the half dozen terms that had been marketed to wake mankind up to the destruction he was doing to himself, had not yet even been heard of.

The flooding from the melting of the polar caps hadn't yet claimed the coasts of the world. Methane potholes, some the size of cars, some the size of college campuses, had not yet emerged in Russia or northern Canada. The super hurricanes the likes that New Reykjavik had been designed to withstand hadn't begun and their matching typhoons in the Asianic oceans hadn't devastated the lowlands of India.

But, that didn't mean that bazaar manmade disasters hadn't been born out against the Earth – disasters that would scare the land for centuries. The wasteland that was once known as Centralia, Pennsylvania was one of those scars.

I had never heard of Centralia. I'd experienced pop cultural references experienced by it though – video games, old style movies, and refreshed holovids. I was surprised to discover how engrained into my consciousness the place was, having never heard its name until I'd investigated it during my flight back to Earth from Arcturis Major.

Centralia, like many townships in Pennsylvania, was a coal town. The spread of the American Industrial Revolution needed fuel. Middleastern oil hadn't taken off yet, nor even had Texan oil. No one had even considered solar power of devised efficient wind power. Nuclear power was sloppy and cold fusion was still close to a century away from the dropping of the first Atomic Bomb.

So, man dug into the earth, digging black rock out and accelerating the events that lead to the flooding of the Old Coasts. It wasn't the last nail in the coffin for Earth's ice caps; just the first of several big nails.

In 1962, a year after Yuri Gagarin became the first human to fly in space, a fire was discovered by the residents in their landfill. Their borough's leaders had failed to meet deadlines to line each layer of their landfill with protections from possible fire. This landfill fire, growing increasingly hotter, eventually allowed the hot coals to penetrate a vein of coal underneath the pit and start a subterranean fire.

But, legend says that a coal fire at the Bast Colliery from thirty years prior had never been fully extinguished and that the fire came from under the ground into the landfill, not the other way around. Some of the First Peoples tell that the fire came from the Earth itself, fighting back – the first volley in a war between Man and Nature that ended with a truce, the clean ups of the oceans and skies, and entire cities under water.

But if that's the case, then the truce is a tenuous one. That fire still burns today. Scientists in the in the 1990s predicted that the fire, which spread from coal vein to coal vein, would continue to burn for as much as another 250 years. That was ten years ago and that fire is still burning slowly outward from the old township, which has long since disappeared into the wilderness that has grown up around it.

Everywhere the fire had touched had cracked the ground and, in many places over time, has released smoke and steam that occludes parts of the area for days at a time. Superstitious locals, until there were no more locals, suggested that the devil lit the fire and that toxic gas, steam, and smoke was proof that the devil or some ancient evil sleep under the surface.

Or at least, that's what some iterations of pop culture references to the imagery would have you believe they thought.

I don't know the truth of the start of the fire. I don't know the supernatural implications of a quarter-millennia old subterranean fire, but I do know that somewhere in the midst of the old town Conner Blooming-Star, Druid and Cleverman, Totem Master and Shaman, hid something called the Dagger of Augury.

And I was going to find it. I was going to find it for the paycheck. I was going to find it to wrap up the job. And I was going to find it before Angus Blooming-Star beat me to it.

I don't believe in prophecies or destiny or spirits. But, I know weird things are afoot and the younger Neridah Blooming-Star thinks she can set them right with that knife.

Things getting back to normal and a decent payout, is all I wanted.

I explained all of this to Velma as she piloted our repulsor rental from the Starport, another expense tacking onto Neridah's bill...and in the meantime, out of my dwindling cash.

We sat in silence for a while for a while after the explanation, following the northwestern road from Philadelphia that skirted the edge of the remnants of the borough that once housed Centralia. When she finally spoke, Velma wasn't her normal bouncy self.

"That's pretty heavy, Einar." She said from behind the controls. "You have any idea where in this town the Dagger is?"

I looked out at the woodland beyond the borders of the Philadelphian metropolis. Most of the major cities on the new coast had grown more than doubled in size as the old populations had retreated from the rising waters – those that couldn't afford to move off planet to better prospects anyway.

Most of the rich went up into the stars. Most of the poor went inland.

But despite Philly's growth over the last two centuries, there was a definite barrier where that development simply stopped in the Northwest. That was the woodlands just outside of Centralia. The fire wasn't expected to continue spreading that far south. But, as if by design, mankind had simply not bothered to grow in that direction – like it knew that whatever lurked under the Earth wasn't worth taking the chance on.

"According to the old records," I mused aloud. "There are supposed to still be a handful of buildings intact in the old township. I'm hoping that whatever motivated Angus to hide it here and then wipe the record from his own database didn't involve hiding it in some hollow of a tree. We'll start with the buildings."

"Makes sense." She agreed. "Any idea which one?"

I chuckled. "No one goes there and I don't think has in decades aside from Angus. I don't even know how many buildings are actually left. My details aren't exactly new."

"Great." She shook her pink and porcelain head frowning pale lips where she'd washed off the smudged lipstick from her interrogation. "Needle in haystack."

I listed to the final message from Tora's communication burst, all arriving on the same ship's download despite all leaving at different times.

"Einar." It was Neridah this time. "Good news. Someone bought up all of the band's merchandise at the last show on Caleron and even donated a huge chunk of credits – the purchase listed him as our 'Biggest Superfan.' Nefiri says we have enough to cover the flight all the way to Earth. We'll be getting there early. Hopefully, you've had smooth sailing getting the Dagger. We'll be in touch when we hit Sol Prime."

Someone bought all the merch? "That's....convenient."

"How many credits do you think they needed to haul to get the rest of the way here that quick?" Velma said. She had the same cynical tone to her voice. She learned well enough working for me that good things always come with a price.

"Yeah...more than all their merch." I eyed the centuries old concrete barrier that blocked the overgrown exit from old highway as we approached it. "Think this rental can get above the tree line? I don't think we're going to fit it onto what's left of that road. I'd like to hurry and not walk."

Two centuries of overgrowth, outside the zone of the burn, had turned the old road into something more like a foot path through red maple trees and yellow birch, all leaveless with the winter weather. Intermixed were evergreen hemlock trees and pine. A light dusting of snow covered the mulch of fallen leaves.

Velma tested the height restriction of the repulsorlifts of the rental vehicle. We made it nearly twenty feet up before the limiters kicked in. "Nope. They're pretty restricted."

"Yeah, to keep anyone for flying a rental up too high into restricted space." I rolled my eyes in irritation. "Looks like we're going to have to walk in."

"Good thing we bought the jackets, then." She padded her heavy winter coat. It was black, bulgy and full of warm padding, and had stylish orange inverted chevrons on the arms for that faux-military aesthetic that remains popular regardless of the latest trends.

Mine was less warm, but more my speed. I had bought a winterized rain coat. It wasn't real leather like the trench coat I preferred. But, it was in my preferred color, black. Also,, it allowed me to conceal the classic aluminum baseball bat I'd bought at the Phillies Fan Store outside the security gate at the Starport. I also picked up a pair of Gravball gloves for the local triple A team that the Phillies helped support; the Philadelphia Phantoms.

The Gravball gloves were leather-like padded fingerless gloves that allowed your palms to take the sting of grabbing a fast traveling heavy metallic ball with a ceramic shell. Th ball was easy to throw in zero gravity free of inertia. The blue and red gloves matched the Phillie's baseball colors, but had a white ghost floating and holding a yellow gravball. They also had metal inserts at the knuckles for the extra oomph needed to be felt by the armored Gravball members of the other team.

The armor padding they wore, along with the caged helmets, was supposed to protect them from the fast moving heavy ball. But it was an unwritten rule that every Gravball game was going to see a fight break out.

Hey, Gravball's an aggressive sport, okay? Humans are mean enough at bloodsports without having some alien fighting team game mixed in. But, aggressive was what I needed a little of, considering I had to toss my holdout blaster before we went into the Starport back on New Reykjavik. My Detective License lets me travel with my weapons as long as I had the right carrying cases. I hadn't had time to stop by the apartment to grab mine and be off the city sized platform before the Ambassador could turn the encounter at the Embassy against us.

I slung the baseball bat's handle onto a small sling of shoe lace I'd tied up inside the long jacket and, together, Velma and I hopped the old concrete barriers. The overgrown barricade was probably put there before the import of repulsortech, meant to stop standard automobiles.

The path was actually made up of two parallel footpath leading into Centralia. Combined the paths used to be a major road with two lanes in each direction and a small median between, with the center of each side of the road making up each path. Even in the most worn portion of each path, the dead winter grass and wilted weeds were ankle deep at best as they protruded from the inch deep old snow. No one had been down that way in months, if not years.

The virgin looking path was occasionally graced by the tracks of local wild life. I'm a city boy and lived on a walking robotic island. I couldn't tell you what track meant what.

About a half mile into the walk chunks of paved concrete and old road lay out against the trunks of trees along the sides of the path. It was as if someone had taken the time to rip them up and put them on display a long time ago – a memorial of sorts. Even those had weeds and growth over them in spots.

"Sarah Alayna, 2016." I had stopped at the large chunk asphalt leaning against a tree. It was spray painted on with yellow paint in all capital letters, over even older graffiti. "Whoever you were, you were here...two hundred and thirty four years ago. And so was Mikey Wells, 2200."

Velma put a Gravball gloved hand on another asphalt memorial at the next tree. "Tracey, 2011. You people hadn't even been to Mars, yet."

"Not for another decade or two, nope. But, it looks like Aaron was in 2193." We walked on past the display with the two oddly paired markings. We read each label as we went – Derek Wagner, Ziggy, the face of a pot smoking green eyed man (an alien?), Goodwin, and Andy hearts Alicia. Joe was there on 3/16/16 and so was Sue on 4/11/2111.

As we went farther along the graffiti got older, the asphalt chunks got more covered and less legible, and it became obvious that salvaging some of the old road and adding your mark had been a tradition that, like the old city, found itself dying about fifty years ago.

The farther along the old road we got, the less even like a path it became. It was then that the smoke and steam began to be obvious. The little bit of snow that had settled on the ground was melted there and the air was clearly about a full degree Celsius warmer.

At first the smoke and steam was a mix ankle high ground fog and wisps of acrid smoke that hovered like ghosts as high as a man, to disperse as they rose. But, the farther and farther we got along the road, the fog and smoke increased.

The ground became more craggy, with exposed earth and smoke rising out.

"I read that this was all easing up." I said through my gloved hand. "All the pictures and holo-vids showed it clear here."

Velma knelt down, her denim knees on the ground and she touched some of the exposed earth with her exposed fingers. "The ground is warm...and soft."

"Soft?" I knelt beside her, my dress slacks settled into the moist earth. I touched the dirt. "Yeah. Really warm and that's freshly exposed dirt."

As if on queue the ground shook a little and a plume of steam burst from a distant crag. "Geological activity. This place getting unstable you think?"

Her pink eyes looked at me wide, "I think we should hurry up and find your knife."

We made our way deeper into the fog and smoke along the road, the smells irritating my throat and sinuses. Finally, we came upon a cross between our path and another. The remnants of an old red sign, with the word Stop written in English, crept out of wilted overgrowth. Up and down the road, the debris of old buildings stuck out of the undergrowth and collapsed stone walls could be made out along the sides of what were once the town's road – just tall enough to stop a car.

"Looks like we're definitely here." I said, pulling up the old satellite images of the town. "Last time they mapped this area, there were only a few in tact buildings left. Follow me."

I turned right and we moved deeper into the wasteland of wilted winter shrubbery, cracked roads, and steam infused smoke. The fog grew thicker as we move deeper into Centralia. It was like a the town itself didn't want visiters and I could see why this natural hellscape could be the inspiration for horror video games, Wellington's *Vampire Zero* novel, and the feature story of Koontz's *Strange Highways*, as well as the holo-horror classic *Damned Rising* by Bruno Snatcher. Man, that thing gave me nightmares as a teen – jump scares in full emersion holovid?

I shivered as I relived the memory of that nightmare film with looming buildings in the holographic fog...especially when one of those buildings suddenly loomed out at me for real.

I half expected the Demon Pumpkin to rise out right in front of me like in my childhood.

"Did you just...meep?" Velma said in shock.

"Wh..?" I cleared my throat. "What?"

"You made a sound." She sidled up to me and looked at me with that wicked smile of hers. "You...meeped. You aren't scared of this place are you?"

"Some people think it's a doorway to hell." I reminded her. "And no. I'm not scared."

She followed me as we approached the aforementioned looming building in the fog.

The building was in disrepair, but intact. The faded white lettering for the Municipal Building was mostly missing. Their absence left the outline shapes of each letter, in English, like a reversed suntan upon old the brick walls. The flag pole in front was bare, only the tattered threads of an old rope hung from the pully at the top. The old wooden electricity pole had long ago fallen over and lay broken against the exterior wall of the building.

The nearby garage, that had once doubled as a fire station, had broken glass revealing a dilapidated and rotted old yellow vehicle. I'm guessing it had once been a fire truck.

All along the exterior of the buildings centuries of graffiti marked the success of the adventure seekers who dared to break the invisible borders of this forsaken town.

"This is one of the more prominent buildings in town." I told Velma. "Lets get inside and see if we can find any clues."

Together we forced the old glass and metal framed front door open, not the first to ever have done so. But the first to likely have done so in years, if not decades. It was the same building exterior as the horror vids, except for the colorful old graffiti. That more human touch was all that gave me the fortitude to take that first step through the door.

And then we entered the town hall from Hell.

XXII

~~~

CHAPTER
TWENTY-TWO

Load Playlist Track: Chainsmoking, Jacob Banks

The Municipal Building was one of the last functional buildings before the population of Centralia died out or moved on. It acted as a final police station, fire department, court house, and administration building for whatever remained of a government of about ten people at the time that Sarah Alayna scrawled her graffiti on the old road into town, most of them elderly.

Years before that girl made her mark, the former United State of Pennsylvania had decided to secure the area around the town and abandon it. The only allowance was for those who still lived in the fumes and cracks of the old town to stay until they chose to die or move away. Eventually, one way or another, the town lost its final residents – and the Municipal Building was there to save them from fires, arrest them if there was a crime, and tell them how much to pay in taxes.

Even when there's almost no one left, we feel a need to have someone telling us what to do. We're all self-fascists in the end, I guess. Freedom is a madness in the eyes of many.

And I felt more than a little "free" with my wits inside the former symbol of the State. The building's windows, what few there were designed into the institutional square of a building had been either smashed out or boarded up. Very little light crept into the dusty, smoke filled, structure.

I used my wrist computer as a light, turning my forearm so that it projected outward like a shield. Neridah didn't have a light on her, but something about her human-like species allowed those bright pink peepers of hers to see better in the dark than me.

"Anything?" I asked Velma.

"Other than the smell like something died in here?" She wave her mechanical hand in front of her nose as she wrinkled it up.

Sure enough, we found the rotted corpse of a medium sized cat curled up under the rusted aluminum desk that probably doubled as a reception area or a desk sergeant check-in. It must have wandered in there knowing it was going to die. It was curled up like it had laid down to sleep, but it was rotted out it's side and crawling with maggots. The weather outside was too cold for flies, but the fresh body gave them somewhere to keep alive for the moment.

Something shifted along the ground behind me and I spun to turn the light on it while I raised a gloved hand into a fist.

"What's up?" Velma startled, her two hands, flesh and metal, were up in fists beside me.

"You didn't hear that?" I asked her.

"Nope, just those bugs buzzing around."

"Hmmm." I looked up and down the ground in case it was some kind of rodent. Nothing.

"Einar." She said with a little urgency and pointed to the wall at the back of the old office. I turned my light up to the wall and it reflected back some from an old glass case with a red circle marked on it and a name next to it.

"Neridah." Velma read aloud. "That's...creepy."

"Yeah." I moved to the display. "Like someone knew she'd be coming here."

We looked at the circle, and then through it with the light. Inside the case was an impossibly pristine copy of the municipal map of the town. It had to be a copy. The circle was around a particular building.

"What kind of building is that?" I put my finger on the glass. "Velma, I don't read English very well. What does it say?"

"You know it used to be one of the most prominent languages of your planet, right?" She looked at it. "It's not a building. I assume you understood the names Peter and Paul. You do use mostly the same alphabet in Iceland right?"

I shrugged, "I can barely read Icelandic these days. I haven't had to since I was a kid. I'm usually using GCT."

She shook her head, "I at least know the language and alphabet of my nation of my homeworld."

"You guys have more than one nation?" I was taken aback. "More than one language?"

"Yes." She seemed offended. "It's not like I mistake every one of your people as speaking 'Human', right? Human isn't a language."

"No," I countered, "But most of the time I encounter aliens speaking just one language."

"Well," she said, "You definitely haven't been paying attention. They're probably just speaking whatever the most common language of their species is. Like English used to be for your world. An entire species losing their identity to take on GCT isn't exactly unheard of, but many of us have a little homeworld pride."

"I guess if humans had homeworld pride we wouldn't need New Reykjavik to go around cleaning up the trash of a ruined Earth." I frowned.

"True." She agreed shaking her head. "You are a very solipsistic species. You don't even take each other into account half the time."

"Anyway," She pointed the glass, placing her finger up against mine and moved a little closer. "That's not a building. It's a cemetery."

"Actually buried people?" No one really did that on earth anymore. Not enough room to waste on cemeteries. Skyscraper sized mausoleums existed in many cities to accommodate generations of the dead, with the structures managed by the Planetary Trust and funded by the Parliament. System Lord Sch'Gwenish, the great slug himself, recently attended a ribbon cutting for the latest Necropolis within the Ring of Hong Kong, a fortress designed to hold back the rising seas. "Creepy."

Velma moved in closer still, I could feel an almost electricity between us and she lowered her voice and her eyes and put the hand at the glass on mine. "Thanks for coming to save me. I tried to get them away from you, but once they caught me and I saw their faces, I knew they were going to kill me."

"You're my secretary." I cleared my throat. "No one steals my secretary."

She didn't raise her head all the way up, but her big pink eyes did turn up to me, haunting in the half light of my wrist computer. "Just your secretary? We've been working together for a while now, ever since you saved me from that thing. You've always protected me."

It suddenly felt a lot warmer than a cold winter in there. Maybe the increasing geothermal activity from the coal fire had become more unstable.

Velma seemed to shift closer without moving. I could tell what was going to happen next. I wanted it to. I'd wanted it to ever since I first rescued her. But she was a victim and that wasn't professional. Then, she was my secretary and *that* wasn't professional.

And now she was my partner, a junior partner, and that...wasn't professional. I felt myself lean in.

Definite geothermal activity.

Her eyes half closed and her lips parted just a little. Even without her usual bright pink makeup, and despite being ruddied up from Angus' slaps, they were inviting.

I'm a professional...I was going to kiss her like a professional...

beep beep my wrist computer went off indicating I had a call and I stepped back to answer it, shaking off the sudden confusion of doubt, but relieved of the chance to think about what was about to happen.

"Galbraith, go." I said into the light of my wrist. I could see her disappointment as she turned her head and stepped away. I felt bad not following through on that, but it was arousal, not romance stirring me. I'm a professional and I didn't see her as more than friends, colleagues, and someone I had to look out for. At least that's what I told myself.

I'm a professional, I swear.

"Einar," Captain Tora's voice came over the comms. For her to be speaking to me with that kind of response time meant that they weren't just in the solar system, they were close to Earth. "We're on approach to Earth. Have you found the dagger yet?"

"How did you get clearance to land planetside?" I said baffled. Usually private ships were made to park at Earthport Staley and then shuttle in on commercial flights. There were exceptions, plenty of them, but they were prohibitively expensive, illegal, or governmental.

"I'd say Luck." Barked Tree in the background, and then changed tone as if he'd stopped facing the microphone. "The statistical odds of your plan working were three hundred forty five to one."

"What?" I said, confused. "What is that little ashtray talking about? What plan?"

"This is an old ambassadorial ship." Tora said. "It never got decommissioned, so I tried the old landing codes that authorized us planetside to the embassy."

"And it worked?!" Tree was right. There's no way they didn't shut down those old codes after that much time.

"Well," Eight's voice came up. "It worked well enough for them to not immediately deny us. They told us the codes were valid but expired and asked us if we had updated codes. So, Roadie used her ambassadorial codes to see if they would work."

"Who's Roadie? The new drummer?"

"Ha!" He laughed for a good long moment. "No, we hired and dumped six back on the last burb of a planet. He asked too many questions about the club and really kind of sucked. We really need to hire someone with four arms next time."

"So. Who's roadie?" I asked again, perplexed.

"She's not part of the band, but Neridah likes to be helpful. So, she's been doubling as our roadie and one of our dancers. Anyways, she's just a Paige, but her codes were valid enough. I guess they didn't look too close at it. They just saw a lot of ambassadorial noise from us and let us through."

Didn't look too close at them? I guess that's possible. I'd think that the ruckus I caused at the Embassy on New Reykjavik would have put them on higher alert. But, they would have been looking to go after someone leaving the planet, not coming in. Maybe they were just too distracted looking for us.

Or, maybe Angus approved their way in. Could be he was getting whispers in his ear again. Could be he was trying to get to Neridah now that I was close to getting the Dagger.

"Yeah," I came off more dubious than I wanted to. "I'd still come in careful. And don't land at one of the Embassies, even though you used a code for that."

"Why?" Tora said, drawing out the word with concern. "What happened?"

I didn't want to tell them over their comms that Angus was working for the Nether. I didn't want them telling Neridah like that. I wanted to tell her in person, in case it upset her. Besides, she'd believe me better after they looked at Velma's slowly swelling lip.

I flashed back briefly to those lips for a moment, before shaking it off.

"I'll tell you when you're planet side." I said. "We need to move fast and get back off planet. Come down to the coordinates I'm transmitting to you now. We're close to the Dagger and we can get it the rest of the way together."

"Have to get off planet fast, you say?" Eight's tone became more serious. "Are we going to need to gear up?"

"Wouldn't hurt." I said. "Also, if you have a spare blaster or two, we could use them. We're only armed with a baseball bat and some gravball gloves."

"Jesus Human Christ, Galbraith." Vixiri's voice approached as she cursed. "What have you gotten into?"

"Hell." I smiled at Velma as she returned to the conversation. She couldn't help but smirk. "We're in Hell. You'll see. We've sent coordinates for it."

XXIII

CHAPTER
TWENTY-THREE

Load Playlist Track: Time Bomb, Rancid

The Saints Peter and Paul Cemetery was on the southwest end of what had been the town. The journey to it wasn't far, maybe three or four hundred meters through the smoke and steam and through the woods that were criss-crossed with wide paths that used to be roads. We passed some remaining markers to find our way, rusted out old street signs. We walked down Locust Avenue, an appropriate name for a city that was a plague to its own world, and paste Centre and Park Streets.

Finally, we had to break from the cracked and steaming dirt path of Lucust and into the woods proper. Through the trees and underbrush, dried brambles of half-dead thorny bushes and dried waist high brown grass, we tried to keep our bearings.

At one point we walked through the bottom of an old house sticking up through the bushes and grass. It's old stone walls rose almost to our knees, but we'd somehow missed it as we passed through a wall that had long ago given into the vines that had crept up and pulled it down with the vengeance of an offended Earth. It wasn't until we were in the center of the building that the smoke gave way enough for us to see it around us.

It was, in a warped way, still furnished by a pair of black rusted wrought iron chairs around a petrified wood table whose lacquer survived the centuries of rain, smoke, snow, and sun.

Velma jumped up on the table and put a hand over her brow to block what little sun was breaking through the grey clouds that blanketed the region. Like ashes the snowflakes fell into her hair, melting there and matting down her alien hair. Her exceptional night vision wouldn't help her now and she was clearly turned around.

So, I jumped up on the table beside her and looked around as well, comparing my location on the global positioning system with my recollection of the map in the municipal building.

Suddenly, the table began to feel like a surfboard underneath me as the two metal chairs broke free from the turf that had grown around their feet. Some of the stone walls of the house shifted and fell as the ground shook and rolled below us. Velma and I were both tossed from the heavier table. I lost her in the smoke as I landed on my upper back against a stone nearby.

"Ugh!" I groaned as the rest of my body caught up to me on the ground. The earthquake continued for another full minute before it jerked me once off the ground and, like some gargantuan belch, a plume of steam burst from the direction I was certain we were heading. I groaned as I called out for my apprentice, "Vel! You ok?"

"Owww." Was her answer. Her voice was diffused by the smoke and fog, directionless and muted. "I think I hurt my leg a little."

"Great!" I sarcastically failed to sound up beat. "At least that means you're alive, right."

"Yep." I saw her gloved flesh hand appear above the smoke with a thumbs up. "At least I'm not dead...yet."

I got up and made my way to her. She was laying in a wet pool of mud and the right leg of her jeans had torn open and she was bleeding. There was a piece of rebar sticking out of the ground next to her and it had some blood on it. "You're going to need a tetanus shot, I think."

"Add it to the girl's tab." She said bitterly, taking my hand and pulling herself up. The way she said 'the girl' sounded quite bitter. "Let's just find this cemetery okay, boss?"

"Well, I think it blew up." I pointed to the white and black pillar rising about fifty meters away. "But that's where we have to go."

She brushed mud off her legs and hips. "Great."

We made our way through the rest of the overgrowth. In a copse of trees we found some grown over tombstones and knew we'd found the edge of the cemetery. The smoke and steam plume wasn't far off at that point, but the trees the old residents had no doubt planted there to make a final resting place look serene had long ago taken over and turned into a small forest.

As we went deeper into the woods, we found more and more gravestones, many of them toppled by the rising trees and roots. Finally, in the center of the graveyard, we found the source of the smoke and steam.

The sinkhole had swallowed a few trees and lit them afire with the heat. But, the majority of the vapors rising were from some sort of underground stream that had boiled over and popped the very ground beneath it. The fires from the trees were more at risk of spreading to the woods around it than down into the cavern below.

"Boss." Velma pointed between a small mausoleum and the cavern. A moment later I saw what she spotted first. There were stone stairs rising up from the collapsed cavern up to the mausoleum above. "That's the only actual structure we've seen in these woods. If I was going to hide something here, it'd be in there."

I nodded. "Yeah. Good thinking. You check out the exterior of the tomb above ground and see if you can get in from the outside. I'll climb down and check out the area underneath."

She acknowledged the order and set off around the cavern as I started sliding my way down into it, trying to avoid the boiling steaming water of the stream. I doubted that anything would be in the stone structure above, that was too obvious. But, I didn't want Velma going down in that hole until I was sure it was safe. She'd already been kidnapped, roughed up by Pyqeans and had her leg injured thanks to an earthquake. This case was getting rough on us both, I didn't need to make it worse on her.

The broken soil and earth was warm, but not quite enough to be muddy. As I climbed down I looked to my left at the steaming stream of shallow water bubbling up from among the sediment and smoothed rocks that had once lived among dirt that had long ago washed away. To my right and above loomed the back of the crypt which acted as an entrance to this underground cavern of the now long dead. If it weren't for the limited light coming in from the hole that the rupture had produced, the cavern would have been eclipsed in a permanent shroud of darkness.

Hopefully the break in the ground would double as a blessing and make it easier to find the dagger.

My wrist computer started beeping with a signal again. I activated it through voice control while I searched around inside with the cracked stone ceiling as the only thing holding the tonnes of stone and cement of the crypt hovering above me.

A growling sound burst through my ear piece followed by a robotic woman's voice. "Kliff would like you to know that we've reached orbit and are making our way to the entry window to bring us down to the Embassy on North America. From there, we will veer direction and head to you. However, there is concern among the crew that this deviation in our flight plan will alert authorities."

"Yeah, Kliff." I answered the Grothrark instead of his mouthpiece. "We'll have to act fast when the team gets down here. I'm at the location now and trying to secure the artifact. With luck, I'll have it before you arrive and can just break for atmo as soon as we're on board."

"What do you mean 'We?'" inquired the droid over Kliff's voice.

"My secretary is with me." I said. "She needed some field work experience. We'll try and be ready by the time you're here."

Something moved in the shadows in the back of the burial catacomb. I didn't hear anything. I wasn't even sure I saw it, when I think about it. I just...felt it.

"Hey Kliff." I said cautiously. "I'm going to have to let you go. I've got to deal with something."

I readied my baseball bat and switched off the wrist computer so my eyes could adapt to the limited light without being blinded by the display. Carefully, I all but tip toed along the side of the stone steps that led back up into the Crypt proper.

I saw it that time, a subtle shift of shadows at the farthest point of the cavern. It was, again, absolutely without sound.

The hair on the back of my neck perked up and I could feel a light chill slide down my spine. I took in a slow breath and steadied myself. Even slower, I let the breath slip out of me as I disappeared into the blackness of the far end of the crypt.

After a moment, I was certain that my eyes were starting to adjust and I could begin to make out a light blue outline of something, or someone, near where I think the back wall was.

"Einar..." a man's voice whispered my name quietly. Something inside me wanted to jump straight out of my skin. "Einar..."

I froze in place. Something about it was terrible and wrong. I knew it wasn't a place I should go.

I closed my eyes and clenched my teeth and ground my feet, perhaps too loudly, into the dust and dirt of the catacomb's floor. When I opened them I was certain I could make out the ghostly shape of someone looking at me. "Einar..."

"Einar!" a woman's voice yelled at me as someone grabbed me by my shoulder and pulled me away. I jolted and spun at the voice, winding up my bat to strike.

I was halfway into the swing to crack her head in when I realized it was Velma. She had recoiled down to her knees and had her arms crossed over her head as she looked away in fear. She hadn't been prepared for her boss to attack her suddenly or she might have had the sense to get away from me.

"Vel?" I said startled. Anger swelled up in me that she was so stupid to sneak up on me like that in the dark. "Where the hell did you come from?!"

"What?" she looked up between her arms. The confusion on her face stood out. Her skin was so pale that it reflected what little light was getting to the back of the chasm. Her face was like a ghost with a pair of very lightly bioluminescent pink eyes, irises wide with fear, glaring at me in terror. "I...I was calling you my whole way down the stairs. What the hell were you doing sneaking toward that tunnel without some back up?"

"Tunnel?" I looked back to where I'd seen the spectral form and saw only blackness. "What tunnel?"

She pointed right to where I'd been heading. "The tunnel entrance right there at the end of the room. You had your bat up and were sneaking over to it."

I still couldn't see it. She had better dark vision than me. Her race didn't have the level of sunlight our world did. It's part of the reason why those that lived on New Reykjavik stayed in the Low Down. They passed well enough for humans, were generally more attractive on average than us, and functioned perfectly well in most educated jobs. They just preferred staying out of the light and that resulted in living in parts of town that forced a false impression on them by humans.

"I didn't see the tunnel." I said. "I still don't. But I saw something move over there."

She looked again. "I don't see anything except..."

She squinted. "...some kind of graffiti or writing? There wasn't anything like it in the crypt upstairs."

I switched the flashlight on my wrist computer and illuminated the direction Velma had pointed out and we approached a tunnel that looked like it had long ago been either washed out by the underground stream or been an old coal vein that had burned out. I wasn't a geology type, so I couldn't tell.

City boy, that's me.

"Most of those are definitely Earth letters." Velma approached carefully painted writing on the old stone walls around a crack leading into the tunnel. "Western hemisphere...lasin..latis..."

"Latin." I corrected her. "But that's not latin. Just using the source alphabet that is shared with English, French, and the like. I recognize it, somehow."

"You know what language it is?" She said. "What about these other ones?"

A second set of writing was outside the first and I definitely recognized it. "Those are runes. They were used by people long before we picked up the other language. It was used a lot by the early Norse and other Germanic and Icelandic people."

That gave me an idea. If they used Runes, whose meanings were interpretive based on how they were being applied – folkloric use versus an actual alphabet of a couple different languages – then that probably meant the latin letters were from a language that was culturally similar.

"Translation search." I said into my wrist computer and aimed its camera at the wall. Software for translating language and displaying it differently had existed on Earth since before we even left it. By the time we got operating systems and artificial intelligent systems from other species, we had the technology down. But, it was usually used to translate more common languages.

"Language match undetermined." Text appeared in my holo display. "Refine search."

Conner hid the dagger down here. He was Scottish. "Language search. What is the name of the language the ancient Scottish spoke?"

"Scots Gaelic" the words replaced the previous text and offered some other suggestions for articles and language examples.

"Translation search, Scots Gaelic to GCT." I voice commanded. Despite the massive databases of the Sol System to work from, which synchronized with data from every other system in the galaxy over time, as ships performed required data dumps to system navigational buoys upon arrival, it took a full minute for the search to work.

I watched through the holographic display of the wrist computer as GCT font, far more fluid and elegant than Alpha-Romanic letters of any font, appeared over the original text.

"Through the Vale between here and the Dreamland, We shall watch over you." I read the words out loud.

"What does it mean?" Velma said, walking between me and the words, the augmented reality of the lettering disappearing wherever she blocked the view...as if they were always written in Galactic Common Tongue.

"Um..." I said the hokey thought that came to mind. "I think it's a spell."

"We shall watch over you?" Velma said. "Who is 'we?'"

"We are the Guardians of the Watchtowers." A man's voice said from the darkness of the tunnel as a translucent Conner Blooming-Star slowly faded into view, his body glowing with a blue hue like a hologram. "At least, that's what the Druids called them."

"What the hell?!" I shouted at his appearance. Velma continued to stand there oblivious to his appearance and not reacting at all to my exclamation.

"Detective." Conner motioned me to him. "I told you I could reach you easier, now. And here of all places, we can finally speak clearly."

I felt myself slip forward like I was falling through my hologram until I was on the other side of it. I looked back and saw myself shaken and cloudy eyed, kneeling and looking through the hologram at, no...through, me. "What the hell is going on?"

"Time is short, Detective." Conner encouraged me to him. "I was hoping to explain this all to Neridah when she came here – but she sent you."

"Well, not every plan works out the way we want it." I tried to go back to my body but I felt myself drifting toward Conner like a leaf on a creek headed down stream. "Why can't I move?"

"Because you aren't experienced enough to." He said with a fatherly voice of encouragement. "But don't worry. I'm here to keep you from drifting off. Come with me...into the *Dreaming*."

XXIV

CHAPTER
TWENTY-FOUR

Load Playlist Track: Hotel California, Eagles

I remember walking toward Conner, forward to the tunnel entrance. I know I saw dirt and rock walls about me. I shouldn't have seen them. There wasn't any light, but still there it was, visible. The darkness of the space was its own thing, present in a way I knew would block my eyes if my body had stood in that spot.

I lack the right words to describe how I saw the darkness there, but I'll try. It wasn't simply an absence of light, as in physics. It was a palpable material essence that changed how I saw the space, but didn't occlude it in any way. As if Conner and I were lights, shadows as dark as black holes sat behind crevasses and rocks, right where they belonged. Yet somehow the material surfaces in those shadows were completely visible, just veiled in some sheen of milky void that declared its presence and was somehow absent in the visible sense.

As for the source of our light, neither Conner nor I glowed. When I saw him in the dark back in the crypt Conner had been translucent, like a reflection on glass, but as if he'd been dry brushed with a blue hazy glow. There in the tunnel, which we walked down farther into, he was as solid and real as I remembered from my dream.

"The darkness isn't reacting to a light from us." Conner said in response to what I realized I was thinking about it all aloud, at first. "It is reacting from the presence of our existence. The darkness is absence of elements of our reality that your living mind has trouble comprehending, so it pushes it away."

"It's avoiding us both." I pointed out. "Are you sure?"

We made a right at a fork in the tunnel, moving slowly downward along an old water flow that rolled along as an illusory mist of itself as soon as I realized how much water it would have taken to chew away at the dirt there.

"Careful." Conner touched me on my shoulder, causing the water flow to disappear. "You're focusing on the past of this place and that's what you'll start seeing. There's time for that, sure. But you can get lost in it. Yes, its avoiding us both – to you. To me, its just their and I see it and know its avoiding you. Your perceptions are all that matter to you here."

"What is all of this?" I finally regained control of my surreal fascination enough to ask such an obvious question. "This is the Dreaming, you said?"

"That's the English name my wife's people called it." Conner said as the walls became painted with living murals, true to their color, but absent of details that told you it was a projection of reality. Somehow, I understood it was a Story – particularly a Story of a memory. It was a tableau-vision of a pregnant aboriginal woman with eyes the color of Tasmanian Seas inside shells of Coral and deep welled irises of the darkest night. She was in a blue dressing gown for a hospital. Conner was holding her hand, somehow both before me and part of the mural at once. "My people, Druids with ancestors from the old British Isles, tend to call it the Otherworld. But in the language of my wife's people, she would call it..."

"...*jukurrpa*." She finished his sentence with a distinct Australian accent in an English I somehow understood better than I should. She spoke to him through labor contractions, her breath heady. She appeared to be looking him in the eyes, but she was looking beyond him – at me. "Aye see it, Conner! Aye see her. She'll be true to ya family name, a real blossom; a *neridah!*"

She was looking right at me and it was unnerving. She couldn't have been looking at me. I looked to my left and my right and saw myself, smeared mural from my feet and onto the opposing wall behind me like a shadow itself. I was standing beside Neridah, Captain Tora, Kliff, Eight, and the Vixin. I couldn't see where we were, but it was obvious we were protecting her on all sides, weapons drawn.

"She's gotta part ta play after your Fate." Neridah's mother was saying. "You'll hand it all off to her. She'll fight a sky war with the *bunyips*. And she'll find help ta do it. They're'ill be a war in a great celestial *billabong* an' she'll ascend an' become the Rainbow Serpent."

"You an' Angus both 'ave a role ta play, husband." And as she said his name, a mural of Angus Blooming-Star, younger than I'd seen him, was on the tunnel wall near her and somehow beside Conner. "You'll both have ta keep her safe. The bunyips'll want her to spin the spiral dance, and she just might. But you gotta keep her from it or I don't know what'll 'appen."

Like a fade in an old projection movie, the mural slithered into a nothing of that blackness and shadows that kept away from me the way it had before and Conner continued down the path of the side tunnel.

"The barrier between our reality and this one is weaker." Conner uttered a new exposition. "This fire is so old and so known that it's made an imprint in Hyperspace. I hid the dagger here because I knew I'd be able to keep an eye on it."

"But, you're dead." I started to worry if I was dead too. "How are you even here?"

"Well," he shrugged. "I'm not quite the man I used to be. Do you know how Hyperspace shadows work?"

"You mean gravity wells?" I knew the theory well enough. An object in real space that has enough size and mass exerts a force that reaches even into Hyperspace. One of the advantages of travel through Hyperspace is that you don't have to worry about the same laws of physics, because there's nothing to be relative to. Time doesn't exist in the same manner there and there isn't a possibility of paradox that would pull someone back in time. An Alcubierre bubble does something similar, but it still has real space to contend with, so it requires increasingly more power to fight off the effects of relativity. Hyperspace does it naturally.

But, when you combine the two you get some truly mind-boggling speeds. It's a step down from hypothetically folding space.

"That's a good explanation." I didn't remember saying anything, I'd just thought about it quickly. "Well, Hyperspace shadows are as close to an equivalent to matter as there is in Hyperspace. You don't have to worry about your speeds in that dimension between our own and whatever else is out there because you don't have to worry about hitting anything. But, hyperspace shadows will exert enough real space on an object that belongs there and pull it back to our reality."

I nodded. "And that means suddenly you find yourself flattened into a medium sized planet, burned up by star, or getting sucked into a black hole. How does this explain your being here?"

"I can't speak for Totems, Gods, and whatever Divinities are out there;" he raised his hands apologetically and looking about him like someone might be listening. "But we spirits that a Shaman can interact with are just the hyperspace shadows of the living. Sentience and belief are powerful things and merely being conscious of the world around you has at least a small influence on it, because what you wish and believe exists on this side exerting a sort of spiritual gravity back on real space."

"Are you saying how we perceive reality effects what actually is real?" I was about to say bullshit, maybe I did – he reacted like I had.

"Almost as much as reality affects your perception, yes." Conner and I entered a small antechamber that had been manually dug out of the tunnel. It was humming with the power of a small fusion generator connected inside a small glowing half domed plasma shield. The emitters were all located on the inside of the dome, safe from being damaged by an attack. The only exposed portion was a cipher pad with a biometric sensor.

"That's impressive." I kept back from it. Plasma energy, like those from a blaster, could be deadly and just getting close to that much could burn you. "Is the dagger in there?"

"We'll get to that." Conner waved a hand at the plasma shield dismissively. "I need you to hear the rest of the story. Angus was supposed to have told Neridah all of that when she was old enough, but I don't think he did. There's more he should have told her and even more he doesn't know – thank the Divine."

"You better hurry then." I said impatiently, watching in shock as he stood entirely too close to the plasma dome. "Neridah will be here soon."

"Yes." He said, "Even here, Time has some meaning – though not as much as you are used too."

Again the weird realist drawings warped their way along the walls all around the antechamber. As if the room were square, four beings stood with their arms outright toward the center and slightly up. I didn't recognize two of the species, definitely alien (one extremely so), but the other two were familiar.

One was a human woman, Japanese I think, dressed in some sort of ritual robes adorned with a symbol of the rising sun on it. She seemed elderly, but deep inside her I could feel a passionate youth and vigor. The other was a young lady that seemed like she wasn't even Velma's age. She was an Ara'lonian, the near-human elfin species of the royal house of the Expanse. Her robes were resplendent, bordering on angelic.

The two species I didn't recognize consisted of some sort of reptilian being with short stubby forearms, like a T-rex, and a gelatinous green thing I could tell took a humanoid form out of respect for me – its floating pinkish brain bobbed up and down roughly where a head would go. The reptile's yellow beak was open in a noiseless scream and the motion by his claws toward the point everyone was focused on felt more ceremonial than effectual."

In the ceiling center, a blurred painting of Conner floated splayed with each arm and leg pointing toward one of the others. He wasn't dressed in his nice ambassadorial robes as he was in front of me. He was naked entirely and, I suspect, his projection gave him either more credit than he was due or I was feeling slightly less masculine in his presence.

"When the betrayal happened." Conner's eyes were closed with concentration, as if he were fighting something. "I knew it was coming, or something like it. I didn't know what the Nether were; my wife's *bunyips*. I had spent a few years hunting for prophetic artifacts to help me See what my wife had warned me about. She had died giving birth to Neridah."

Between the beings a muddied funeral pyre illuminated as if in water colors. "We hadn't even had a day to mourn her absence when High Priests from the Imperial Shamanic Council came to see me and Angus. They said they had foreseen her value to the Hegemony and it was ordered that she be raised under the protection of the Expanse. Angus was already an Ambassador, but they made me one too and gave me assignments that kept me from my daughter. They gave me no explanations and worked against me being close to her. So, I asked Angus to raise her as his daughter, so she wouldn't feel the absence of a father in her life."

"Did he help the Nether in the Betrayal?" I broached the subject and for a moment all of the guardians about the room shuddered. "Did he help Lord Archimedes?"

"No." Conner clinched his fists. "He was a great Dad and he helped keep me involved as best he could. I used my time away from her to seek out omens and knowledge about what the Expanse knew about her and what her mother foresaw. That led me to the Dagger."

"It's used for Augury." Looking up the word was the first thing I did on my ride to Earth from Arcturis Major. "It helps see the future?"

"If you're strong enough." Conner acknowledged.

"And what did you see?" I had become captivated in the Story swirling around me, images appearing to match each element of his tale as he told it, even if I didn't see the details and nuances, I felt the Horror Conner did as he'd looked through the blade.

"I knew I was going to die." He looked at himself on the ceiling.

"That I would forego being reborn in the Otherworld until I'd fulfilled my role."

"To give the dagger to Neridah?" I could almost see inside the Plasma when I thought about it. "What is she supposed to do with it?"

"I don't know." Conner looked at me tired. "I only saw I was supposed to help her get it. Whatever she's going to do with it, she needs to hurry. We're getting weak."

"Weak protecting the dagger?" The beings had been surrounding the plasma shield on all sides. "Are you all Shamans protecting the dagger?"

"No." And suddenly the plasma dome became a plasma sphere and swooped away from me until it was a single star among many. The five guardians were still along the walls and ceiling. But in the center, slithering around the stars, shadowy tendril nightmares corrupted the life force of the universe itself. "It is we, more than the Expanse fleet, that contains Nether forces within the space they took in the war. There were so many of us that died, so many people knew it happened, that we gained a...permanence...from those who were shocked at our deaths. The Nether are as much creatures of hyperspace as our own. When we died fighting – we continued to fight. We have used almost all of our shadows to contain a Shadow that threatens to swarm out across the galaxy."

I saw the shear scope of the threat in a way the Imperial Expanse news reports never could – if they were let loose, we didn't stand a chance. And these men and women of every species in the galaxy, these people I called kooks and charlatans were cut down by it in the most horrible ways and somehow, when given the choice to cease suffering, chose to face it.

"Four. Two. Three. Seven. Nine." Conner said. "Remember it. The code and the sensors are keyed to my genetics. Anyone closely related to me can open the shield with the code. I think that's why the Nether have sought to influence my brother. And from that they know about her role...and yours."

He pointed to the terror lurking in the stars. "She has to stop...this."

All of the lights of the stars went out, the plasma shield faded out. I found myself in darkness on my knees, tears streaming down my face.

XXV

⟨✦⟩

CHAPTER TWENTY-FIVE

Load Playlist Track: Sheena is a Punk Rocker, Ramones

"Einar!" Velma's voice shook me out of what felt like a hallucination, all the while she shook me by my shoulders. "Einar!"

"Yeah..." I shuddered, goosepimples rippling across my body starting at my base of my skull. "I..I'm...I'm ok."

"Like hell you are!" She held my wrist computer up to my face to get a look at me even better than her acute night vision allowed. "You were shaking and talking to yourself. Then you started crying and screaming numbers over and over again."

"Four. Two. Three. Seven. Nine." I whispered to myself like from a distant memory and the sight of the giant chaotic masses, their tendrils groping hungrily in the darkness of space, rushed back into my mind. They were unknowable horrors and I knew they could see me. My stomach turned and I found myself wretching in the catacomb below the tomb that hung dangerously above us.

Velma stepped away as I vomited on the floor, her voice muffled from covering her nose and mouth. "Eww. Damnit, Einar, what happened to you?"

I shook my head trying to reason with what I had just experienced.

It didn't make sense. It wasn't possible. But it wasn't a hallucination. I'd had those before when experimenting with drugs...for a case, I promise.

"Doesn't matter." I waved my hand at her dismissing the question. "But we were right. The dagger is here. I know where it is."

"How?" I didn't have to see her face to know the look it was giving me...that I had gone crazy.

I was saved the indignity of sounding like a religious nut by the sound of my wrist computer beeping at me that I had a communication coming in. It was the *Legacy's Façade*. I raised it to my face and said "Einar...go."

"This is Tora." The Captain's voice came over the communicator. She sounded very stern, the way that military and cops sound in the holovids when they're talking on their communicators. "We got planet-side using Neridah's codes and changed our course to you. We were immediately contacted by the Ambassadorial service ordering us to land at the nearest Starport. We didn't respond and then they warned us to comply or they would be sending out Sensuo fighters to intercept us. We're almost on you, so we won't have much time before they're on us."

The Ambassadorial service had threatened to call the Sensuo? They were the Hegemony's cross-system pseudo-military law enforcement branch. The Sensuo were divided into five segments of the Galaxy with Earth and the Sol Systems being part of Sensuo Alpha and each Sensuo effectively ruled by a member of the Hegemony. That's why they were nicknamed the Five Sensuo Kingdoms by anti-monarchists. If the Ambassadorial service were bringing the Sensuo in this, they were doing it very officially.

That could have worked out in our favor. That would mean that any arrest, if we were caught before leaving with the dagger, would have been public and on record. That also would mean the dagger would be registered as evidence and we'd have an opportunity to report on the activity of Angus Blooming-Star.

That's why I was sure they were bluffing. Ambassador Blooming-Star had worked to keep things in the shadows that long. He wasn't about to blow his cover as an agent of the Nether.

"Just get down here." I said on the comms. "I know where the dagger is now. We'll get in and get out. They're just trying to divert you so you can't get to me before..."

"Before what?" Tora's voice got tense. "Who's after you, Galbraith?"

"I'd rather tell you in person." I still couldn't bring myself to tell the crew, and thus Neridah, about her uncle over comms. She deserved to hear it from me directly, as well as the whole story – if we had time. "Just get here. I'm going to have my comms send you regular pings so you can zero in on my location in the town. Don't land too close to the crypt you'll see. The ground isn't stable."

I flipped off the communication link and triggered the location ping after a few simple lines of code.

"You're trying to protect Miss Blooming-Star's feelings, aren't you?" something was off with Velma's tone when she asked the question.

Was I doing the wrong thing keeping her from knowing the truth about her uncle? I kept telling myself I was waiting until she was there in person, so I could soften the blow. But, I think Velma was right, I was having trouble breaking it to Neridah that the man who had raised her as his daughter was actually using her to get to the dagger.

I knew it would crush her, my client, to learn that Angus served the Nether and Lord Archimedes – the forces that murdered her real father. She was a good kid and I didn't want to see her hurt. Maybe I'm just a softie when it comes to seeing women cry, but was it more than that?

I'd only spent a little time with her aboard the *Façade* between Arcturis Minor and Arcturis Major, but despite my protestations regarding taking the job, I felt compelled to not just help her. I felt compelled to be near her.

Sure, I had what I called "Knight In Shining Armor Syndrome" when it came to a damsel in distress. And, certainly, I felt an attraction to Velma, the last damsel I saved. She was a gorgeous neon pink beacon that you'd have to be dead not to be aware of. But there was...something...about Neridah Blooming-Star I couldn't explain.

"She's an innocent kid." I told Velma, playing off what was going on in my mind. "I hate giving up the bad news to good people. But it's best to tell her in person, to soften the blow."

Her eyes narrowed at me. "You're a terrible liar."

Velma was right. I was lying as much to myself as to her. But that didn't change how I was going to handle it. "Let's enjoy the break before they get here. The air at the bubbling stream is warmer. We can wait for them near it."

Less than ten minutes passed when the spot lights on the underbelly of the Legacy's Façade flooded the entrance to the cavern as the blocky medium sized transport hovered over us. Apparently satisfied they'd seen me and the scene was clear, the spot lights shut off and the transport flew sideways just beyond the clearing to another not far off in the woods.

In the distance I saw the glowing neon words "Mouse Club" in Galactic Common Tongue, written in the alphabet of the Hegemony.

Before long I saw lights swaying as a group moved toward me, scanning the woods as they went. The fog had lightened up some since the ground had let it escape, but the beams of white light still made for an eerie reminders of the danger of the woods around the crypt - a reminder of the fire that crept just below the surface and that blew up the ground around the crypt.

The lights shown down the hole I'd climbed down and illuminated Velma and me.

"Space Dick." Eight said in greeting from behind one of the lights at the rim of the hole.

"Space Punk." I tried to come up with something witty, but I don't think it was nearly as cool. "It's easier to come down through the stairs in the crypt. We'll meet you down here and go the rest of the way to the dagger."

A moment later, we met the crew at the base of the stairs. They had to come down single file through the stairwell.

Eight had taken point and scanned the catacomb with the light mounted to the base of his blaster rifle before lowering it to shake my hand. He was dressed in his old Colonial Trooper heavy armor, minus the helmet. It was white and hardened to handle most small arms fire. His was faded in spots and scored from occasional blaster shots. He'd also painted the logo for the Odds on the breastplate, a human skull with a percent sign on the forehead. He said, "You look like shit."

"He's had a rough day." Velma said as they shook hands. "I'm his apprentice, Velma."

Vi'Xiri flowed in behind him, seemingly dancing as she moved and dressed in completely impractical armor. It was ablative gear, like what I usually wore under a shirt – flexible and absorbs a couple shots from a basic blaster pistol. Only the Vixen's armor consisted of knee high boots, a patch of armor that covered her crotch in the shape of a g-string and an armored vest that only covered her breasts, chest, and upper back. The armor was all worn over a red tight fitting bodysuit that closely matched her skin tone and left very little to the imagination. A small glass visor covered one of her eyes, most likely synchronized with the small hunting blaster pistol she was carrying. I'd seen them before and they augment your view of reality and probably displayed a target and helped define the space around her in low light.

"'Allo Einar." She hummed to me as she floated over to me and pecked me on the cheek. Her head tendrils all flowed disjoint from her movement, keeping their tips facing Velma until she turned to see her as well. "My my, aren't you a colorful one."

"Aye can see why you keep 'er around." Vi faked whispering to me, followed by a wink at Velma – eliciting a shocked blush.

Tora swaggered down the steps in the same orange jacket she'd worn last time I saw her. Her right hand rested on her hip holstered blaster pistol and her left hand carried a flashlight she used to illuminate us. She was kind enough not to flash it right in my face. "Einar."

"You bring me a piece?" I asked her as I nodded a greeting.

She thumbed a gloved hand over her shoulder past her pony tailed black hair. Neridah stood there, her dark curls tied back in a pair of thick pig tails. She was dressed in an outfit that matched Vi'Xiri's and was clearly uncomfortable in it. She was looking down and blushing so brightly that she almost matched the reddish-orange jump suit. She carried a pair of blaster pistols, each with a small flashlight mounted under the barrels.

"Neridah." I said her name as if it meant hello. She looked up almost bashfully with those ocean blue eyes, which stood out from her lightly umber skin. A small sheepish smile flickered on the edges of her lips. She was beautiful. I knew I'd seen it before, but I hadn't realized how affected I must have been the first time we met.

She was looking me in the eyes, and then with sudden confusion, she looked over my right shoulder. I turned my head and thought I saw someone there just briefly. Conner?

"Hi!" Velma burst in between us with her hand extended and far more perky than made sense. If you could be aggressive with your good attitude, she had found a way. "I'm Velma, Einar's partner. You must be our *client*, Miss Blooming-Star."

Neridah was taken aback and the gaze between us had been broken. Velma was right, though, she was the client and we were on the clock – especially if Angus and security from the Embassy were potentially about to be on me.

"Y-yes." She shook Velma's hand politely and formally. "I'm Neridah Blooming-Star, Paige for the Sol Embassy to the Parliament of System Lord Sch'Gwenish of the Expanse."

Kliff growled something from behind Neridah as he squeezed his way by her, ducking the otherwise reasonable ceiling height of the catacomb. Everyone's lights played off the metal plate on his head. His fur was covered in a pair of ammunition bandoleers across his chest, each a power pack for the repeating blaster rifle he carried. It had an axe blade mounted under its barrel instead of a flashlight.

Could he see well in the dark? I didn't know much about Grathraks except their world was heavily wooded and they worshipped their most elder trees as totem spirits that guide their Shamans.

"Kliff recommends we dispense with the introductions and collect the Dagger." Diva's voice translated for the large being.

"Right." I said as I took the spare blaster pistol from Neridah with a "thank you. Follow me. The dagger is this way."

I led the way to the tunnel entrance that I had walked with Conner in the weird vision I'd had. It looked very different in the light of everyone's flashlights and pistol lights. But, I could still feel the Darkness lurking in the shadows and I shuddered.

"This place is strong with spirits." Neridah said suddenly. "I can almost see them. I've never Seen while outside the *jukurrpa*."

"Jukurrpa?" Eight asked from just behind me. "What's that?"

"It has a lot of names." She said. "One common among my people is also The Dreaming."

"So you're saying the jurkpa..." Velma stuttered on the word.

"Jukurrpa." Neridah corrected.

"You're saying its real?" Vel finished her thought, clearly annoyed at the clarification.

"It's what led me to Einar, Captain Tora, and the band." Neridah confirmed before lowering her voice to Velma, who wasn't much older than her, as if trying not to be heard. It carried in the small space. "But, it really feels like it was leading me to Einar even moreso than anyone else. I've felt very disconnected from the prophecies since he left. There's some kind of bond there."

Velma snorted derisively, "He gets that a lot – and there are plenty of broken hearted women to show for it. I wouldn't, hon."

Wow. That was really uncharacteristically rude for her. Still, Neridah felt that connection too?

"Were you one of them?" Neridah's tone indicated she was standing her ground.

"AND here we have the antechamber with the dagger." I said louder than necessary to cut the conversation short.

We entered the last stretch of tunnel that held the shield generator. In the center, on a small altar with long dead flowers, lay an ornate dagger. It was hard to make out the details behind the flicker of the blue energy shield.

"How are we supposed to get it?" Tora said, flicking a small loose stone at it. The stone evaporated into carbon.

Velma and Neridah were still standing in the tunnel, with Kliff crouched uncomfortably behind them, in a defiant and silent stare off.

"Ladies." I called them. "Can we get the magic dagger now and get here before the bad guys do?"

They both turned death glares at me and I actually felt myself quail a little. "Okay..."

"You know what?" Velma said taking a deep breath for self control. Her porcelain cheeks were flush with embarrassment. "I'll go back out and keep an eye out for trouble. I'm the assistant detective after all."

She made her way, barely, through Kliff's hanging fur and disappeared up the tunnel.

Velma leaned in. "She is quite feisty. I like 'er."

I rolled my eyes. Telarians are known for their libidos. It's part of the reason why their women are sought out in the sentient trafficking circles. But, for once, I wasn't in the mood.

"This is an older model shield system." Eight said checking out the controls. "We could blast it, but we'd probably lock in the on position if we did anything less than severe damage."

"Rawwrr-roar-ruuuuh. Grr grr grr." Kliff barked something.

"I could do severe damage to it." DIVA said in a flat generic robotic tone of voice instead of her normal feminine snark.

"I know the code guys." I walked over and punched it in. "Neridah. You'll need to touch the biometrics reader. It's keyed to Conner's genetics, but yours should do."

She walked over to it swiped the small scanner with her thumb. Suddenly, the shield disengaged and the room went from a dancing flicker of blue light to the creepy darkness of a few flashlights in a cave under several thousand tonnes of earth. It was disconcerting.

"How did you know the code?" Tora said.

"Four. Two. Three. Seven. Nine." I said almost reflexively.

Tora paled. "April twenty-forth, twenty three seventy nine. Conner's birthday."

That would make Conner about sixty or so when he had Neridah, if my guess about her age was right. He didn't look it. Even with modern medicine, the average human lifespan was in the mid-hundred and people past natural development tended to take supplements that slowed genetic decay. So, we aged significantly less than we had just a century before. Still, he didn't look that old.

"He waited a while to have kids, then?" I asked Tora.

Tora nodded. "Said it was his wife's decision. He said she only wanted one child and not until the stars were right."

"You haven't said much about Conner while we flew here." Neridah interjected, almost hurt. "I asked and you avoided it or said it wasn't your place to say."

"This was clearly significant, kid." Neridah nodded to the dagger. "So, are we going to do this?"

XXVI

CHAPTER TWENTY-SIX

Load Playlist Track: Anarchy In the U.K., Sex Pistols

Neridah nervously approached the small altar-like table in the center of the disengaged shield's center and tentatively touched the dagger's hilt before finally picking it up. The dagger was almost long enough to be considered a small sword. The edges were visibly sharp and the blade made of some odd white metal I'd never seen before.

It was almost as if the dagger had been crafted from some metallic version of bone. Although clearly sharp, the blade was slightly warped everywhere between the edges, with the thickness non-uniform except along the blood groove in the center. I never got close enough to see it, but there was clearly etched writing inside the groove.

The cross guard was a silvery metal that curled upward toward the blade at the tips with smaller opposing curls dipping back toward the wielder. Along this smoother and more refined metal were intricate carvings of letters in High Ara'lon, but not in a configuration that made sense to me – clearly it wasn't Galactic Common Tongue. In the center of the hilt, above the grip, was a bright red jewel that made me think of a massive ruby. The stone was as thick as the hilt itself and in the center of it, a wriggling blackness, that reminded me of the shadows I saw in the Dreaming, was trapped. I could almost feel it trying to break away from the jewel. All together, the stone looked like the bloody eye of some large predator.

Neridah examined it all more closely than I ever had a chance to. "So, this is supposed to be the key to saving the Galaxy?"

We were all just standing there looking at it, as if we expected it to do something.

"Any idea of how you use..." I started to say.

"No." Neridah cut me off. "I wish I knew what it was even for. Look around. Let's see if Uncle Conner left me anything."

"An instruction manual would be nice." Eight muttered as he examined the small table and Vi'xiri and Tora started looking around the small outcroppings of rocks in the stony antechamber.

Neridah shifted a glance at me when she realized I hadn't taken my eyes off her while everyone committed to the search. We locked eyes and it felt like the irrational connection I'd felt building since I had come to Centralia electrified. I watched her lips purse as if she wanted to say something to me when her eyes suddenly dilated and she quietly went rigged. I felt paralyzed with fear and the warning that something was wrong caught in my throat. She had stretched out almost fully before I overcame the feeling.

"Neridah!" I heard myself saying as if in slow motion. I watched everyone turn and shine their lights on her as Eight pulled a brown paper wrapped package out from under the table, drop it and rush over to catch Neridah before she fell over.

"What happened?!" Tora yelled as she checked the girl's pulse.

"I don't know!" I said finally moving to her myself. Her eyes hadn't moved off of me, but her pupils had begun to return to their normal size. "Neridah! Are you okay, kid?"

"Angus." She whispered eerily. "He's coming. We're out of time. Why didn't you tell me...?"

"Tell her what?" Tora looked to me angry. "What did you do Galbraith?"

"Her father...or uncle...whatever." I blurted out. "I didn't get to it. He hired me to retrieve her, not save her. He did it to ensure I was there with all of you. He knew about the prophecy some how. He wanted us to find her, to bring her to the Dagger. He's after it."

Kliff grabbed me suddenly and pulled me up to his crouched height, causing my head to smack into the low stone cave ceiling. Diva, with an almost sadistic tone in her voice said "Kliff says if you have betrayed Miss Blooming-Star then your soul will suffer far longer than your body is about to."

"No...no no no." I said raising my hands non-threateningly. "He tried to steal the dagger from me thinking I had it. He'd gotten to me too soon. We escaped and came here to get it. I didn't tell her because..."

Neridah cut me off again, her voice ghostly as her body relaxed from full rigidity. "...you didn't want to hurt me by telling me my father had betrayed me."

"He's under control..." I tried to explain.

"...of the Nether." Neridah finished. "Yes. I know that now. Kliff, he's ok."

She eased herself out of Eight's grip and patted the Grathrak's furry arm reassuringly. "He's ok. But that doesn't change things. We're out of..."

Captain Tora's comlink went off on her belt and she tapped the white cylinder. "What is it Tree?"

"Ma'am." The little robot said in his polite butler voice. "I'm detecting a small ship landing in the town. It did not appear on the ship's sensors as having an identification."

"Angus." I grunted from the ceiling. "Can you let me down? He's probably got..."

"...Pyqeans?!" Neridah said in shock. "What are Pyqeans doing helping him? They're trained to be loyal to the Hegemony. They would never help the Nether."

She was a member of the ambassadorial core. Pyqeans were advisers to the government. The government she had been groomed to serve her whole life. They were considered absolutely loyal to their offices, even when they conflicted with other Pyqeans. Her shock was full of heart-break as much as disbelief.

But, how did she know?

"How many Pyqeans does he..." I started to ask her only to be cut off again.

"How should I know?!" She looked at me terrified. "You're the one who said he had Pyqeans."

"No he didn't." Tora said thoughtfully. "He..."

"Oh." Neridah looked distant. "Yeah, he didn't say the whole thing did he? You're right. I keep finishing sentences for people."

"How, sweet thing?" Vi'xiri put her hands on the girl's shoulders and guided her to sit on the table. "How are you doing this?"

Neridah didn't answer, only looking increasingly distant, her grip on the Dagger tightening.

"The dagger." I answered, my conversation with Conner's ghost starting to all come together. "Conner used it to see the future, to understand a prophecy about her. He said she would need it to basically fulfill her destiny."

"He said?" Tora looked at me with accusation. "I told you, he's dead. He might have found some way to reach out to her but..."

"...you saw him." Neridah's eyes had welled up and begun to dribble tears down her perfect dark skin. "He took you into the *jukurrpa* and gave you a Story. You saw my mother. She was gifted, but as a woman she wasn't allowed to be our Cleverman. But she could see the *nyuidj*. The dead spirits were with her and told her stories of the Everywhen. And they whispered you to my father and he whispered you to me."

Kliff lowered me to the cavern floor at last and ran a clawed hand over my head growling lowly and reverently. The metal droid around his throat spoke dispassionately. "You have seen Beyond. You have been blessed."

"Thanks big guy." I shrugged off his grip and pulled my head back from his pawing. "But that doesn't change the fact we're about to have company. We need to get moving."

"What about this?" Eight raised the small package up from the table. "Should I open it?"

"It's a tongue of the Rainbow Serpent." Neridah answered the question. "It contains the spirit of Daramulum and protects Shamans. Some people call them bullroarers. But it's only supposed to be used by the men folk. We women are forbidden to use it."

"So...should I open it?" Eight repeated the question.

"But you did." Neridah looked to it finally. "Didn't...you?"

Eight started to open it and I stopped him. "If you saw him open it, then you're right. But if he doesn't open it because you already know what it is, that means you can change the future you see...right?"

She thought about it. "But if I don't actually see it, does it change?"

"I think your father was trying to tell me just that with the Dreaming." I said. "How we perceive the universe can influence it and how the universe is can affect our perception."

"So..." her eyes went wide and she lifted the dagger and peered at it amazed. "...this Dagger allows me to See the everywhen and change what hasn't happened yet."

"Think about it." Vi'xiri's head tendrils were rattling with excitement. "Focus on it and tell us what happens next."

Neridah pulled the blade up and I watched as she peered over the hilt, her eyes gazing through the curls that reached up to the blade. "I...see....I See. Oh no..."

"What?" I asked her just as my comm link went off on my wrist communicator. Velma's voice came on without me telling the system to answer the call, a code I'd given her to bypass it and reach me in emergencies.

"We have company!" She said, her voice was rough and I could hear the sound of gravel and shuffling as she ran.

XXVII

CHAPTER
TWENTY-SEVEN

Load Playlist Track: Kaleo, Way Down We Go

"Kliff!" Eight barked orders. "You protect the girl. Tora and Dick cover the far entrance to the room. Vi and I will cover your assistant and we all fall back here!"

He raised his rifle and ran out of the antechamber with only the slightest pause from Vi'Xiri as she processed his orders. Kliff barked an affirmative and moved himself between Neridah and the entrance tunnel, kneeling to brace his large rifle.

Tora pulled her blaster pistol out and I followed suit and we moved up to the cross tunnel, cursing. "Shit. I'm not a soldier, Tora. And they've got us trapped if we go in there."

She crouched down onto one knee and braced herself against the tunnel wall, hoping to use any cover from it she could get. "You're right. But until we know how many we're dealing with, fighting our way through that tunnel's choke point isn't an option. Trust Eight. He knows what he's doing."

The sound of blaster fire started getting closer and red and green flashes of light could be seen where the plasma bolts were hitting walls just out of sight. "Hey Kliff! I yelled into the antechamber. Any chance you can get that shield ready to activate once we're in there?"

He growled something long and the Diva answered for him. "As long as the code is the same to turn it on, yes."

"Test it." I yelled. "If it gets too ugly, we can at least hide inside until they bust their way in. It could buy us some time!"

He growled an affirmative that I didn't need translated by that point. But, the Diva did anyway with her usual snark. "He'll probably just break it!"

"Coming in!" Vi'xiri yelled ahead as she and Velma hustled their way between us. Velma collapsed against the stone wall behind me out of breath and holding a stitch in her side. "They are too many. We can not fight our way out."

Eight walked backwards down the tunnel firing deliberately and with an even calm pace. As he turned the bend fully he reached to the utility belt on his armor and pulled out a metal cylinder with a bright red button at one end and then pressed it.

I wasn't a soldier, but even I knew what that was. I turned and covered Velma with my body as Tora looked away and covered her head with her arm. Vi'xiri winced but kept her guard up with her target pistol. I watched as her tendrils wrapped tightly over her ears.

The grenade flew down the hall and Eight got his rifle slung over his shoulder just in time to cover his ears with his gloved hands.

I didn't look away in time. It wasn't an explosive grenade. Instead it was a flash band, meant to disorient an enemy. The flash blinded me instantly as we fell back into darkness. I felt dizzy as my ears rung from the concussion. I think I fell down on top of Velma and I'm pretty sure I felt her grabbing at me.

A million dangerous moments passed as I was dragged and pushed along before I got my feet under me and obeyed the nudging that directed me to move.

I still had my pistol in my hand, so I wasn't captured. I also wasn't moving very fast, so we were running. But we definitely weren't in the antechamber. Even with the white spot in my vision blinding me, I could tell it was too dark to be the room with the shield generator.

Unless I'd gone blind, that is. Shit! Had I gone blind? Did that grenade burn out my retina?

No. I wouldn't have the white spot in the middle of the darkness if I did. My eyes worked. There just wasn't any light. I couldn't hear myself ask where we were, but someone put a finger up on my mouth to silence me. The ringing was high pitch and still painful.

As I was bumbling along, I panicked with a thought somehow more unsettling than my brief fear of blindness – Where was my hat?!

I patted my hair, realizing it wasn't on my head. Had it fallen off in the tunnel near the shield generator? If so I could go back and find it. Was it lost in this maze of underground tunnels I'd been blind through?

"Relax." Neridah's voice somehow whispered through the ringing in my ears and comforted me as the familiar tightness of the felt fedora slipped onto my head. "I didn't leave it behind. You were screaming for your hat the entire way to the floor."

At some point in our endless shuffling we stopped and I was propped up against warm stone. I had started sweating a while back, but I thought it was just exertion. Now I realized, we were closer to the fire. I could smell acrid air from freshly made carbon. The hat's brim must have been catching the sweat from my brow – I'd have to have it cleaned professionally when I got back to New Reykjavik.

I heard mumbling in the midst of the ringing and then some shaped began to appear around the white spot. They weren't the right color, but they were there.

"I said are you alright?" Velma said worried as sounds came rushing in like a flood against my throbbing ear drums. "Einar. Can you hear me?"

"Yeah." I felt out toward the shapes and gripped something supple, yet firm.

"Hey now, Boss." Velma giggled as she pulled my hand away. "That's sexual harassment."

"Whoops!" I jerked my hand back. "What happened?"

"Stun grenade." Eight said in a matter of fact tone. "Covered our retreat."

"I mean after that." I said and began to realize the little bit of red shapes I could see were because of a light on his belt. "And what's with the red? How can you see clearly?"

"I'm Genetically Engineered." Eight answered, his face barely visible in the low light. "My eyes see this color fine in the dark. It gives us an advantage in a fight against a lot of species in a fight if they don't have low light gear."

"We fled down the passage away from the Pyqeans." Tora answered. "I still can't believe they're on board with this attack. All of my years transporting diplomats and I never heard of a pyqean going bad."

"Vel clearly zis group has." Vi'Xiri retorted. "Everyone has a price."

The spot in my vision started to clear up as I also adapted to the red light. We were still in the tunnel system, but we were on a slope of some kind. "Where are we headed?"

"Not sure." Tora answered. "We're following the kid's lead. She's the one who told us to run."

"What about the shield generator?" I think I was legitimately hurt they didn't use my plan of hiding inside. It wasn't a way out, but it was a known quantity. Now we were stuck in a tunnel in a flaming hell hole, lost in the dark and being hunted by digitally uploaded robot people.

"This is the right way." Neridah assured me. "I'm not sure how I know. It's just a feeling; like a whisper."

A whisper? Her father was still here helping a little. "Ok. I can get behind that."

"Really?" Velma was taken aback. "You can get behind her having a 'feeling' and leading us into the dark unknown?"

"Yeah." I responded maybe too defensively. "I've seen way too much weird on this job to think she doesn't have something going on."

"Oh she's got something going on, boss." I could see Velma's head look up and down on Neridah. Her eyes were good in low light as well. "I'm sure you could see that in the dark. But that isn't a good enough reason."

"Why don't we have lights on anyway?" It occurred to me that aside from Eight and Velma, the rest of us were probably struggling.

"Pfft." Velma shook her head and muttered under her breath. "Nice deflection."

I let that slide. We didn't need to be having a spat at the moment. We needed to get out. "Why can't I turn on my flashlight or wrist computer?"

"We're not sure what the Pyqeans can do visually." Eight answered. "Neridah is telling us which way to go and your assistant and I can see well enough to guide everyone. Best we stay unnoticed as long as possible. We're on our way uphill at the moment, so I think we're headed back to the surface somewhere."

Scuffling and scraping sounds echoed behind us in the tunnel and everyone tensed. "We changed tunnels a few times. They may not be heading toward us."

"Yeah." I rolled my eyes as I got myself upright. "That's exactly the luck I've had so far. We need to assume they're in the right one."

Neridah closed her eyes and tightened the grip on the dagger. "This way I think."

She moved up the sloped tunnel and we all followed, with Eight close enough to almost step on the backs of her feet. His rifle was over her shoulder as he peered ahead. I followed directly behind with Velma behind me. Tora lagged behind just enough to watch out for us as Vi'xiri and Kliff kept up to us.

"T-intersection coming up." Eight said in a low voice, more to Neridah than the rest o fus.

"We'll take a left I think." She answered him. The heat was reducing a little. We were headed away from the subterranean fires. Still, it wasn't cool. Sweat dripped down my face and I'm my shirt was soak in the pits and on the back.

"You girls came dressed for winter." I chuckled lightly. "This can't be comfy."

"Shh." Eight hissed as we made the turn. "Figure up ahead. Can't make him out."

"Don't shoot." I whispered. "We don't want to draw attention to us."

Cool air moved toward us from the figure's direction and, even in the dark, I could kind of make him out in a circle of light blue. There was night ahead and not like the dark of the tunnel. "I got this."

I slipped the aluminum baseball bat off the makeshift sling I'd hung it on inside the jacket and put my blaster pistol in the back of my pants. You never want to tuck it into the front of your pants. You're just asking to shoot off your pecker. I knew this one thug who used to keep his blaster there and – well, you don't want to hear that story.

Safety first, I slipped ahead of the group as quietly as I could and tip toed my way toward the tunnel entrance.

Sure enough, there was a figure there. He wasn't watching the tunnel exit. He was standing by a bush looking down into the collapsed catacombs from above. I hadn't even seen the smaller sinkhole that made the tunnel when we investigated the graveyard earlier. Clearly, he hadn't paid it much mind either.

I felt a rush of adrenaline as I knew I was about to hurt, or possibly kill, someone. It wasn't like killing directly in self defense. This guy wasn't immediately trying to end me. But, I knew that he likely would once he saw us. So, I steeled myself to do what I had to do.

I rushed out of the tunnel, upward at a slope, and swung the bat up over my head with all my might and tried to do my best impression of Mook the bouncer. The Pyqean was wearing a hooded robe over his robotic form, so I hadn't been sure at first if I was going to be connecting to robot or flesh. The dent in the aluminum bat as I over extended my swing told me I'd guessed right. But down the Pyqean went to the ground onto its hands and knees.

My forearms burned from the effort of the strike. They say there are stories of human mothers flipping disabled repulsor cars over to save their children. That's the kind of adrenaline being in fear of your life gives you in a fight. Still, I knew that strike wouldn't have done him in the way it would have to a human skull with a meat brain.

I grunted over and over as I bashed into the head and back of the robotic man. Meanwhile, the group must have made their way up to me.

Eight pulled me off as Kliff, now free of the short passage, grabbed the Pyqean by its robot head and pulled it from it's torso in one mighty tug.

"Good job, Space Dick." Eight said jovially, patting me on the shoulder. "I knew you had it in you."

"Vell," said Vi'xiri nervously. "Ve should 'ope that it didn't attract any attention."

As if on queue, a dozen figures made their way up from the catacombs in a hurry with blaster pistols drawn.

"Kill everyone but the girl!" yelled a shadowed man chasing behind them. I recognized the voice as Angus Blooming-Star. "Lord Archimedes will want her alive!"

"Dad?" Neridah quailed at the words and backed into Eight. "No...nooo..."

"Snap out of it." Eight hissed to her. "We have to get to the ship."

Blaster fire from below emphasized the urgency of our departure.

"Which way?" I yelled to the group. "Where's the ship?"

Kliff pointed across the sinkhole that had been the catacombs of Centralia and growled.

"Oh great." I knew it couldn't be that easy. "Other side of all the guys trying to kill us."

Eight stepped forward and started blasting robbed figures, driving to be more cautious after the first two went down. He took a hit to his armor, which knocked him on his back and scorched his chest plate right in the band logo.

The wheezing sound of a heavy blaster pistol escaped from Angus' weapon.

Kliff roared and stepped in, lowering his weapon so the barrel was vaguely in the direction of the attackers and a volley of standard blaster pistol powered plasma bolts erupted in the direction of our attackers. His blaster rifle began to wheeze like a heavy blaster, but he just disengaged the power supply and replaced it with a new power magazine and returned to firing.

Everything seemed to slow down at that moment. Eight rolled up onto one knee and raised his rifle and continued to fire, more deliberately than Kliff. Tora took cover behind one of the dead trees and fired away. Velma and I grabbed Neridah at the same time and began the circuit around the crypt's sink hole. She was our client and we both protected our client.

That's why I was doing it, I told myself.

And then suddenly, the heavy blaster from Angus wheezed again and I noticed Velma wasn't with us. My heart dropped as I looked behind us for her.

She was on the ground and her robotic arm, the one holding her pistol, was laying three feet away from her. But instead of gripping it in pain, her off hand was holding onto her leg as she screamed.

Angus had taken her arm, but someone else had hit her in the leg. We had been flanked by a pair of pyqeans that had been watching the sink hole from other vantage points. The team had made some advances to catch up, but we had two coming right on us and Angus and another pair making their way up the last climb of the sink hole.

That sense of time slowing increased. It was like I could see everything going on all at once, but despite my racing heart I was frozen and unable to decide what to do. I needed to protect Velma, but I couldn't leave Neridah unprotected.

Then she raised the dagger to her eyes and Looked at Angus. Her eyes dilated and the black pupil like thing inside the ruby warped and twisted inside, filling the gem. She side stepped a fast moving pyqean that had reached for her and she severed its arm.

"Eight!" She yelled. "Grenade in the stream, now!"

Eight pulled out his second grenade from his belt and flicked the red button. This grenade was black.

By the time he threw it Neridah was barking more orders. "Vi, behind you! Kliff, focus to your left!"

Vi'xiri spun in her heels the way only a dancer could and place two blaster shots into the head of a pyqean. Kliff turned to his left and let loose another volley that dropped a pair of the robotic assailants.

The grenade went off in the stream as instructed. This wasn't a flash bang. It was highly explosive. Like a zit, the ground under the stream popped with heated fury, lifting the remaining pyqeans and Angus up and into the woods. The pyqeans likely didn't feel the damage, if they felt anything at all. But Angus had to have gotten burned and beaten up, if he survived at all.

Neridah looked through me distantly before her pupils contracted back to normal. I could see something wriggling in the white of her right eye. Then she shuddered and passed out.

XXVIII

CHAPTER
TWENTY-EIGHT

Load Playlist Track: Arch Enemy, The World is Yours

Time rushed forward for me, back to normal speed. I felt like I was moving through knee high mud as I had to choose who to go to, Neridah or Velma. They each lay a dozen feet from me in opposite directions.

Velma's pale eyelids fluttered over her vacant pink orbs. She started to go into shock from the leg wound and Neridah was laying on the ground twitching as if she were having a seizure. I had to triage the situation. I could only help one of them.

I turned back the way we'd come and knelt at Velma's side. Whatever was happening to Neridah, I wasn't going to be much help to her. Whereas Velma was bleeding out from the shot to her leg. Most of the wound had been closed by the plasma blast, but it had put a hole straight through her upper thigh and she was seeping blood and ooze. It had hit her artery and despite the fused meat, the wound had already cracked open like the blackened skin of a chicken, letting the blood out through the crevasses.

I pulled off my jacket and stuffed one of the sleeves almost entirely in the hole while covering her with the rest as best as possible to keep her body temperature up in the cold. The jacket was built for rain and wasn't doing a very good job and I felt panic begin to set in.

"Help!" I yelled to the team as they started to make their way to me, finally unhindered by the scattered pyqeans. They caught up to me quickly. Some of Kliff's fur was singed where he'd taken a few glancing blows in the fray. Vi'xiri had enough grace to keep from getting hit and it looked like Eight had a couple new scorch marks in his heavy armor.

"She's bleeding and something's happened to Neridah." I pointed to Neridah urgently.

Tora responded by heading to her as quickly as possible and saying "I've got her. Take care of your partner."

"We need to do a better job of stopping this damned bleeding." Eight instructed calmly and handed me a knife as he fumbled with his utility belt. "Cut that pant leg off. We'll need it."

I slipped the knife into the denim where it had fused with Velma's skin and watched her wince. I sliced at it as carefully as I could, lifting her leg gently as I went around underneath it.

Meanwhile, Einar pulled out a half dozen tampons, a small roll of gauze and some kind of small pneumatic-injector.

"Holy utility belt, Batman." I joked as I slid the pants leg down to the top of Velma's combat boot before cutting the fabric off at her ankle. Humor, it's how I deal with a lot of problem situations.

"What?" Eight paused, confused. "Batman?"

Apparently, it is also how I waste my coping mechanisms in problem situations. I rolled my eyes and held out the pants leg for him. "Nevermind."

"Cut it into two long thick strips, quickly." I followed his instructions as he pulled the jacket sleeve out of the gapping hole in her leg. Then, one at a time, he inserted each tampon into the wound one at a time and retracted the biodegradable housings. The cotton wads expanded and contacted the seeping blood and clear fluids, absorbing them better than my water resistant rain coat. "You done with those strips?"

I held them out to him and he tossed them onto his shoulder. "Check on the girl. I'll get this wrapped up the rest of the way."

"Can you save her?" I held Velma's gloved hand with my own. The Gravball plates in our gloves were clunky and I couldn't give her the grip of support I wanted. "Tell me you can save her."

He popped the injector into the area around her wound and then began wrapping the gauze around the leg to cover both ends of the hole. "I've seen worse. Go check Neridah."

I left him to finish his work and made my way over to Tora as she re-strained Neridah by straddling her and placing her knees on Neridah's upper arms. She had found a thick stick and managed to force it into the young woman's mouth so she wouldn't bite off her own tongue.

"What happened to her?" The Captain said to me as I got there. "I don't know what else to do."

"She used that Dagger." I said trying to pry it out of her hand, but she had a death grip on it. "Something happened when she did. It went into her."

The dagger's gem was still black, but it kept fluctuating at the edges with red, like it was fighting being contained.

"Went into her?!" Tora looked at the gem as well and curled her nose in revulsion. "What do you mean 'went into her?'"

I pried Neridah's eyelids open. There, in the white of her right eye was the black smoky thing wriggling at the edge of her blue iris like it was trying to break through a wall.

"What the hell is that?!" Tora almost jumped off of Neridah, but kept her composure.

It was a hunch, but somehow I knew in my heart it was true. "A Nether."

As I said the name of the black malicious monstrosity trying to in-vade Neridah, she looked directly at me. Her pupils contacted as tightly as they can for a human and her mouth let go of the wooden bit that Captain Tora had placed there.

"Hazzzsssaaasshhhhhaaaaaa---reeeeaaaaaarrrraaaarrrr!!!!" She spoke with a mix of growling and hissing that was like some demonic mix of a Tibetan monk or a Voltch'I singer, but without any sense to the sound.

This time it was my turn to jump back. I lacked the Captain's courage and I had to come back down off my feet. "Fight it Neridah! Don't let it take control of you!"

Her eyes were still open and looking at me as she growled and hissed like some possessed person from a horror holo, just like the ones that made me uncomfortable with Centralia as it was.

"Fuck..." was all I could get out at first. Then I slapped her right across the face, stunning her. "Fight it! Listen for Conner! Listen for your father! Listen to the totems! Fight it!"

I don't know if it worked, but she closed her eyes and stopped hissing and resumed shaking and twitching. I kept repeating the words "fight it" over and over in her ear for a several moments before the blasterfire resumed.

The pyqeans that had been knocked clear by the heated geyser explosion had clearly regrouped and were firing at us from across the giant sink hole. On the other side an enraged Angus Blooming-Star was missing half of his shirt and was covered in red splotches and giant blackened welts. He was unarmed but yelling commands to the pyqeans and pointing his exposed arm and hand at us in rage.

Kliff gave his retort to their interruption by opening up a hail of blaster fire from his repeating rifle, forcing the pyqeans that remained to duck behind cover. The cover didn't help one of them as Vi'xiri picked one off with her target pistol by aid of her sighted eye piece.

The Ambassador only grew more enraged. He barked more orders at the Pyqeans and it was almost as if his black and red splotches grew more pronounced with the anger. But, that could just have been the fact he'd just been burned and his body was starting to figure it out faster than his brain.

That was going to smart in the morning.

Eight finished tying the last of the two denim clothes around the wound on Velma's leg and then picked up his blaster rifle and joined the fray, downing one of the pyqeans.

That second loss got the Ambassador's attention. He looked around and must have realized that although we were down two through the hole fight, he was down more than half of his contingent. Some pyqeans could be truly ancient sentient machines, but they were advisers – the Odds were clearly fighters.

After a second look around to measure his situation he appeared to yell several curse words. I couldn't hear them over the blaster fire, but the expression and way he mouthed the words told me exactly what was about to happen.

He ran.

He was no doubt headed to wherever they'd landed their ship. His run was sloppy, like he was favoring a busted leg. He was slow.

"I still have a chance." I said under my breath.

I looked to Velma possibly dying from her injury and looked to her cybernetic arm slagged on the ground near her. I looked to Neridah who was laying there fighting off a Nether possession with Tora stuffing the stick back in her mouth. That bastard was responsible for all of this.

Unlike the Ambassador, my legs were fine.

I chased after him.

XXIX

CHAPTER TWENTY-NINE

Load Playlist Track: Skillet, Monster

I'm not a fitness freak. I don't go to the gym. I don't run on a tread-mill. I do live in a city where you can't just drive a repulsor vehicle around anywhere you want and its common to foot it at least from wherever you are to the hyperloop and then again to the next part. I also do a fair amount of sneaking around in my job. So, I was in reasonable shape and hyped up on adrenaline from a fire fight and watching my secretary...I mean apprentice...or assistant, whatever title works, almost die and a girl I was clearly way too attached to for a client go through some reality changing horror.

So, I ran pretty fast after Ambassador Angus Blooming-Star. Still, he kept a good clip for a guy running on a hurt leg. He also had the advantage of being pretty far out and closer to where I'm guessing they'd landed their ship than me.

I crept closer to him as I ran, enough to keep from losing sight of him in the smoke and fog that had begun to occlude the trees he was running between. Still, his speed extended the time before I was going to intercept him – and my side was starting to hurt from the run after a while.

How he managed to have the stamina to press on was beyond me, even if he was feeling his own adrenaline pumping through him.

What mattered for my chances of catching him was that he didn't see me running behind him yet. I would have fired off a shot from my blaster, but running all out is a sure fire way to miss someone and I didn't want him to notice me until I was at a better range.

At one point he faded from sight in the white smoke. I didn't slow down because I had his vector down. He had been bee-lining it to somewhere and if I kept the same trajectory I would intercept with that spot soon enough.

A break in the smoke above me revealed dim stars and I considered how rare it was to see stars at night on earth at all. The light pollution from all the cities and the high population of the world living on less land than there used to be before the rise of the tides had made sights like this rare for me. I'd seen alien skies aplenty on my cases throughout my end of space.

If I weren't trying to kill a man, and avoid dying in the effort, I would have liked to have paused to appreciate the moment.

Behind me the sound of blaster fire became less frequent and considerably muted by the absorbent nature of the mist. Only faint flashes of green and red silhouetted the trees closest to the sinkhole. Everything else had begun to slip into the dark smoky night.

Creeping over the fog layer, through the break, I caught glimpse of the red blinking light of a ship's transmitter antenna. It wasn't from the direction of the *Legacy's Façade*. I adjusted my course and picked up the pace as best as I could through the bramble of dead underbrush.

Before long, I found myself breaking into a clearing at the base of an expensive looking luxury small transport ship about half the size of the Façade. It probably was hyperspace capable, but wasn't designed for long hauls. It was long and sleek, maybe 15 yards long and half as wide. Based on the number of portholes along the sides, its interior was more like a passenger transport for interplanetary travel for groups – much like what I'd flown on from the *Earthport*. Except I'm sure this was first class with leg room. The ship had a fashionable arching spoiler on the back containing the engine in the center and away from the main body of the craft. I think some ships used that to protect the passengers from engine radiation instead of adding heavy and more expensive shielding.

Gotta love government budgets. The ship wasn't as expensive as it was made to look.

Like the Façade's faded paint job, this ship had the deep red color of the Ambassadorial corps – indicating it had diplomatic immunity and that it was an act of war with its home System Lord to accost the ship by any other System Lord. That would get the Hegemony and the *Sensuo* fleets involved in trying to restore the peace. This paint job was new and fresh.

It wouldn't protect him from what he'd done to my people.

The kidnapping back in New Reykjavik was still fresh in my memory. He'd beat Velma for information. He'd attacked us. He'd shot her. He almost killed her.

I stood at the base of the boarding ramp. It was still down. I pulled the blaster from my pants and balanced the baseball bat in my off hand and started up as quietly as I could. There was no way I made it there before he had and he hadn't seen me chasing after him.

Then I heard a stick crack behind me and I froze.

"Shit." I cursed under my breath knowing I'd been out foxed and he had me from behind. I raised my weapons submissively to show I knew it too. Maybe he wouldn't shoot me and I could talk my way out of it.

"Is he inside?" Tora panted behind me. I spun in surprise and saw her hunched over with her gloved hands on her knees barely keeping her breath. She obviously didn't spend much time at the gym either.

I heart was pounding with relief. "I think so, yeah. I had him in sight most of the way."

"What was wrong with him?" Tora said and waved her hands over her shoulder and pointed at her back, too out of breath to get more detailed about what she saw.

"The explosion?" I asked without the confidence I'd had in that assessment while chasing him. Now that I thought about it those hives and welts were huge and really dark. If those were burns, he'd have been dead. "We'd better be careful...just in case."

"I *has* been a weird day." She agreed and pulled her blaster from her hip holster.

I pointed back to the woods. "What happened to Neridah?"

"She stopped having her fit." She answered. "I don't know what...huh...that shit in her eye is, but it didn't seem to have control of her. I gave her to Vi' and followed you."

"I can handle myself." I said defensively.

"You're the one who said you aren't a soldier." She responded. "This is a war and I'm invested in it now."

I nodded my thanks and we returned to my previously scheduled stealthy approach up the loading ramp and made our way into the ambassadorial transport. The first room we entered was the open airlock, with nothing fancy to it except panels to open and close doors – which we didn't need thanks to a careless guest.

"He didn't secure the hatch." Tora whispered to me. "He's not planning on flying off. What is he up to?"

I put my gloved finger up to my mouth, trying not to hit myself in the face with my pistol at the same time. I pointed to the floor of the airlock. There was a small black pool of what I can only describe as rotten blood. Another smaller pool was inside the ship, where the flight crew would greet you if they'd brought one as a witness. It was very nicely appointed and had a secured display rack full of expensive liquors, dark liquors and a bottle of actual Russian potato vodka, and a food printer.

The next blood spot wasn't backward into the passenger section of the ship, but forward into the small passage containing doors to where the crew likely slept and eventually into the cockpit. The door to the cockpit was open and I could see some movement against the backwash of instrument lights. It was talking.

"She has protection." A gravelly voiced Angus argued. "And those useless pyqeans won't hold out much longer. They've probably all up-loaded to the hypernet and back to Pyqea for new bodies as we speak."

"That will raise questions, Ambassador." A haughty British accented voice replied in GCT, distorted like it was over a communications sys-tem. "When that many of them upload into replacement bodies, the Hegemony will question the sudden expense from so many sources all at once."

"There wasss no choicccce!" Angus began hissing his words and coughed between sentences. "I faccccilitated the girl'ssss arrival in the ssssystem asss you inssstructed, but we had been expossssed. Now....cough....there is no...cough...hope of taking her..."

Tora and I each stood on opposite sides of the hatch for the cockpit with our backs to the way and braced to turn and fire in. I nodded that we go, but she put a hand up to hold me off and was clearly interested in listening in.

"I disagree." The voice seemed amused. "You no longer need the pyqeans. Those we can conceal will return to their missions. The others will be deleted. You can retrieve the dagger yourself now. It's a pity you won't be in a state to control taking her alive. She seemed like quite the trophy – but the dagger will do."

"Gaaarrgllle..cough." Angus choked out before stopping his fit of coughing and gaining a deeper and more guttural control of his own voice. "Yes, master. I will retrieve her..."

"Now!" Tora yelled and turned to fire into the cockpit. I was a split second slower, and good thing too. Her shot went into the ceiling as she was thrown back by something colliding with her.

That left me standing with my blaster pointing at a mutated Angus Blooming-Star.

XXX

CHAPTER THIRTY

Load Playlist Track: Radiohead, Creep

From the waste down, he was still the same man, as far as I could tell. He even moved in on me with the limp from the injured leg. The black welts of his torso had coalesced into one large black swelling mass which had overcome the majority of the left side all the way down his left arm, doubling its mass. Where his palm had been was replaces with a hissing fanged mouth with a lapping black tongue. His fingers had swelled into inky black prehensile appendages of their very own, each about a couple feet long.

The black mass had also crept up over the side of his neck and completely overcome his lower jaw, extending his teeth and sharpening his canines. His eyes were fully dilated and I could see the same slithering mass I'd witnessed in Neridah's whites. It had fully broken the almost nonexistent iris and broken into Angus' pupil.

He hissed as he stepped through the doorway and made a swing at me with his newly nethered limb. I backpeddled as quickly as I could and fired a shot that hit him right where his heart should be.

Ichor like the bloody pools we'd tracked into the ship spurt from the impact, but the wound simply sealed itself over as he screamed at us with a wicked hatred in his guttural voice. "You! You made this so much harder! You've made it so I have to kill her! She was going to witness so much beauty! She could have been one His brides! You did this!"

He extended his palm at me and it hissed, drooling ichor from its fanged mouth. Then the fingers-turned-appendages flew out at me, elongating to me faster than I could back out of the hallway to the food cabin. Theses...tentacles...grabbed at my forearm as I managed another shot that severed one from his arm.

The Nether mutated Angus Blooming-Star winced in pain and screamed. He pulled his arm back and the tentacles retracted to their former size with the severed one sputtering the black ichor on the floors and walls, and Tora and I, as it went. The tentacle, minus the one that flopped around on the floor as it shrank down, also had ripped the gun from my hand.

The fanged mouth hand bit into it and crushed the barrel between its teeth. Fuck! If that thing got a bite into one of us...

Captain Tora managed to snap out of being stunned from the hit that had knocked her to the floor of the passage hallway. She fired a pair of shots into Angus' chest.

"You raised her as her father!" She yelled as she rose from the floor, her back to the wall, and she kept firing into him with each free breath. "You were his brother! You betrayed them both! Die you son...of...a....bitch!"

Her brutal barrage pushed him back into the cockpit of the ship before her blaster went quite.

click *click* *click* Tora pulled the trigger a few times before she realized her power pack was empty. Still determined, she reached to her hip holster and felt for a replacement power magazine. She patted it twice and then looked down to see she was out. The ferocity of the fighting at the sinkhole must have used all of her other ammunition.

"Shit." We managed to say in unison before NetherAngus roared and burst at us from the cockpit, his remaining tentacles flying forward down the tiny hallway.

"Run!" I yelled as we both took off back the way we came. I cleared the airlock first and was halfway down the ramp when I heard Tora scream behind me. She was only a pair of steps behind me, but she was a foot off the ground. She clawed at a black tentacle wrapped around her throat. Each ankle had a matching pair lifting her off the ground. The fourth remaining one was wrapped around her rib cage.

"Erk..." was all she could get out as she began to choke. Angus emerged from the ship, the left side of his face had completely turned black, replacing his eye and ear with biting little mouths and his hair on the side had turned into thousands of little wriggling...things.

NetherAngus retracted his tentacles again, faster than I could move to grab at her, and the palm of his former hand, teeth and all, disappeared into the flesh of the Captain's lower back.

Tora went rigid with the pain. I saw her eyes roll back in her head and her eyelids flutter as she tried to scream with no air coming through her choked larynx.

Then she simply went limp.

I went in swinging with the baseball bat and caught his arm where the wrist should have been. I had enough effect for his remaining human eye to look at me with a dilated mania. He simply tossed her aside to the ground beside the ramp before stepping forward and swiping at me with short blood-ichored talons that had split through his pink fingertips sometime during our engagement with him.

I took the gash across the chest as he knocked me over the side of the ramp. I landed beside Nephiri Tora's dead, or hopefully just unconscious, body – I didn't know which, but I feared the worse. Red blood trickled into my torn shirt from the stinging deep scratches in my chest. I looked up from laying there and NetherAngus loomed over me on the ramp making a hissing guffaw.

"I should have given into it sooner." He growled at me. "The freedom is tremendous. The power to change, to kill, and to...consume."

His palm's mouth lapped its tongue at Tora's blood from its fangs gleefully as he lowered his tentacles at me, ready to unleash them toward me again. "And now, pathetic little Terran. Your part in this is over."

I was out of breath from the run and the fight. My adrenaline rush had drained out of me when I saw Tora slip away. The gash in my chest hurt and I knew I couldn't move fast enough. I winced, ready for the end as the tentacles flew out at me.

Instinctively, I tried to back away, wishing I could push into the very Earth to my back and move the world to get away – and the tentacles never reach me. Inches from me, the hideous black monster fingers stopped and shook.

In the darkness a whooshing, roaring, hollow sound rose and fell and rose and fell. Angus' attention had shifted to the sound coming from just inside the clearing, at the edge of the woods.

In the center of the sound, spinning a rope over her head with something attached to the end was Neridah Blooming-Star. The sound was coming from something at the end of the rope, which she twirled with the motion of the wrist of her left hand. She was using the bullroarer. In her right hand she held the Dagger of Augury, it's ruby now pure and missing the black wriggling horror within.

Her eyes were the color of a starless night and had the feel of the shadows of the Dreaming. Her lips moved with a chant in a language I'd never heard before – which isn't saying much even on Earth, let alone in a galaxy as vast as the Milky Way.

Angus took a step away, up the ramp, as the tentacles recoiled back to their reduced, but still horrifyingly distorted, length.

I was alive – a fact I wasn't going to waste. I rolled upright and brought the metal baseball bat as hard as I could into NetherAngus' still all too human ankle.

My hit snapped him out of his shock and as he fell off the opposite side of the ramp his tentacles lashed back, wrapping around my arm again. He hit the ground like a stack of bricks, pulling me behind him. I hit the side of the ramp hard with my gut before being pulled by the black fleshy ropes back up onto the metal walkway.

He let go of my arm to prop himself up, but managed to pry my baseball bat out of my hand in the process. The hit against my gut had knocked the breath out of me and I found myself on my hands and knees panting as I looked down at NetherAngus.

I found myself in a moment of clarity despite my injuries and fatigue from the night's adventures. Looking over NetherAngus while he was stunned, I realized his change had been in proportion to his injuries. He survived the explosion in the sinkhole because he'd absorbed the burns and the concussion by changing. He survived my shots and Captain Tora's blasts by changing more.

I looked to the ankle I'd certainly broken with the baseball bat.

Nothing. He hadn't continued to change. He was moving sluggishly, clearly averse to the chant from Neridah and the sound of the bullroarer she spun with an air of command above her head.

She had him restrained, somehow.

He stood up slowly, fighting her power over him.

Then Kliff, Eight, and Vi' emerged, running, from woods behind Neridah. They looked to her wide eyed. She pointed the Dagger toward the ship and they followed it with their eyes.

Seeing NetherAngus rising up and lurking slowly toward Neridah from the ramp, they all became suddenly serious. They all looked to one another and nodded with understanding before raising their blasters.

Collectively, they fired everything they had left into him. Against the Odds, he managed to stay upright through most of the onslaught. But, eventually, he succumbed to the burning plasma and fell back over. The blasters went silent as they all ran out of ammunition.

NetherAngus lay on the ground looking up at me, fatigue and hatred burning in his remaining eye. He wasn't healing from the wounds, but he wasn't dead...yet.

I jumped off the ramp at him. Well, I fell off the ramp at him, really. I landed on my knees atop his oozing and plasma burned chest and then just started punching him.

The metal plates of my gravball gloves connected in full with that angry eyeball until I caved it into his skull. When he stopped twitching, I think I should have stopped. But, I didn't until Eight and Kliff pulled me off of him and to my feet.

My throat hurt from the screaming I had been making as I hit him. The bullroarer had stopped some time ago and Neridah was kneeling over Nephiri Tora's body brushing the Asian woman's sleek black hair off of her eyes.

XXXI

CHAPTER THIRTY-ONE

Load Playlist Track: Waidmannsheil, Rammstein

We all gathered around Neridah kneeling by Tora's body. She was on her side, her wound exposed through the shredded orange leather flight jacket. The creature had taken a chunk out of her lower back. Now that I was out of the fight, I could see that she was still breathing shallowly.

Still, there was no way she was going to survive. The hand thing had bitten into whatever internal organs were back there and she'd already lost far more blood than she could hope to recover from. Vi'xiri started crying and pressed her head into Kliff's fur.

The sometimes feral seeming grathrak ran his meaty paws gently over the tellurian's red head tendrils, brushing them backward. He was whimpering what a sound I'd imagine a sad bear must make.

Neridah placed the Dagger up to her face and look through the crossguard with those empty black eyes. I don't know what she'd hoped to see in the future with that thing. Tora's fate was clear. She was going to die.

Eight quietly came to attention and saluted the Captain. He was grim, but you could feel his respect for the smuggler virtually pouring out of him. He might have even gotten misty eyed. He might have shed a tear. Maybe.

Then Neridah touched her eyes and plucked out a wriggling small piece of darkness as she muttered a chant. Before any of us could say a word she slipped it into Tora's gaping wound and touched it with the Dagger, raising the volume of her chant and the pitch of her words. Threads of black ichor spread began spreading quickly where muscle and sinew should be.

She was turning her into a thing like Angus!

Eight realized it at the same time as me. His knife came out, blade down, and both of us raised our hands getting ready for another fight. The nether had taken control of Neridah and she'd just infected the Captain.

We were going to have to kill her.

"I'm fine." Neridah said putting up a hand toward us, foreseeing our reactions before Kliff and Vi'xiri could figure out what had happened. "It isn't in control of me. It tried, but it failed."

"How do we know?" I said with trepidation. This girl who had invaded my life, my dreams, and my desires had been infected by a horror that had terrified a generation and killed millions. Could she really have resisted it? "Prove it."

She looked up to me, the blackness gone from all but her pupils. The blue rings of her irises were nearly invisible, but they were there. "It was my purpose all along. It's what my mother Saw. It's what I've Seen."

"Is it still in you?" Eight asked with his dagger ready and Kliff slowly began extending his claws.

Vi'xiri's head tendrils 'sniffed' in the direction of the kneeling Shaman girl. "Aye think she iz telling us ze truth. Or, at least, she believes what she iz saying."

"You can smell that?" I asked the dancing girl. "And you're sure?"

"Oh yes." Diva spoke independent of Kliff. "Miss Vi'xiri's gifts of scenting out lies have gotten us out of a tremendous number of poorly decided business situations. Her credentials as a lie detector are second only to her ability to detect an overly aroused teenaged boy."

With that the tension popped as we all burst into laughter. Even Neridah facepalmed herself and shook her head. Perplexed, the operatic voice box asked, "What did I say?"

Tora coughed as her breathing improved. Her eyes flittered open at the laughter and she blinked up at as. "What did I miss?"

Eight pointed to Tora's side cautiously, his dagger still ready despite the supposed break in his foul demeanor. The Captain tilted her head to glimpse what she could and saw the black mass forming in the hole that had been her lower back. "Ohmygod...no..."

"It's alright, Nephiri." Neridah reassured her. "I'm resisting it for both of us. I can't get rid of it from either of us, but it won't take hold of you any farther – and I still need you alive."

"Thanks?" Captain Tora said disturbed. "What do you still need us for?"

"Not all of you." Neridah turned and looked each at Eight, Kliff, and Vi'xiri. "The Odds have done their part. Thank you, friends."

She then turned her eyes to me. "Your final part in fighting the Nether hasn't played out yet. I'm not sure when it will. But, you're done for now."

I felt my eyebrows raise up along with the hair on the back of my neck. There was more?

"What about me?" Tora asked Neridah. "Why do you still need me alive?"

Neridah turned her eyes to the Captain. "I don't know how to fly a ship. And I'm not strong enough to keep the Nether in you under control with you far off. I need you to come with me."

"Where you going?" asked Eight. "We can help."

Neridah shook her head. "No, Eight. You've done your direct part in this. If you come with me you will die. I can See things. I can change them. But when I do, I have to See them again. But if you come with me now, all of you will die."

"Will I die?" Tora asked her and Neridah sighed and prepared to speak. "Don't. I don't want to know. If you can change fate, so can anyone's choices. I'll come with you and I'll keep myself alive...and you too."

They nodded to one another and helped one another up.

"I don't like it." I said, feeling a sinking feeling in my gut. They were going to leave us all behind. "This thing in you can't be controlled forever. You saw what it did to Angus."

"It can be." Neridah countered. "Free mutants exist throughout various parts of space."

"Those are offspring of those Nether things and victims." I argued. "Everything I've heard says that those the Nether turn never turn back. We need to get this out of your before you go too far."

"It can't be taken out of me." Neridah shook her head, the tone of her voice like what a mother would say to a crying child to help it feel better. "At least not yet. And no, before you ask, my tribe's Cleverman can't help and my father's clan's Druids can't either. None of them are strong enough to do it."

"There has to be someone." I begged, taking her hands and pulling her close to me. "It's a big Galaxy."

"It's a big Galaxy I have to protect from the Nether." She answer me and kissed me on the cheek. "But this thing in me is my connection to holding them back. And, the dagger you all helped me find is my key to staying ahead of the Nether – to continue my father's work and the work of those Shaman Masters who's spirits have grown too weak to continue."

"You're going to hold back Lord Archimedes and his Nether all by yourself?" I disbelieved aloud. "That's a tall order, Neridah."

"Do you know what my name means, Einar?" I shook my head and she smiled. "It means 'Blossom' in my tribe's language. My mother chose it because she Saw I would Blossom. And when I finish doing that, I won't just hold back the man who Betrayed my father and the Galaxy..."

Her face grew grim and her eyes narrowed. "I will destroy him."

"Wow." I believed her. I had no idea how she could do it, but she meant it.

Within an hour we had all returned to the *Legacy's Façade* and the Odds had moved their belongings off the ship. Velma lay on a gurney hooked up to lifesaving equipment from the ship's emergency medical equipment.

I watched as Kliff and Eight pushed The Snowball down the loading ramp that had been the front entrance of the Mouse Club and despite its damage still present, my heart jumped a little at seeing my old mini-pod safe and sound.

We then all stood around the entry ramp to the ship one last time to say goodbye.

On Neridah's orders, Tora gave me possession of their service droid RT-3. The little butler, clearly offended, was using his drill sergeant voice to command the band on organizing their instruments.

"MOVE THOSE BOXES YOU GIANT MOP!" He barked with more snarl than you'd expect out of something that small. "WE'VE GOT TO CLEAR THIS DECK!"

Halfway through the off loading process of the equipment before Vi'xiri decided she'd had enough of the half-pint white robot.

"Jesus Human Christ." She marched over to him. "Shut up or I will shut you off."

The little robot went rigid and then switched voices. "My sincere apologies ma'am. I was just trying to help."

"I've ordered a transfer to your account." Neridah told me as we all hugged one another in farewell. "You've completed my case. But, I'll be calling on you again someday...free of charge."

"Free of charge?" I mocked disapproval rather obviously. "Why would I do that?"

"In minutes the Hegemony is going to lock down my assets." She rolled her eyes. "The Imperial Shamanic Council has heard through the Totems many of the events of today. They'd been watching me since I was born knowing something was going to happen. The Betrayal disrupted their attention so I wasn't directly followed after that. But, I've got their attention again. Even now a ship of the Sensuo has been sent by them to investigate. Before they get here a ship containing Sol System Colonial Troops will arrive under order of System lord Sch'Gwenish. The Hegemony will have informed him by way of his Pyqean advisor."

"Is the advisor one of the Nether loyalists?" I said, worrying that we had more trouble coming. "You can't really kill a pyqean. All of those that were here will have survived somehow."

"I don't think he is." She shook her head. "Most of them are alright, I suspect. But yes, there's a group of them working within the government to help Lord Archimedes. I can't see what he promised them for their help. Maybe you'll have to figure it out."

"Maybe?" I was surprised she was preternaturally foreseeing my involvement.

"I can see a lot." She answered. "But not everything. Not yet anyways."

She laughed in a way that told me that innocent girl was still in there somewhere and it brought a smile to my face.

She was right, about five minutes after the *Legacy Façade* tooko off into the sky, a military troop transport was hovering over us barking commands that we drop our weapons and raise our hands. How they missed the *Façade* was a mystery to me. But, between the smuggling skills of Captain Tora and the Sight of Neridah Blooming-Star, I supposed anything was possible.

We, on the other hand, all found ourselves immediately surrounded by Earther colonial troopers and then promptly arrested.

EPILOGUE

Load Playlist Track: Dropkick Murphys, Amazing Grace

In a seedy nightclub in the lowest depths of the Low Down of New Reykjavik, a band played a sound that was like old earth EDM and Dark Matter Death Metal had a baby that grew up to be a transgenre mishmash of Dubstepped Swing and InterWorld Gypsy Music. It was some intense fusion of raw primal rage and happening Jazz they called the Deep Djugga.

The Odds sang and roared a slower than average Dirge, but with the same virulence they were known for. While camping out in my living room for the last week they told me all about their new album. It was a Deep Djugga rock opera of sorts telling the story of a heroine rising out of the darkness of the Nether to destroy them. They'd only written the first song, a ballad, that loosely told of the battle in Centralia. They sang it in traditional Voltch'I.

It sounded really good, but most likely no one in the club understood its story. Still, they flailed to it passionately in the mosh pit.

"So, boss," Velma yelled to me across our drinks after checking a display that projected from her new cyberarm, a built in wrist computer. "I've received word from the Magistrate that they've dropped all charges thanks to an investigation by Lord Sch'Gwenish's office."

"Yeah." I took a sip from my glass of real scotch. "It hasn't been reported officially, but word is getting out in the shadier parts of the Hypernet is that all five Sensuo Kingdoms have gone on alert and increased patrols of the areas of space controlled by Lord Archimedes."

"Any word on Neridah?" She said sheepishly in a gap the band put in the music for effect. Her jealousy was still showing, but she actually seemed to care about the answer. I adjusted my fedora a little and used the motion to obscure some of my face while I tried not to give away how concerned I actually was.

"Eight says the bounty hunter boards have her unofficially placed on a hit list." I leaned in to tell her, rather than yell it. "Seems someone in the Expanse doesn't want her doing whatever Neridah and Captain Tora left to do."

"And what about us?" She yelled over the music. "What next, boss?"

"The money covers a couple months of rent." I shrugged and finished down my drink. "So, we need new cases. But for now..."

I stood up and offered her my hand. She took it and stood up. She was wearing one a short sleeved French cut bodysuit with the The Odds written on it in glowing pink letters. Over it she wore a pair of jeans with only one leg, exposing her new cybernetic leg.

I looked at it and almost said, for the thousandth time, that I was sorry. It was the second time I was supposed to be protecting her that she lost a limb. She put up a mechanical finger to stop me before I could.

"...for now we rock out." I finished the thought.

"What's with the hat?" She pointed a mechanical finger. "I thought you only wore that when you were on a job. Besides, we're deep inside a walking machine city. It's not like you have weather to worry about."

I laughed and shrugged off the question as we waded into the flailing army of the Low Down's alien underground scene and lost ourselves in the primal electric energy of a deep growling Grathrak paired with the melodious voice of a dancing Telarian – both in sync with the operatic voice of the Diva and a heavily scarred old Clone Trooper.

I had the hat on because as far as I was concerned, this job wasn't really done. This case wasn't closed, I told myself as we started thrashing with the rest of the crowd.

I looked up to see the four armed amphibious drummer keeping pace for the best set The Odds ever had. His bright red shirt was emblazoned with a yellow number "Seven."

CPSIA information can be obtained
at www.ICGtesting.com
Printed in the USA
BVHW061314181121
621927BV00008B/389